The Husband

...id

A Regency Novel

CATHERINE KULLMANN

Willow Books

Copyright © 2023 Catherine Kullmann

All rights reserved. No part of this book may be reproduced or utilised in any form or by any means, electronic or mechanical, including photocopying, filming, recording, video recording, photography, or by any information storage and retrieval system, nor shall it by way of trade or otherwise be lent, resold, or otherwise circulated in any form of binding or cover other than that it which it is published without prior permission in writing by the publisher.

The right of the author to her work has been asserted by her in accordance with the Copyright, Designs and Patents Act 1988.

This historical novel is a work of fiction. Names, characters, places and incidents are the products of the author's imagination or are used fictitiously. Except where actual historical events, locales, businesses and characters are described for the storyline of this novel, all situations in this publication are fictitious and any resemblance to actual persons living or dead, businesses, events or locales is purely coincidental.

Cover image: antique engraving from the author's private collection.
Cover design by BookGoSocial

ISBN: 978-1-913545-90-1

First published 2023 by
Willow Books
D04 H397, Ireland

Regency Novels by Catherine Kullmann

The Duchess of Gracechurch Trilogy   *The Malvins*

The Murmur of Masks

Perception & Illusion   →   The Potential for Love

The Duke's Regret

The Lorings

A Suggestion of Scandal

Lady Loring's Dilemma

The Husband Criteria

Stand Alone

A Comfortable Alliance

Novella

The Zombi of Caisteal Dun

For my granddaughter Rosalie, with love from Granny

List of Characters

Cynthia Amelia Glazebrook — **Young lady embarking on her second Season**

Amelia Glazebrook — Cynthia's mother, cousin of Sir Julian Swann-Loring

Jonathan Glazebrook MP — Cynthia's father

Martin Glazebrook — Cynthia's brother

The Nabob Glazebrook — Cynthia's paternal grandfather (off-stage)

Lord Ransford and Lady Ransford née Loring — Cynthia's maternal grandparents

Chloe Loring — **Debutante in her first Season**

Sir Julian Swann-Loring, né Loring — Chloe's half-brother

Rosa, Lady Swann-Loring, née Fancourt — Julian's wife; Chloe's former governess

Kate Swann-Loring	Rosa's and Julian's daughter, Chloe's niece
Robert Kennard	Rosa's half-brother
The dowager Lady Loring	Chloe's and Julian's grandmother, Cynthia Glazebrook's great-grandmother
Lord Swanmere	Julian's maternal grandfather (Julian is his heir through his mother)
Delia, Lady Stephen FitzCharles	Chloe's mother
Lord Stephen FitzCharles	Chloe's stepfather
Alexander FitzCharles	Delia's and Stephen's son, Chloe's half-brother
The Duke and Duchess of Gracechurch	The duke is Lord Stephen's nephew
Lord Stephen and Lady Tabitha FitzCharles	The duke's and duchess's younger children
Rowland, Lord Stanton	Heir to the Duke of Gracechurch, Oxford student

Ann Overton	**Debutante in her first Season Julian Swann-Loring's cousin through their mothers**
Henry (Hal) Overton	Ann's younger brother, schoolfriend of Robert Kennard
Charles Forbes	Ann's musical mentor
Henrietta Forbes	Charles' wife
Cecilia and Ambrose Forbes	Charles' and Henrietta's children
Messrs Bradley, Hayes and Dennison	Fellow-musicians who also work with Mr Forbes
Mr Prescott	Organist
Sir Frederick and Lady Overton	Ann's aunt and uncle

Select Ladies and Gentlemen of the *Ton*

Lord and Lady Benton	Earl and Countess Benton
Rafe, Lord Marfield	Lord Benton's heir
Sir John and Lady Anna Devenish	Lady Anna is Marfield's sister
Jack Devenish	Sir John's and Lady Anna's son

Lady Georgina Benton	Lord Benton's maiden aunt
Francis and Caro Nugent	
Matthew Malvin	
Lord Rastleigh	
Lord and Lady Needham	Earl and Countess of Needham
Lord Hope	Heir to Lord Needham
Lady Elizabeth Hope	Daughter of the Needhams

London Residences with Employees and Servants

Swanmere House	Julian, Rosa, Chloe, Kate, Lord Swanmere, The dowager Lady Loring and Ann Overton
Parker	Chloe's maid
Morris	Butler
Benton House	The Earl and Countess, Lady Georgina, and the dowager Countess
Dover Street	Lord Marfield
Bates	Valet and major-domo
Mrs Paxon	Cook/housekeeper
Park Place	The Glazebrooks
Cotter	Cynthia's maid

Gracechurch House	*The Gracechurches and Fitzcharles*
Thomas Musgrave	Lord Jasper's tutor and son of the Rector of Swanmere
Miss Barlow	Lady Tabitha's governess

Chapter One

Swanmere House, London, February 1817

It is the undisputed ambition of every mother to see her daughters and, to a lesser extent (for a daughter-in-law may well one day supplant her) her sons, suitably married. The eligibility of potential matches is determined by an arcane logarithm setting his station, wealth, and personability against her beauty, fortune, and station. Although there is no Euclidean exposition to assist in the application of this tool, matrons of all classes are expert in evaluating a man's worth, and the likelihood of their daughter successfully attracting his attention.

There are, of course, exceptions to the rule. Some two years previously, Miss Rosa Fancourt, a governess of modest fortune who laid no claim to beauty, had captured the heart of Sir Julian Loring, heir not only to his father, Sir Edward, but also to his maternal grandfather, Lord Swanmere, and had in due course been presented to her Majesty as Lady Swann-Loring, Sir Julian having marked his marriage by combining his paternal and maternal surnames. Now Lady Swann-Loring was about to launch her sister-in-law, Chloe Loring and her husband's cousin, Ann Overton, into the *ton*.

"Although it might as well be the blind leading the lame, for all the knowledge I have of the *beau monde*," she said candidly to

13

Sir Julian who lounged in a chair in her dressing-room, enjoying the spectacle of his wife being arrayed in full court dress, hoops, feathers, lappers, and diamonds. "We must be grateful to Chloe's mother for the FitzCharles connection. I am sure Lord Stephen will be able to advise us, and you must keep your ear to the ground for any hint of unsavoury habits—women or gambling—you know what I mean."

"Not from personal experience."

The twinkle in his eye belied this solemn profession and she shook her head at him. "Julian, you must take this seriously."

"I do, I promise you." He leaned over to kiss her, careful of her finery. "Good luck, my love. I look forward to hearing all about it."

~~~

In the hall of Swanmere House, the three ladies gathered their trains over one arm and stood patiently while maids swathed their finery in wide, black cloaks, carefully drawing the capacious hoods over their plumed headdresses.

"In your dominos you are more suitably attired for a masquerade than a drawing-room," the dowager Lady Loring remarked. "Only the loo masks are wanting."

"Apart from protecting us from smuts and soot, they will keep us warm while we wait our turn to be admitted," her granddaughter-in-law Rosa, Lady Swann-Loring answered. "We'll leave them in the carriage, of course."

"And they will be useful if we are invited to any masquerades," Chloe Loring pointed out.

"I should like to see you dance an entire evening with that over your gown," said Lord Swanmere, a gentleman who, like her grandmother, would not see eighty again, and in his youth had made the grand tour. "Dominos for masquerades and *ridotti* were made of much lighter stuff—silk or taffeta."

"Hmm. You could have a coloured one, to match your gown," Chloe said. "Maybe we should have a masquerade instead of a ball, Rosa."

"Not this Season," Chloe's brother, Sir Julian Swann-Loring, said firmly. "How much longer do you intend to stand here in the hall?"

"What was it the gladiators used say?" Rosa asked.

"*Morituri te salutant*—those who are about to die salute you," her husband supplied. "It will not be so bad, I hope."

"Just a dead bore," Rosa said, "but it must be done, I suppose. Come, girls."

Chloe and Julian's cousin, Ann Overton, obediently followed her out to the new barouche-landau. Lady Loring had insisted on making Rosa a present of it, saying there was no suitable carriage for a lady of fashion at Swanmere House and that if Rosa was to be put to the trouble of bringing out her sister-in-law and Julian's cousin, she should at least be properly turned out when driving in the Park and on other outings. "These things make all the difference, my dear," she had said, "and you will allow me this small pleasure."

The twin carriage hoods enclosed the occupants of the carriage in a dim cocoon. The day had never brightened, the gloom increased by the tendrils of fog that crept from the river through the streets and across St James's Park, blending the smoke and soot from thousands of chimneys into a malodorous, thick vapour that irritated the eyes, nose, and back of the throat and left a black deposit everywhere.

"Will it really be so tedious, Rosa?" Ann asked as they moved away.

"It depends. The first time is more interesting, I suppose, just being in the Queen's House and so close to the royal family. But there is a lot of waiting, first a very slow procession until our carriage reaches the entrance, then we must make our way up the stairs, and then wait our turn in the throne room, one behind the other. It all depends on how many presentations there are, for they delay matters; other ladies simply pass the throne with a curtsey."

Chloe closed her eyes, letting the conversation wash over her. She wanted to concentrate on this moment of setting out for the Queen's House, of stepping onto Society's stage fully recognised as an adult, eligible to take part in all the Season's activities, not only accepted as marriageable in every sense, but also as actively seeking a husband. It was the first step on a new journey leading away from her familiar loved ones towards a new family of her own. Only Heaven knew how long the road might be, what hazards, twists, and turns lay ahead of her, whether she would finally reach safe harbour. Safe harbour, as in finding the right gentleman; a kind, honourable gentleman who would love and cherish her, whom she would love and cherish in return.

She had no idea what he might look like but she knew she would recognise the loving look in his eyes, a look that could not be feigned or counterfeited but must spring from the heart. She wanted that secret meeting of eyes, the exchange of little smiles that she had seen between Julian and Rosa, the sharing of quiet family moments and the setting aside of private time, just for them. Above all, she wanted their children to grow up surrounded by love.

"Have you fallen asleep, Chloe?"

"No. I was just thinking how momentous an occasion this is. Do you not feel it too, Ann?"

Her friend nodded. "It is very ungrateful of me, but I am so happy that my mother has remarried and left for India. Just imagine if she were here—we would be alone in the carriage; which would be worse—the flutterings, the exclamations, the reproaches, and reminders. She would have me in such a state that I would be bound to trip over my train or turn my back on a prince..." She broke off as the others laughed.

"I think she would be just as grateful that she did not have to admit to an adult daughter," Rosa said. "Judging by her treatment of you, she wished to imply that you were younger than you are, and by extension, shave some years off her own age."

"Why would she do that?"

"From what Julian says, your mother was an attractive, appealing child who was adept in coaxing adults to give her what she wanted, so she may not have wanted to grow older. Also, many women fear their prospects of marriage dwindle as they age."

"That would explain why she did not take you with her to Bath, or on her other journeys," Chloe said. "It would be easier for her to flirt and make eyes at gentlemen, without a grown daughter by her side."

"I never thought of that," Ann said, startled. "She always said I was too dull and gauche, too prone to saying the wrong thing."

"You mean in not saying what she wished you to say in support of her flights of fancy," Rosa said. "Perhaps I should not say such things about her, Ann, but I would not like you still to suffer under the effect of such remarks. Believe me, they reflect much worse on her than they do on you. Do not be afraid to be your true self, my dear, and you will do very well."

Ann smiled brilliantly. "Thank you, Rosa. I had not realised how engrained they were in me. I suppose you are right; they might say more about her than about me. I hope Mr Lambole is good to her. He seemed very proud of her at any rate, and very generous."

Chloe pulled the cloak closer around her shoulders and pressed her scented handkerchief to her nose. "What a miserable day. I had not thought that London would smell so badly, but between the fires and the horses…"

"Not to mention the tanners, the brewers, and the other manufacturers," Ann added wryly. "It makes one long for a good, breezy day where everything is blown away and there is a blue sky."

"And white, fluffy clouds like we see at home," Rosa said with a sigh. "We must hope that spring will reach London one day."

The rhythm of the horses had changed to stop and walk, as the line of carriages paused to let passengers alight and moved on again. "The footman will alert us when we near the head of the line," Rosa said. "Remember, we must leave our cloaks here. Be sure you have your fans, carefully gather your trains, and duck your heads as you alight so as not to knock your feathers askew."

Soon they heard the double rap on the roof, and began to divest themselves of the warm cloaks. The carriage stopped under a portico and the footman opened the door and let the steps down. Chloe was grateful for his proffered hand to steady her as she extricated her unwieldy hoops and long train from the confines of the carriage. All three negotiated the hurdle without mishap. It was a relief to emerge from the gloom into the brightly-lit entrance hall and take their place in the procession of ladies slowly ascending the grand staircase; their voluminous skirts and draperies requiring a free step to be left between each one. At least this dawdling progress gave her the opportunity to admire the wonderful paintings and spectacular ceiling.

It was a pity Mamma could not present her, but she would not for the world have Rosa think she regarded her as second-best. They had all agreed that it were better not to provoke the scandalmongers who might wonder at Lady Stephen FitzCharles presenting an adult daughter from a previous marriage. She glanced at the diamond bracelets on her wrists. They had been a wedding present to Mamma from Papa's great-uncle. 'You should have them now,' Mamma had said last year, 'and the other jewellery I had from your father and grandmother.' Well, the bracelets would remind her of Mamma today.

They reached a sort of ante-chamber; through a doorway she could see the red and gold awning over the throne. There was a stir and the Queen appeared, accompanied by the royal family and attendants. Chloe took a deep breath. She caught Ann's eye and smiled encouragingly. Ahead of them, the first lady to be presented let her train fall to the ground where two lords-in-waiting spread it out behind her.

"It is just as we practised," Ann whispered to Chloe.

"Yes."

One by one, they moved forward. Time seemed to stretch and shrink at once; it was an eternity until they reached the throne and yet Chloe suddenly stood before the aging Queen.

"Miss Loring, presented by Lady Swann-Loring."

At the Vice-Chamberlain's announcement, she removed her right glove and sank into the deep court curtsey, gracefully extending her bare hand. Her Majesty touched it with hers and it was over. She rose to her feet and began the sideways withdrawal, curtseying to each prince and princess as she went.

At last she could gather up her train again and look about her. It truly was a dazzling spectacle. The vast room was illuminated by three enormous crystal chandeliers, the light reflected in four tall gilt-framed oval mirrors. The hooped skirts might be cumbersome, but they displayed the rich fabrics and ornamentation of the gowns to perfection, gleaming and shimmering as if a flight of exotic butterflies had suddenly spread their wings. Here and there the silks and satins were punctuated by dark court and bright red military uniforms, and happy was the gentleman who could display a well-formed calf and trim ankle in his white silk stockings.

A dark-haired woman at the far end of the room caught Chloe's eye and beckoned quietly with her fan. She looked like—it couldn't be, yet it was—Mamma! Full of incredulous joy, she edged through the throng even as Mamma came towards her.

"Why did you not tell me you were coming?" Chloe whispered as they touched cheeks. Of all the places to meet her mother, the Queen's drawing-room was the most unlikely.

"I thought to surprise you—I could not resist when the duchess wrote and said she was coming to London early this Season and would we not join her. At her suggestion, I had left my court dress at Gracechurch House, and we were able to re-vamp it with different-coloured draperies and train. You look delightful, my love. I love the little posies of forget-me-nots. The blue matches your eyes exactly."

The Husband Criteria

Chloe laughed. "I was terrified I would catch my foot in my hoop or trip over my train."

"Everyone is, but I have never heard of it actually happening, have you? You made your curtsies with great aplomb, at any rate. I am so proud of you."

"We practised and practised. Grandmother had Ann and me come to dinner in hoops all last week. We had to pretend that she was the queen, and make our curtsies to her and Lord Swanmere."

"Come now and make your curtsey to the duchess," Mamma said. "You will like her, I think."

Chloe did like the petite lady who held out her hand with a friendly smile. "I am happy to meet you, Miss Loring, and I hope we will see you soon at Gracechurch House. You will wish to visit your brother, I know."

Chloe, who had been wondering whether she could simply call at a ducal residence, could only smile and stammer, "Thank you, your Grace. You are very kind."

~~~

"Tea, tea, my kingdom for a cup of tea," Chloe chanted when they had regained the sanctuary of the carriage. "My back aches from standing in this wretched contraption, my feet are sore, my face feels it will crack if I smile once more today, and if I have to make another curtsey, I shall topple over like Kate used when she was learning to walk."

"What is more important, release from that contraption, or tea?" Rosa asked. "Which should come first?"

"Release, if we may just put on morning gowns. We can be changed in ten minutes, can't we, Ann? It will take them that long to bring up the equipage and a tea-board."

Julian came out to the hall as soon as he heard the women's voices.

"Tea in the blue drawing-room, Morris," Rosa said to the butler after receiving her husband's kiss. "And inform Lord Swanmere and Lady Loring that we have returned and do they wish to join us there. We can then tell you all together," she added to her husband. "We first want to remove these hoops."

Fifteen minutes later, they were all assembled in the blue drawing-room. Court gowns had been replaced by morning muslins, and feathers, lappets, and diamonds plucked from the modish hair-styles that would take longer to dismantle.

The two grandparents, who had insisted on coming to town with the rest of the family, were agog to hear every detail of the drawing-room, including a detailed description of the queen and princes and princesses whom they both remembered from past years. Lady Loring raised an eyebrow at hearing that her former daughter-in-law was in town but made no comment.

"She acknowledged me openly and presented me to the Duchess of Gracechurch as her daughter," Chloe said. "I am relieved; I had wondered would we have to pretend there was no connection if we met."

"But why?" Ann asked.

"Oh, I forgot you did not know. She went to France with Lord Stephen while she was still married to my father. Only his aunt, Lady Mary, was with them and they contrived to make it appear that Mamma was her companion. But they married within months of my father's death. It all happened around the time of Napoleon's

The Husband Criteria

escape from Elba and it was almost two years before they returned to England, and nobody questioned anything. Only the immediate family knows the full story, but if you are to live here, and meet her frequently, I think it best that you know too. But don't say anything to Hal or Robert."

"I liked her, and the duchess," Ann said. "It was kind of her to ask you to call."

Chapter Two

Chloe jumped as rain hit the window panes with a staccato rattle. "Another storm. How long are we to be confined to the house?"

"At least it will have cleared away the fog," Ann replied. "Everywhere will be refreshed after the storm has passed. Chloe, the duchess has children, doesn't she? Older children, I mean, not babies."

"Yes."

"Do you think you could ask her if she would recommend a music teacher? I would love to have some lessons while we are in town."

"I'll ask, but you need a real musician, Ann, a musician in their heart and soul, as you are, not someone merely proficient like most of us."

"Yes," Ann whispered, "if only I knew how to find him."

"Do you want to marry such a gentleman?" Chloe asked. "A marriage of true minds?"

"Yes, no… I can't really explain. I could not marry a man who did not enjoy music or understand what it means to me, but I don't know if he should be so involved in music as I am." Ann blushed and laughed. "One of us should live in this world, I think."

"You need someone who will remind you to eat, or that you are supposed to be somewhere in an hour's time?"

"Yes, and who will understand that his household will not be my first concern."

"What about his children?"

"I don't know, Chloe. I would not want to neglect them, but would also not wish to devote all my time to them."

"He must be willing to take on some of your duties and well-enough circumstanced to pay others to do the rest."

"Maybe it is better if I don't marry. My father left me some money, and I could earn more with my music."

"Would you not be lonely?"

"You can be lonely even if you are surrounded by people," Ann said simply, "and content when you are on your own. Even my grandmother says I shall have to put my music aside when I marry, but I honestly don't think I could."

As soon as the storms abated, a note came from Gracechurch House inviting Sir Julian and Lady Swann-Loring together with the Misses Loring and Overton to a dinner *en famille*. Arriving at the appointed hour, they were shown to a pleasant parlour where the duke and duchess chatted with Mamma and Lord Stephen while a boy of about thirteen and two younger girls knelt on the floor with baby Alexander.

As soon as Alexander spied the newcomers, he scrambled to his feet and toddled towards them, his arms raised. "Chlo, Chlo!"

Chloe laughed and lifted him so that he could sit on her hip. "You're getting heavy," she said, then smiled at the boy and girl who were introduced as Lord Jasper and Lady Tabitha. Mr and Mrs Forbes were the parents of the other girl, Cecilia, and a neat, pleasant-faced woman who sat near them was presented as Miss Barlow, Tabitha's governess.

"You are Alexander's sister," Lady Tabitha said. It was a statement, not a question.

"Yes."

"His father is our Great-Uncle Stephen, so he is our cousin," Tabitha informed her, "and his mother is now our Great-Aunt Delia. She is your mother too."

"Yes." Chloe wondered where this was leading.

"Then you must also be our cousin," the girl said triumphantly.

Not knowing what to say—it seemed quite forward to claim kinship with a duke's daughter—Chloe looked to the duchess for guidance.

Her Grace laughed. "Tabitha has always regretted the fact that our family is so small, Miss Loring. You will do her and us a favour if you agree to her proposal."

"I should be very happy to, ma'am," Chloe assured her, then said to the girl, "If we are to be cousins, you must call me Chloe."

Tabitha nodded approvingly. "Alexander wants to get down, Chloe. Come, we are playing with the Noah's ark."

Chloe's lips twitched as she complied; here was definitely a *grande dame* in the making.

"I generally do not come to town with the children until after the first of May," the duchess was saying, "but we are transforming Stanton; opening up the lower level so that we can go directly into the gardens from our rooms, and building a new wing with a ballroom, so we decided we would all come up when Parliament reopened."

"Must you move the kitchen and offices as well?" Julian asked. "That is quite an undertaking."

"Indeed, but they are sadly out-dated. It will be easier to build new ones than modernise the existing ones."

"That is true," Rosa said. "We refurbished the kitchen at Swanmere two years ago. Cook is now delighted with the Rumford stove and roasting oven, but at the time she was not at all happy."

"Make lion roar," Alexander demanded, handing Chloe the yellow-maned beast.

"Will Noah not object?"

He shook his head. "Lion roar."

Chloe cleared her throat, and took a deep breath. "**HROOAARR!**"

The tall young man just entering the room recoiled theatrically. "Good heavens! Are we about to be eaten al…Chloe! I mean, Miss Loring."

He was not as angular as when Chloe had seen him last; his shoulders had broadened and, although his waist was still narrow, his trousers were moulded to muscular thighs. His fair hair was trimmed in a modish cut but his crooked smile was just the same.

"Thomas! What a lovely surprise."

"Indeed," he said, bowing to Julian and Rosa. "And here is Ann, too."

"I see you are all acquainted with Jasper's tutor," the duke said.

"And with all his family," Julian said, shaking hands with Thomas. "His father is vicar at Swanmere."

"Almost three years ago, I was the summer tutor for Lady Swann-Loring's and Miss Overton's brothers who were staying at the Castle," Thomas Musgrave explained. "It was that experience that made me consider seeking a position as tutor when I came down from Oxford. How are the boys, ma'am?" he asked Rosa.

"Very well, thank you. They are to stay with us here in town during the Easter vacation. You must bring Lord Jasper to visit them—they seem to be about the same age."

"May I not come too?" Tabitha demanded.

"You must come and visit me and my baby niece," Chloe said promptly. "Kate is six months younger than Alexander. She is just starting to crawl."

"Can I bring Alexander so that the two babies can play together?" Tabitha asked. "He must get bored in the nursery by himself."

Tabitha got bored in the schoolroom, Chloe suspected. It probably wasn't as easy to go for rides and walks here in town as it would have been in the country. And the weather had been so miserable, too.

Lord Stephen looked at the clock and knelt beside his son. "It is time the animals went to bed. Say good night to the lions."

Pair by pair, Alexander wished the animals a good night and handed them to his father who tucked them away in the ark. He then made the rounds of those present, collecting good-night kisses, before his father picked him up and carried him out of the room.

Lord Jasper had his mother's black curls and grey eyes. He was more reserved than his outspoken sister, Chloe thought, observing how he came to lean silently against his mother's chair while she chatted with Rosa.

The Husband Criteria

The duchess touched his hand gently, as if to say, *I know you are here.* "Are the two boys Mr Musgrave mentioned at school?" she asked Rosa.

"Yes, although I have the impression from Hal and Robert it is something more to be endured than enjoyed."

"That's about right," Thomas Musgrave said, with a grin. "It toughens boys up—accustoms them to the vicissitudes of life."

"I suppose it does," Julian said, "but I don't think a boy who is naturally of a studious bent, is necessarily well-served at a large school."

"Especially if he is not very interested in sport," Jasper said suddenly. "At least, that's what my older brother, Stanton, says. And I find all ball games a dead bore. Perhaps it is because I am not very good at them," he added honestly.

"Sport is like anything else; you won't improve if you don't practise," Thomas said mildly. "It is important to exercise the body as well as the mind; *mens sana in corpore sano,* after all."

"What does that mean?" Tabitha asked.

"Jasper?" Thomas said.

"A sound mind in a healthy body," the boy translated. "But exercise need not be ball games, need it? Did the Romans play football and cricket?"

"I don't know about cricket, but they certainly played with balls. But riding, walking, dancing, and fencing are all good exercise, as well as being part of a gentleman's education."

"You continue to improve with the foils," the duke said, and Jasper looked pleased.

"A good dancer is welcome everywhere," Lord Stephen said. He had returned to the room and stood listening quietly to the conversation.

29

"Papa loved cricket," Chloe said. "Remember how we had a cricket match when he was sixty, and how pleased he was when his players won? Julian and the undergardener were the last strikers and needed six notches to win. I overheard Sir Jethro Boyce bet a pony they would not do it, and Papa took the bet. I was so furious."

"Why?" her mother asked. "You never told me of this."

"My old Firefly was the only pony in the stables."

The others began to laugh but Tabitha looked both puzzled and angry, either because she did not understand the joke or resented the poor pony's fate.

"Rosa explained that pony also means a certain sum of money—twenty-five pounds, she thought, and that Firefly was safe," Chloe added quickly and was happy to see the girl smile and nod.

"Have you any entertainment for us this evening, Tabitha?" the duke asked.

"A song," Tabitha said, "but you must sing too."

She sat at the pianoforte and plunged into the introduction to "*A Frog, He Would A-Wooing Go*", sharing the different roles with her brother who gestured imperiously to their listeners to join in the chorus. By the time poor Mr Frog met his sad end, the impromptu choir was smiling broadly and gasping for breath.

"Splendidly *con brio!*" Mr Forbes said. "My compliments to you all."

"That was as good as your chicken song, Ann," Thomas said.

"My chicken song? Oh, *Il est Bel et Bon*, you mean?"

"What is it? Will you sing it for us?" Tabitha asked.

"You need several people to get the full effect," Ann said. "Why don't I teach it to you when you come to Swanmere House?"

Tabitha beamed. "Thank you."

At dinner, Chloe found herself sitting between her stepfather and Mr Forbes. There was the usual polite hubbub and passing of plates until everyone was served but then Stephen turned to her.

"So, you have made your curtsey to the Queen. What did you make of it all?"

"It was a magnificent occasion, but best to all was to see Mamma there. That was a wonderful surprise. She looks so happy, and Alexander has grown so much. How long do you plan to remain in town, sir?"

"I'm not sure. I hear Kean is to play Macbeth and Othello this month in Drury Lane. I have only seen him play Richard III. I should like to see him in another role."

"I would love to see Macbeth; it is so dramatic—just imagine the weird sisters and Banquo's ghost." Chloe shivered theatrically.

"We must endeavour to get seats. Perhaps you will be our guests."

"That would be wonderful. We have received some invitations to routs and balls, but I would like to see more of London than ballrooms and drawing-rooms."

"If Rosa and Julian will spare you to us one day a week, I'll engage to take you anywhere you want."

"Thank you! I shall consult my guidebook and draw up a plan."

"How is Lady Mary?"

"Aunt Mary," he corrected her. "She would be sad if she thought you had repudiated the connection."

"No, of course not," Chloe hastened to reassure him. "Will she come to Town this Season?"

"Yes, to stay with her daughter, Lady Qualter. You must meet her, and her daughter, Anna. She is a year older than you, I think."

"You and Mamma will come to our ball, will you not?"

"We wouldn't miss it for the world," Stephen assured her.

"What are your plans for the Season?" Chloe's mother asked Rosa when the ladies had withdrawn after dinner. "Apart from your ball, I mean."

"I have been wondering how to go about it. Two years ago, when I was presented, we only stayed in Town for a few weeks. We were not long married and happy not to go into society more than was necessary."

"I'm afraid you will need to do more than that now," the duchess said sympathetically. "You must pay and receive calls, see and be seen at the theatre and the opera, give some little parties at home. If Chloe can develop her own circle, she will find it a real support later on."

"She has Ann and her cousin Cynthia Glazebrook. The three girls get on very well together."

"That is an excellent start. I am always sorry for those girls whose mothers feel compelled to send out their invitations as soon as they arrive in town, instead of letting them find their feet first. They are such nervous creatures, and do not enjoy their Season as much as they might. I suggest you wait to give Chloe's ball until after Easter, when Parliament has reconvened? Chloe will by then have made friends and have some established partners to rely upon."

"Will that not be too late?"

"Not at all. Many families do not come to Town until then and you will have the advantage of having come earlier and being more settled. I hope you will come to my *soirée* next week, and you will find that matters progress quite naturally from there."

"That is very kind of you, Duchess," Rosa said.

"I'll send the Glazebrooks an invitation. Is there anybody else you would like me to invite?"

To Chloe's surprise, the young ladies were not bidden to the pianoforte once the gentlemen had joined them. Instead, Mr Forbes took his seat there, with the duke who carried a strange sort of wooden flute—a recorder, Ann whispered to her—at his side. They would play a sonata by Handel.

"That is a new departure for you, is it not?" Lord Stephen said to the duke when they had finished.

"Yes and no. I played the traverse flute until I broke my wrist some years ago. Afterwards, I found the grip difficult. When I met Forbes again last year—we knew each other at Oxford—he suggested I try the recorder."

"You picked it up very quickly," Mr Forbes said.

"Only with your help," the duke retorted. "But then you have always lived and breathed music."

"Like Ann," Julian said, with a smile at his cousin.

"Really?" Mr Forbes looked at Ann. "In what way?"

"She plays and sings excellently, but it is more than that. Her interest in music is all-consuming; when she stayed with us a couple of years ago, her greatest pleasure was to delve into the unsorted archives in the music room and catalogue them while trying out both the pieces and the instruments."

"The first time we met, at Lady Ransford's," Rosa said, "she, Chloe, and the Ransford's granddaughter, Cynthia, sang a collection of Mr Moore's Irish Melodies. Ann accompanied them on the piano, playing charming interludes to link each song. Later she admitted that she had improvised them on the spot. They just came to her, she said."

"Do you like to compose?" Mr Forbes asked Ann.

"Yes, but I fear I do not know enough about it. I was hoping to find a teacher here in London, but it must be the right person."

"Right, in what way?"

"I want to express myself in my music; not be tied into sonata forms and parlour songs."

"Beethoven more than Haydn?"

"Yes. Not that I don't like Haydn, but there should be more…" Ann broke off, clearly dissatisfied with her explanation.

"I see. Is there anything you would feel happy playing for us?"

"Now?"

"Play some of *Summer at Swanmere*," Chloe suggested.

"What is that?" Mr Forbes asked

"A sequence of short pieces. I was trying to capture the different moods and days that made that summer so special," Ann said as she moved to the pianoforte. "Arriving, getting to know one another, our walks and outings, the wet days where we worked together on the Dread Secret, our evenings together. I'll play two. The first is *Sun and Clouds over the Mere* and the second is *Evening Song*."

She began a gently rippling melody with her left hand then, with the right, added clusters and phrases of notes that gathered and broke apart.

"Beautiful," Rosa said when she stopped. "It was easy to let your thoughts drift with the music, just as if you were lying in a punt on the Mere."

Ann looked pleased. "That is what I was trying to convey."

Evening Song was not the solemn, prayerful melodies that the listeners might have expected but a confusion of voices that, little by little, changed to individual lines and finished with a thrilling four-part canon.

"A very neat fugue," Mr Forbes complimented her. "What is the main theme?"

Ann laughed. "It is what Thomas called my chicken song—an old French song I found at Swanmere and taught the others one evening."

"Excellent. Well, Miss Overton, if you would like to spend Mondays with us, I should be delighted to help you in your endeavours. I would love to work with a musician of your calibre."

"May I, really?" Ann looked from Mr Forbes to his wife to Rosa and Julian.

"Please do come, Miss Overton," Mrs Forbes said. "Our house is always full of musicians—I think you will find it most interesting, and I shall be glad to have another female about," she added with a smile.

When the tea-tray was brought in, Tabitha went to help her mother pour while Thomas and Jasper handed round cups of tea and coffee. This task completed, Thomas took his own cup and came to the sofa where Chloe sat alone. "May I?"

"Please do, Thomas. It must be two years and more since we last met. I cannot believe that your mother did not tell us you were appointed tutor to Jasper. How long have you been with him?"

"Last July, at the end of the Trinity term. The duke wrote to my tutor, whom he knew from his own days at Oxford, looking for a recommendation. Jasper was due to start at Harrow in September, and they wondered if a tutor might suit him better. They wished to try it out over the summer and it was already mid-July."

"The experiment was obviously a success, for here you are. You and Jasper must have got on well together from the beginning."

"We did. That summer with Hal and Robert helped me plan not only his lessons but also his free time. I knew that it was important to keep him busy, not only at his desk but also to tire him out physically."

"That must be easier in the summer, or at least in fine weather."

"We ride every day unless the rain makes it really impossible, we fence regularly, and the dancing master comes once a week. He also plays battledore and shuttlecock with Lady Tabitha."

"That should keep both of you out of mischief," Chloe said with a little smile. "Do you like it?"

"I like teaching Jasper. He has an enquiring mind and I am free to order any books I think will benefit him. In some cases, we learn together. But I am also aware that it is an exceptional situation and I am unlikely to find another with such an interested pupil and congenial parents. But enough about me. Tell me what you have been doing in the past years. My mother said you went abroad."

"Yes, with my cousins, the Glazebrooks. And later I stayed with my mother and Lord Stephen at his aunt's estate near Nice."

"It was such a nice surprise to see Thomas," Chloe said to Ann after the guests had left. "He was always very easy to talk to. It was as if only weeks and not years had passed since we had last met. Isn't it strange how some people are like that? It was the same with you, but we had been corresponding while we were apart."

"He writes to Hal and Robert."

"Does he? Did you know he was with the Gracechurches?"

"No. Even if he had told them, Hal would not have thought it worthy of mention."

"I suppose not. It was a very pleasant evening, wasn't it? I had imagined a duke and duchess must be very stiff-rumped, but they are not at all."

"It was wonderful! I couldn't believe it when Mr Forbes offered to let me work with him, as he put it. I can't wait for Monday."

"He is not a teacher, is he? Will you have to pay him?"

"I never thought about that. I mean, he was a fellow-guest. Would it not be insulting to offer him money?"

"I don't know. Thomas and the governess were there, after all. Shall I ask Mamma? She can find out discreetly."

"Would you, Chloe, please?"

"Lord Stephen says that Mr Forbes takes select pupils for the love of music," Chloe reported some days later. "There is no question of paying him—he is comfortably off. He seems to be as fanatical about music as you are, Ann."

~~~

"Well?" Julian asked the following Monday evening when, eyes sparkling, Ann burst into the blue drawing-room where he, Rosa, and Chloe sat on the floor rolling a ball to not-quite-two-year-old Kate. The infant's great-grandparents remained seated on chairs but nudged the ball with their feet whenever it came within reach.

"It was wonderful! You can have no idea!" Ann's words tumbled out. "There were four others. In the morning, we took it in turns to play something, then Mr Forbes discussed it with us and made some suggestion as to how we might develop it. Then we each worked on our own piece. At one o'clock, Mrs Forbes called us to a nuncheon. Afterwards, we played our pieces again, but this time without any comment and then, we made music together, 'just for fun', Mr Forbes said. Mrs Forbes and Cecilia joined us. I had brought *Il es Bel et Bon*—of course they all had no problem picking it up. Then Cecilia played—she is very good, and the others played in twos or threes. It was wonderful," she finished.

"Who are the others?" Rosa asked.

"Let me see—there was Mr Bradley; he plays the cello, and has quite a deep voice. Mr Dennison plays the viola, and also the viola da gamba, which is quite an old instrument, supported on the knee, not the shoulder. Mr Hayes plays the flute and the piano. His voice is middling. Mr Dennison has a most unusual voice, more like a woman's contralto. He also plays the harpsichord. They sang a madrigal together; it was beautiful. Mr Forbes gave me the music for a piano trio by Mozart—he, Mr Bradley, and I will play it together next week. And we are all to practise a new madrigal."

"She wasn't interested in them as men, only as musicians," Rosa remarked after Ann had gone to dress for dinner. "We must find out more about them, if she is to spend time with them every week."

"What do you mean?"

"Are they single or married? Are they gentlemen? Should we invite them and their wives, if they have them, to our ball, for instance? I think we should invite the Forbeses to dinner, don't you? It is very good of him to take such an interest in Ann."

Chapter Three

Dearest Cynthia,

Not only has the rain finally stopped, but it promises to remain fine today. What do you say to ices at Gunter's at three o'clock? Ann and I may have the barouche-landau and can collect you at a quarter to if you are agreeable.
Please say yes! The footman will wait for your answer.
    Yours etc.
    Chloe

Cynthia Glazebrook jumped up from the breakfast table to hastily scribble Yes, please on the bottom of her friend's note. She carefully refolded it and readdressed it to Miss Loring before handing it to the waiting servant.

"An assignation, Sis?" her brother Martin asked as he poured himself another cup of coffee.

"Yes, with Chloe and Ann at Gunter's."

"What? Is Chloe in town? How did I miss it?"

"They came up for the drawing-room while you were away."

"Did you go, too?"

"To the drawing-room? Yes, with Mamma. It was interesting to experience it when I did not have to be presented, but it did leave me wondering about the purpose of Royalty. Before, Kings governed and led armies but, when you come to think of it, they have no purpose today other than ordering Society."

"In what way?"

"We all take our place from them; they decree the order of precedence and have the power to advance people if they choose. It is on their say-so that one man is ranked higher than another. Yet rank says nothing about a man's intrinsic worth, does it?"

"No. In fact, one may argue that frequently the one is inverse proportion to the other. You are very observant, Sis."

"Society is such a strange construction, I find. Look how quickly everything collapsed in France during the Revolution. But then they had an Emperor, and now Fat Louis is King again. Was it all for nothing, do you think?"

Martin eyed his sister over the rim of his cup. He had not realised she thought so deeply about such matters. In many ways, she echoed his own reservations about English society. "I don't think so," he said slowly. "Some seeds, or roots, however we describe them, must have remained. The calls for reform grow louder here, for example. Their proponents must be encouraged by France, not to mention the success of the American colonies in breaking away from us."

"Thank you," Cynthia said suddenly.

"For what?"

"For taking me seriously. Mamma would go into fits if she heard me—berate me as unladylike, or a bluestocking; I don't know which is worse in her eyes. And Papa would smile in that condescending way of his, and say something like, 'It is the way of the world, Cynthia. Without structure there would be anarchy'. Both would say I should keep such views to myself if I wish to find a husband. Would you like it if you had to watch your tongue all the time?"

Martin laughed. "In a way, I do. At least when I am with young ladies—be sure to say nothing to alarm them. I can't talk to them the way I talk to other men. It's quite boring, frankly."

"As if you're only engaging a little of your mind and are afraid to go deeper?"

"Precisely. In Weymouth you and Chloe talked about the criteria you would look for in a husband. Is that one of them—to be able to have a proper discussion with him?"

Cynthia nodded. "But it is practically impossible to learn whether you can or not—you cannot go apart with him and, in a group, the conversation rarely rises above the commonplace."

"Especially at a ball or a party, when there is a lot of coming and going. That is one reason why I decided to read for the Bar— I wanted a more substantial occupation than just the society merry-go-round. Besides, a more thorough understanding of the law must always be useful. One could say it is the first step to reform."

"You are fortunate to have such an opportunity."

She didn't sound bitter, more resigned that such a way was not for her, he thought. "But are there no such opportunities for you? Look here." He flipped open the newspaper and showed her an advertisement. "Walker's Lectures on Astronomy at the Theatre Royal, demonstrating the Eidouranion or Large, Transparent Orrery. Would that interest you?"

"Let me see." She took the paper from him. "Oh, it sounds wonderful. But I can't go on my own, and Mamma would not take me."

"I should be happy to escort you."

Her face lit up. "Really? Thank you, Martin. It is very good of you!"

He was embarrassed by her response. He should have paid more attention to her, he thought, and not just seen her through their parents' eyes as an obstreperous daughter unamenable to guidance. She would be twenty-one soon, after all.

"Do you want to marry?" he asked abruptly.

To his surprise, she hesitated. At last she said, "I would like to have my own establishment, but I don't know that I could trust any man enough to hand myself over to him, body and soul. Father has said he will dower me generously; why should I not have the money myself and remain an old maid. I can be aunt to your children," she added with a smile.

"Would you not rather have children of your own?"

"And risk dying in childbed?" She looked at the clock. "I must go. I am to accompany Mamma to the milliners. Martin, you won't repeat what I said, will you? Mamma would be furious. Here she is, going to the trouble and expense of a second Season and I'm not even trying to catch a husband."

He opened the door for her. "Don't worry, Sis. Mum's the word."

~~~

When Cynthia came down the stairs that afternoon, Martin was waiting in the hall. "I must pay my respects to Chloe. I haven't seen her since we left Nice the year before last."

Before she could reply, they heard the rattle of a carriage drawing up outside, followed by the sharp rat-tat of the door knocker.

"Miss Loring, to take up Miss Glazebrook," the footman said, and stood back to allow the brother and sister to pass.

Martin removed his hat with a flourish and handed Cynthia into the barouche-landau. Once she was seated, he bowed to Chloe. "I am delighted to see you again, Cousin."

"And I you, Martin. Do you accompany us?"

"No, no. I'm not so rag-mannered as to intrude where I am not invited. I merely wished to say, 'good day'. It is too long since we met."

"Indeed it is. Pray do join us."

"If I may." He took his seat beside Cynthia, opposite the two young ladies.

"Do you remember Miss Overton?" Chloe asked. "We gathered at Lady Ransford's on our way to Swanmere three years ago."

Martin raised his hat to the quiet girl sitting beside Chloe. "Yes, of course. You're a dab hand at the pianoforte, aren't you?"

She didn't bridle or brush off the compliment, but smiled and said, "I love to play."

Several open carriages had already drawn up in Berkeley Square where waiters were kept busy running across the road from Gunter's Tea Shop with trays of glasses containing sweetmeats and ices. While ladies remained seated, their male escorts lounged nonchalantly against the railings, nodding to acquaintances who strolled past, assessing the occupants of the carriages with a knowing eye.

I suppose we return the compliment, but I hope more discreetly, Cynthia thought, looking past Chloe and Ann to the couple sitting in the curricle behind them. They were the Nugents,

The Husband Criteria

Lord Nugent's heir and his sister. She remembered them from last year. Mr Nugent was well turned-out, as befitted a gentleman of the *ton*, if a little too dandified for her taste. He was talking to a tall man who had to be one of the most handsome men Cynthia had ever seen. He had removed his hat to bow to Miss Nugent, revealing neat brown curls that framed a noble forehead and classical features. His broad shoulders tapered to a narrow waist, his long legs were displayed to perfection in pale pantaloons and glossy boots, his plain dark blue coat and silver-embroidered waistcoat sat just so, with no hint of the dandy or the beau. Lord Marfield, she recalled suddenly from last Season, recognizing his expression of barely restrained boredom. Earl Benton's son and heir had not paid any attention to insignificant debutantes. Would it kill him to smile, she thought indignantly. Really, he epitomised everything she loathed about the *ton*.

Almost as if he felt her gaze, he turned and looked straight at her. Training required her to lower her eyes modestly but some instinct made her meet his eyes impassively. He bowed slightly—the movement of his head was too deliberate to be a nod—and turned away. Just then the waiter arrived with their orders and she gave herself up to the delight of pineapple ice just as the Nugents drove off.

"Mmm, this is delicious," she said after the first cool spoonful had slid down her throat.

"Nectar," Chloe agreed.

"Ambrosia," Ann said. "Do you not agree, Mr Glazebrook?"

"Most refreshing," Martin answered.

"I thought it was you, Glazebrook." The deep voice sent shivers down Cynthia's spine. It was the gentleman who had spoken to the Nugents.

45

Martin turned. "Marfield. I had not realised you were in town. I thought you still in Melton Mowbray."

"No. The going turned very soft."

"It was wet and windy for the last week or so, here too. Today is the first real spring day. Everyone seems to have had a fancy for ices," Martin replied.

"Indeed." Instead of strolling on, the niceties observed, Lord Marfield turned his gaze on the three young ladies and then looked expectantly, at Martin, as if to say, *Why do you not introduce me?*

"Ah," Martin said. "Ladies, may I present Lord Marfield? Marfield, happy to introduce my sister, our cousin Miss Loring, and Miss Overton."

"Ladies." Lord Marfield raised his hat with a flourish and bowed to each in turn. "With three such charming newcomers, the Season looks brighter already."

Cynthia groaned inwardly. She detested such spurious compliments and despised their makers. Chloe and Ann seemed to share her views, for neither reacted with flirtatious flutterings.

After a pause, during which his lordship's expectant smile faded, Chloe said, "I am looking forward to getting to know London. Which sights would you consider are not to be missed, my lord?"

"I am afraid I would not know what to recommend for a young lady, Miss Loring."

Seeing Chloe flush at this snub, Cynthia remarked, "Either you move in very circumscribed circles, my lord, or go about with your eyes closed."

Lord Marfield's dark eyebrows twitched together but before he could respond, Martin said, "A hit, Marfield. You don't have a sister to keep you up to the mark, do you?"

The Husband Criteria

"I do, but fortunately she is too occupied with her nursery to nag me. Will you be at Angelo's in the morning, Glazebrook? I'll see you there, then." With another bow, and a general "Ladies", he left them.

"What an obnoxious man. He as good as called you a nag, Cynthia!" Chloe said.

"I think you took him by surprise, Chloe," Ann said. "He was expecting quite a different response to his remark."

"I never know what to say to that sort of thing," Chloe admitted.

"Especially when you know it might have been said to any lady," Ann agreed. "It's as if they cast a line, hoping that a fish will bite. Older men are the worst; why should they think we should be interested in someone twice our age?"

"It is best not to encourage them," Cynthia said.

Martin looked from one to another. "I can see this is going to be an interesting Season."

~~~

Rafe Marfield shook his head as he continued past the stationary carriages, lifting his hat from time to time to acknowledge a hand raised in greeting or a smiling nod, but he was not tempted to linger. His pace became brisker; as soon as an opportunity offered to pass between two carriages, he crossed to the pavement opposite and soon had left the Square behind him. He didn't know whether he was annoyed or amused, and if his sentiments owed more to his own behaviour or to the three ladies who had so successfully discomfited him.

What had prompted him to stop and speak to Glazebrook? He knew him from Angelo's but, with four or five years between them, they had never been more than acquaintances. They were both tall but the younger man was less powerfully built. They had more or less the same reach and Angelo had from time to time paired them; initially with Rafe as the more experienced partner but Glazebrook had consistently improved until by the end of last Season he could hold his own.

Rafe had assumed him one of the countless Sprigs of Fashion who came to Town for the Season, dividing their time between the purely masculine haunts of clubs, hells, and cribs, the ballrooms and drawing-rooms of the *beau monde* where the ladies reigned supreme, and the shadowed *demi-monde* where a gentleman was welcome but a lady must leave the field to the demi-reps. He had not expected to find him squiring three of the prettiest girls he had seen for a long time.

His interest had been piqued when Miss Glazebrook met his eyes so calmly. All three had responded to his introduction with murmurs of 'my lord', accompanied by polite smiles. Was it their apparent lack of interest that had provoked his compliment? He had not succeeded in fluttering them and Miss Loring's question had caught him so off balance that he had no idea how to reply. He had not intended to put her to the blush and deserved Miss Glazebrook's set-down, he supposed. He liked her for coming to the defence of her friend.

He had automatically turned into Dover Street but hesitated when he reached his own front door. He was too restless to go in; he would continue on to St James's Street, look in at the Chess Club. Francis Nugent was squiring his sister, but surely someone else would be there to give him a game.

Chapter Four

A steady procession of exquisitely dressed guests made their way up the grand staircase of Gracechurch House, bowed and curtsied to the duke and duchess, and continued in to the great drawing-room. This was the first larger gathering of the *beau monde*, the taking stock at the beginning of the Season. Who had not come to Town? Who made their first appearance? Whose situation had changed? For some, the absence of a familiar face made a loss real; for others, the appearance of a new generation brought home the passage of years.

Mothers of marriageable daughters assessed the lineages and fortunes of the Season's bachelors who, in turn, appraised the debutantes for beauty, biddability, and potential dowery. Who would be the successes, who the failures? Would this year see a new Beauty take the stage or a grand match made, one that would be spoken of for years to come? The *ton* drifted and eddied through the room, little clusters forming and breaking apart again.

Last year, Cynthia had felt the *ton* was comprised of numerous intimate circles in which everyone but she had a place. This year, she confidently nodded and smiled at the various groups, pausing now and then to exchange a few words. She no longer felt compelled to trail in her mother's wake; when Mamma became

49

involved in a longer discussion with the wife of another Member of Parliament, Cynthia and Martin did not linger.

"Good evening, Miss Glazebrook." Miss Nugent turned from her conversation with Lady Tamm. "I saw you at Gunter's earlier. There is nothing like that first ice on the first spring day, is there?"

"It seemed as if everyone felt the same urge to be outdoors," Cynthia agreed.

"Precisely. It is the real beginning of the Season." Miss Nugent looked around the long room. "These early parties are the most pleasant, I think. They also give one the opportunity to get to know those who are new in town, like the family with Lord Stephen and his wife. I wonder who they are."

"Dashed pretty, the two girls," Mr Nugent commented. "One so fair and one so dark."

"The fair one is Lady Stephen's daughter, Miss Loring. The other, Miss Overton, is her cousin," Cynthia said, "and the couple are Sir Julian Swann-Loring and his wife. Sir Julian and Miss Loring are also cousins of ours," she added helpfully, "but Miss Overton is not, as the connection is through his mother, not his father."

"Huh?" Mr Nugent said. "That seems very complicated."

"Not at all," his sister said. "It's like us and the Malvins. Julian and Mattie are our cousins, because their mother was our father's sister, but the other four are not—although we have always regarded them as such, for it doesn't do to make such distinctions within a family."

"Talk of the devil!" Mr Nugent said, as an elegant gentleman joined them. "Are you on your own, Matthew?"

"Julian and Millie are over there." The newcomer gestured vaguely to the other side of the room. "My parents are in Gloucestershire."

"With Arabella?" Miss Nugent said. "I miss her—the Season will not be the same without her."

"I suppose not." He bowed to Cynthia. "Good evening, Miss Glazebrook, Glazebrook."

"Good evening, Mr Malvin."

Matthew Malvin. His sister Arabella had made a splendid match last Season. She and Miss Nugent had known each other from childhood and had appeared to be great friends. It must be like losing a sister, Cynthia thought, as another couple came up and she and Martin moved on.

Chloe and Ann were at the centre of an animated group. However, as they neared it, Cynthia noticed that once they had been introduced, people tended to step back and talk to their neighbours, leaving the two girls alone.

Once greetings had been exchanged, she gently urged Martin to change position so that they formed a group of four. "It's as if they are planets orbiting the sun," she murmured. "They cannot remain but are impelled onwards."

Chloe groaned. "That reminds me of the problems from Butler's Exercises on the Globe. *To find the place of a given planet in the Ecliptic for any given time.* It didn't matter how often I tried; I could never do them. In the end, Mamma agreed I need not attempt them. I love to look up at the night sky, and make out the constellations, but I just could not transfer them to the Globe."

"It is as well you were called Chloe, then, and not Urania," Martin remarked.

She looked at him, horrified. "That is not a real name."

"It is," Cynthia said. "She is the Muse of Astronomy."

"In ancient times. Do you know anybody who is called it today?" Chloe demanded. "You might as well be called Hercules or, or…"

"Aesop," Ann supplied.

Martin threw his hand up at the girls' laughter. "I give in. Chloe is a much prettier name; it suits you better."

"A compliment! I thank you, sir."

"Make the most of it," Cynthia advised her. "Martin is not given to making compliments."

"I do, but only when they are deserved."

At this lofty pronouncement, the three girls glared indignantly at him.

"For that, you must pay a compliment to each of us before the night is out," Cynthia said.

"Only if you return the favour," he retorted.

The three looked at each other. "Done!" Chloe said.

When the others nodded, she smiled brightly at Martin.

"Indeed, Mr Glazebrook, you have a very pretty wit."

Martin accepted this with a smug nod, but looked uncomfortable when Ann followed with, "I vow, Mr Glazebrook, your sparkling wit matches your eyes."

Cynthia smirked as she drawled, "With such a charming newcomer, the Season looks brighter already."

"Sis!" Martin said, outraged, at which the three girls collapsed into laughter.

"Rather trite, Miss Glazebrook," a deep voice said behind them and Cynthia turned to look up into Lord Marfield's impassive face.

The Husband Criteria

Engulfed by a wave of mortification, she sharply bit the inside of her lip, hoping to stave off the blush she felt creeping into her cheeks. Forcing herself not to lower her gaze, she said, "Indeed, my lord. I fear my muse has deserted me and I must resort to lesser inspiration."

"That is sad indeed." A little smile glimmered in his eyes; the cast of his features became less severe and he turned to the couple who had come up with him. "Lady Elizabeth, Hope, may I present Miss Glazebrook, Miss Loring, and Miss Overton? And Mr Glazebrook. Ladies, Mr Glazebrook, Lady Elizabeth Hope, and Lord Hope."

"Oh, we know Mr and Miss Glazebrook," Lady Elizabeth said, smiling, "and are happy to meet Miss Loring and Miss Overton."

Her brother bowed. "Now, do tell us what diverted you so?"

"Just a silly joke, not worth repeating," Martin said hastily. "Have you seen Kean's Macbeth?"

Not long afterwards, they were joined by Mr Malvin, and Cynthia was satisfied that Chloe and Ann no longer appeared to be unknown newcomers but were among a group that included four eligible bachelors, two of whom were peers' heirs. First impressions were so important; it had taken her some time to find her feet last year, and she would spare her friends the experience if she could.

As soon as the sound of sedate trios and quartets gave way to the sinuous invitation of the waltz, the first pairs were formed, the gentlemen turning to the ladies nearest to them. Martin danced with Lady Elizabeth, Chloe with Lord Hope, Ann with Mr Malvin, and Cynthia, to her hidden dismay, with Lord Marfield.

To give the devil his due, he had neither hesitated nor let his eyes stray to other young ladies in the group, but had bowed as soon as Hope had offered his arm to Chloe, and said, "Miss Glazebrook, may I have the pleasure?"

Were it not for the lowering thought that this distinction was due to nothing more than proximity and politeness, she would have savoured it more. They were well matched, she discovered. His clasp was neither too firm nor too loose, but secure enough that she could follow his lead and he never lost sight of the other dancers, skillfully avoiding collisions while making full use of the floor space available. With an inward sigh, she gave herself up to the joy of the dance. Although they did not speak, there was an intangible connection between them, deeper than physical touch, arising from the subtle matching and mirroring of steps, the fleeting locking of eyes during a turn or the brief smiles that marked the end of a complicated figure.

When the music stopped, they smiled in mutual appreciation of a pleasure shared. "Thank you," he said as she rose from her curtsey. She wondered what he would do next. Etiquette required him to escort her back to her mother or other chaperon, but she had not been standing with them. He offered her his arm, and they fell in behind other couples who were 'taking a turn of the room'.

"You dance very well, Miss Glazebrook. One has the impression that it is a joy rather than a duty for you."

"Indeed it is, especially when my partner is equally proficient."

He laughed. "Yes, there is nothing worse than a partner who seems always to count their steps or continually supervise their feet, as if they might suddenly declare their independence and embark on a very different figure than the one intended."

"Or who blithely gets the steps of a country dance confused so that one has to tug them into place. Worst of all is the partner who thinks they can dance the quadrille."

"Perhaps we should insist everyone passes a proficiency test," he suggested.

"Almack's could issue badges, and insist that sets are made up of dancers of similar standard, with a separate room reserved for the lowest level. A patroness would have to approve any promotion out of it."

"We, of course, would be in the highest category."

He uttered this absurdity with a completely straight face and she was delighted by the way he had entered into her flight of fancy. "Like a *premier danseur* at the Opéra in Paris?" she suggested.

"Do they have sashes as well?"

"Perhaps, when not in stage costume. I don't know."

They had reached the Swann-Lorings. Chloe had already returned and was chatting to the little group that had again clustered around her. Cynthia slipped her hand from Marfield's arm, saying, "Thank you, sir."

"Thank you, Miss Glazebrook." He bowed and strolled away.

She had done that very neatly, Marfield thought appreciatively. Much as he had enjoyed their dance, he did not want to dance with her twice in succession. A naïve or duplicitous girl might have taken advantage of the situation by clinging to him until he would either have to reject her publicly or let his hand be forced. The Season was young—there would be plenty of opportunities to dance with Miss Glazebrook again.

"You and Marfield got on famously yesterday," Chloe said to Cynthia. The three girls had gathered in Chloe's sitting-room at Swanmere House to review the previous evening's entertainment.

"Yes, he is not as haughty as he appears. We were talking about the horrors of bad dancing partners." The others laughed as she explained their idea of dancing badges. "We should add them to our Husband Criteria."

"Husband Criteria?" Ann looked from one to the other.

"I'd forgotten that," Chloe said. "When we were in Weymouth two years ago, before either of us had come out, we talked about what we would look for in a husband, and how artificial an environment the Season is—the worst place to find the man one would wish to spend one's life with." She went to the little writing-desk and began to flick through the pages of a notebook. "Yes, here it is. The points are not ranked but in a mingle-mangle as they came to us." She took a breath. "He should be good-looking, but not an Adonis, well-dressed, but not a dandy, and definitely not slovenly. A good rider who also respects your riding abilities."

"Yes. There is nothing worse than being treated as a helpless Miss," Cynthia put in, "or having him ride too close to you, as if he must be ready to seize your reins."

"An interesting and interested conversationalist," Chloe continued. "He doesn't hold forth interminably, and expect you just to say 'yes and amen' but listens to what you have to say."

"That's really important," Ann agreed. "He should also share some of your interests. I could not marry a man who detested music, for example."

The Husband Criteria

"Yes. He must be kind-hearted, care about his family and be on good terms with them. If he is a widower, he should be a loving father, not just looking for a wife to whom he can abdicate all responsibility for his children."

"How are you to discover that?" Ann asked.

"That is difficult," Chloe said. "One can observe his behaviour towards others, listen to how he speaks of his family, but ideally one would have to spend some time with him, say at a house-party—long enough for him to let the company mask fall."

"Easier said than done," Cynthia said gloomily. "What about family and fortune?"

"A gentleman, of course. He need not be wealthy, but able to support a wife and family," Chloe said at once.

"Not a fortune-hunter," Cynthia said.

"Nor a gambler or a rake," Ann added. "I suppose we are dependent on our men-folk to ascertain those aspects of his character."

"We must keep our eyes and ears open," Chloe said.

"This is all very well," Cynthia said suddenly, "but what about attraction?"

"Attraction?"

"You know, that indefinable quality that draws you to one gentleman rather than another, has you all aflutter in the ballroom, hoping he will invite you to stand up with him?"

The three girls looked at one another.

"Do you mean love?" Ann asked.

"Not exactly. I think this comes before love. You know what I mean, don't you? The tremulous feeling when he smiles at you, or the way you dance in perfect harmony?"

"It has to be there too," Chloe said, "but it can't be the be-all and end-all, can it? What was that phrase of your old nurse?"

"'There's more to marriage than four bare legs in a bed'?" Cynthia recited. "But at the end of the day, that is what it will come down to, will it not? So it is essential that we do not find him distasteful in any way."

A more solemn silence fell. If pressed, they might admit to having dreamt of a lover's kisses, and were aware that, in the old phrase, a bedding followed a wedding, that this year's bride was next year's young mother. But they had never considered the realities of this natural progression in terms of that shadowy figure to whom 'one day' they would cede complete control of their person, becoming, as the law insisted, a *femme couverte*, subordinate to him in all things.

Chapter Five

It was customary for the ladies of Benton House to breakfast in their rooms and then gather in the morning room to discuss plans for the day. This allowed the countess to consult her guests and assure herself of the welfare of any older relatives. This morning, she sat with her mother-in-law, the dowager countess, the latter's unmarried sister-in-law, Lady Georgina, and Miss Cassandra Benton, an impoverished cousin who was Lady Georgina's companion.

"How goes the Season, Charlotte?" the dowager asked.

"Calmly," Lady Benton replied. "There is a different mood this year, less antagonistic, more harmonious. Instead of various Beauties holding rival courts, everyone mixes together, no one appears to be excluded."

"Most refreshing. I wonder how long it will last."

Lady Georgina snorted. "What a namby-pambical sentiment! Let us hope that some new Incomparable will emerge to stir things up a little. What is a Season without the spice of a lost reputation or a missed chance?"

"What indeed, Aunt? It would never do to disappoint the scandalmongers."

"Rafe!" Lady Benton looked up at this interjection from the doorway.

"Good morning, Mamma, Grandmamma," he said as he came into the room. He kissed them both on the cheek, before saying, "Aunt, Cousin," with a brief bow that included Miss Benton.

Delighted by this unexpected visit, Lady Benton made haste to escape. "Come up to my boudoir, my love. We can have a comfortable coze." Ignoring Lady Georgina's glare, she tucked her hand into her son's arm and led him upstairs to the cosy room where a cheerful fire combatted the March chill. Taking her accustomed seat on the canopied daybed, she waved Rafe to one of the low slipper chairs either side of the hearth.

He sat obediently and stretched out his booted legs. "The old tabby is here again, is she? She does not get sweeter with age."

"She always had a vicious tongue, and dotes on scandal of all kinds. I avoid her as much as I can. But why speak of her? Shall I ring for coffee?"

"No, thank you. I have just breakfasted."

"Now tell me what you have been doing."

"This and that. The usual round. Angelo's, The Park, Gunter's, routs, and balls."

"Gunter's? Why would one want to sit in an open carriage eating an ice now? It is still cold, despite the sun."

He shrugged. "It has become a sort of unofficial meeting-place for the younger set. It is less processional than the Park—you can invite a girl for an ice without anyone raising an eyebrow."

"Indeed?"

"Indeed. It is the latest fashion. The Season gets very tedious, as you know, ma'am, and there are always these little crazes. Who knows how long it will last."

"Much will depend on the weather, I imagine. Almack's balls start after Easter. Shall you apply for vouchers?"

"I don't know. The girls get younger every year."

"In fact, it is you who are getting older. Perhaps it is time you settled down." She had to smile at his look of horror at this pronouncement.

"Please! I beg you, ma'am. I have always valued your lack of interference in that regard. Pray do not spoil your blameless record."

"Not if you do not wish me to. But you must know you can talk to me about anything, Rafe, at any time."

His face softened. "Thank you, Mamma. But do you not find it wearying?"

"Find what wearying?"

"The Season. How many have you had? Did you marry at the end of the first one?"

She shook her head. "I did not have a Season, not to come out in, I mean."

"No?"

"I was the youngest of the family, twenty years younger than my sister Anna."

"The one who eloped with her brother's tutor? Lallie's grandparents?"

"Yes. My father was determined not to suffer another such disgrace, but at least had the wit to select a much younger man for me than he had for her. He approached your grandfather who discussed it with his wife and agreed to make it possible for your father and me to get to know one another through visits and house-parties but insisted we were not to be subject to any form of duress. Well, your father was, and is, very personable, and the first young man apart from my brothers that I had the opportunity to know, as well as being the heir to an earldom."

"And you were very pretty," Rafe offered.

"And came with a good dowry," his mother added with a faint smile. "Matters progressed quite naturally. We married in June, went to Italy on our wedding-journey, and I was presented at the Birthday drawing-room the following January." She looked into the fire, as if seeing something far away. "We danced the minuet at the birth-night ball. We were both terrified—you have no idea what an occasion it was; just the two of you before their majesties and the assembled court and nobility, all judging every step and gesture. But we managed to acquit ourselves very creditably, or so the newssheets said the next day. Then your father had to dance with another lady, because there were never enough gentlemen. I was sorry for her, because they had not had the opportunity to practise together—to dance the minuet properly, you must be really attuned to your partner."

"Like waltzing," Rafe said, reminded of dancing with Miss Glazebrook.

"I suppose," she said doubtfully. "I have not waltzed very much."

"How long were you married when my grandfather died?"

"Seventeen years."

"And you and my father lived with my grandparents all that time?"

"Yes. Of course, before your father succeeded to the title, we did not have to be in Town for the whole parliamentary session. We came after Easter, generally. That gave us some respite. Although your grandfather Benton was nothing like the despot my own father was," she added fairly. "You heard how he treated my sister."

"Indeed. Infamous!" He got up. "I had better go and see Father. Do you know why he summoned me?"

She tilted her cheek to receive his kiss. "He didn't say anything. Thank you for your visit, my love."

"Goodbye, Mamma."

~~~

"You wanted to see me, sir?"

Lord Benton got up from behind his desk. "Come in, Marfield. I trust I see you well."

"Indeed. And you, sir?"

"Well enough." He gestured towards the tray of decanters. "Madeira or claret?"

"Claret, please. Madeira for you, I suppose?" At his father's nod, Rafe filled two glasses and handed his father one. "Your good health, sir."

"And yours. Come over here, to the table."

Curious, Rafe followed him to where a large estate map had been spread out. "Ailesthorpe House?"

"It lies in South Lincolnshire—the Parts of Kesteven. A neat estate."

"Are you thinking of buying it?"

"No. It's ours—came to us through your great-grandmother. It produces about three thousand a year—less now, of course, but I'm sure we'll come about—things cannot continue to go downwards. The house itself has been let on a repairing lease for the past twenty-five years. It ends at midsummer."

"Does the tenant not wish to renew?"

"No. The thing is, Marfield, I was wondering if you would like to take it over."

"The house?"

"House and estate. I would continue your present allowance, of course, but you would have the additional income as well."

"I should live there?"

"With sole responsibility for it. Make it your home. I often wished my father would do something similar for me. There is something very enervating about knowing that your sire must die before you have any real independence or purpose in life."

"I have never allowed myself to dwell on it," Rafe said. "I hope you are good for another thirty years."

"So do I. But you're what? Twenty-seven? Are you going to twirl your thumbs for the next three decades? It's time you were thinking of setting up your nursery."

"Are you conspiring with my mother, sir?"

"About what? To prod you to the altar? No. I will not deny that we would like to see you settled, but we do not have a plan of campaign. I have not mentioned this to her either. I wanted to sound you out first. But it would mean that you have a home to offer your bride where she can be mistress from the outset."

Rafe took a breath. "You have taken me by surprise, sir. I should like to think about it."

"Excellent. I'll have the map and books sent over to you. I'll ask Hancock to inspect the house and send us a report. We would need to go and have a look at it, ride out over the land as well."

An estate in Lincolnshire. An additional three thousand a year. Set up his nursery. A bride. An establishment of his own. This was the most astonishing thing. The lease on the Dover Street house

The Husband Criteria

expired at Michaelmas; he rented it furnished, and had never been interested in imposing his own taste on it. He had wondered about taking a set in Albany or buying a hunting box somewhere in the Shires, but both had a suggestion of impermanence. Neither would be home. And while Benton might be his childhood home, and, as earl, he would later be responsible for it; it was weighed down with the detritus of centuries.

Assheton-Smith had moved last year from the Quorn to take over as Master of the Burton Hunt. How near was Ailesthorpe to Lincoln, Rafe wondered. Would he be able to host a meet? He would have to learn something about farming and land management—it was a bad idea to leave everything to your agent. Get to know the tenants—a wife would be helpful there. Suddenly, the thought of marriage did not overset him—on the contrary, he found himself considering the qualities he would look for in his bride.

Chapter Six

Looking back, no one could remember who had first dubbed them *The Three Graces*, or when the term was first used. It may have been at the Duchess of Gracechurch's *soirée*. All three were pretty girls but there was no doubt that the sum was greater than the parts. But why? They complemented one another in looks, of course; Miss Loring's fair hair was set off by Miss Glazebrook's dark locks and Miss Overton's rich brown curls. They were more or less of a height; their features uniformly pleasing, but each with a defining characteristic—Miss Glazebrook's oval eyebrows, Miss Loring's curved lips, and Miss Overton's hazel eyes. They moved beautifully and, when together, seem to lean in to one another as if to share a joke or confide a secret, but they were not stand-offish. Indeed, they were always willing to widen their circle to welcome another lady or smile at a gentleman who need not fear that he would be kept waiting on their threshold.

They were not coquettes, nor did they indulge in any sort of petty rivalry. Take us as we are, they seemed to say, as we will take you. But we will not play games with you or vie for your attention. Hardened flirts were at a loss in how to deal with a bland smile and prosaic response, while aging gallants who had patted

The Husband Criteria

a generation of female hands prior to slipping an arm around a slender waist found themselves rebuked, and retired abashed.

With their first ball of the Season approaching, the Lady Patronesses of Almack's met to decide who would be admitted to the weekly balls and who would be condemned to linger in the outer darkness.

"Lady Swann-Loring requests tickets for herself, her sister-in-law, Miss Loring, and a Miss Overton."

"Who is Miss Overton?"

"Sir Julian's cousin, I believe. She was presented together with Miss Loring."

"Miss Loring is Lord Stephen FitzCharles's stepdaughter."

"I suppose it is just a nominal connection."

"No. She is seen regularly with him and his new wife."

"Really? Dear Stephen. I cannot imagine him acting as chaperon. I don't suppose they have sought tickets?"

"Let me see. Yes, here is their application."

"We can hardly refuse them, can we?"

"That means we must approve Lady Swann-Loring's request."

"Agreed."

"Mrs Glazebrook has applied again, for herself and her daughter. One would think she would have learnt from last year. Denied?"

"Wait. Is she not—have you heard of the so-called Three Graces? They are all the rage this year."

"No."

"Yes. They are Miss Loring, Miss Overton and?"

"Miss Glazebrook. They are very close, I believe."

"And we should therefore admit the Glazebrooks? Are we to lower our standards for every foolish craze? I think not."

~~~

Mrs Glazebrook's fingers trembled as she unfolded the little note. One glance, and all was over. "They are *sorry they cannot comply with my request*. Pah! I am sorry, Cynthia. I did try, as you requested."

Cynthia put her arms around her mother. "I know, Mamma, and against your better judgement, too. I'm sorry I exposed you to another rejection from those old cats!" She stooped to pick up the piece of paper from the floor and tossed it into the fire. "There. We shall not speak of it again. You only wanted it for me, I know. Well, I shall do very well without the approval of the lady patronesses and have no intention of kowtowing to them, in the hope that they might change their minds."

Despite her brave words to her mother, Cynthia was quite cast down by the patronesses' rejection. Say what you liked, it was a public slight. Chloe and Ann had most likely received vouchers. She would have to get used to being on her own on Wednesday evenings. Her heart sank as she remembered last year's dreary Wednesday parties when those older ladies for whom Almack's had lost its appeal sent out their cards while any young ladies present shared the uncomfortable knowledge that they had been weighed in the balance and found wanting.

~~~

"What do you mean, refused?" Chloe asked indignantly.

The Husband Criteria

Cynthia shrugged. "It was the same last year. We are quite ineligible, it seems. They don't approve of nabobs, or nabob's granddaughters, apparently. Mamma was not going to apply again this year, but we thought we should because we three are together so much."

"If you may not go, we shan't go either. Shall we, Ann?"

"No, of course not," Ann replied just as Cynthia said urgently, "You mustn't do that, Chloe. I would never expect it of you; indeed, I strongly advise against it. You cannot compel the patronesses to change their minds, and it will only harm your own prospects. You would be blacklisted immediately and would never receive vouchers again. Rosa too. She will very likely apply for them when Kate comes out."

"That is seventeen years away. Almack's may no longer exist then, at least not in this way."

"At least consult Rosa and your mother or, even better, the duchess," Cynthia begged. "They will best understand the implications and ramifications of such a decision. I do not mean to be offensive but this is your first real experience of the *ton*. You have no idea how merciless it can be."

"I don't care a fig for the *ton*," Chloe said.

"Nor do I," Ann said, "but Cynthia is right—others will be affected by our behaviour."

"Very well." Chloe went to her writing desk. "I'll send a note to Gracechurch House."

Dearest Mamma,

Our vouchers for Almack's came today, but Cousin Amelia's application was refused. In the circumstances, I do not wish to attend as I fear Ann's and my presence would only emphasise their rejection, especially since some people refer to us as The Three Graces. *Ridiculous, I know, but we are great friends and do almost everything together. Cynthia is adamant that we should go; she says that our refusal would have grave consequences not only for us but also for Rosa. I promised to consult you and, if possible, the duchess—if she would be kind enough to advise us.*

Please reply by return, saying when we may call.

Your loving daughter,
Chloe.

"The Duchess of Gracechurch, Lady Stephen FitzCharles."

Chloe scrambled to her feet at the butler's announcement. "Your Grace, Mamma! How good of you to come at once." She looked at the butler. "Morris, pray inform Lady Swann-Loring that the ladies are here."

Rosa came in some minutes later, carrying Kate. After greeting the visitors, she put the baby down and looked at the three young women. "What has happened? Is something wrong?"

Mamma held out Chloe's note. "This puts it in a nutshell."

"I was waiting until I heard from Mamma to come and tell you, Rosa," Chloe explained. "I had not expected to see her and her grace so quickly."

"I see. Ah, here is the tea-tray. Chloe, will you make it, please."

Once the cups had been filled, milk and sugar dispensed, the plate of little cakes passed around, and Kate was sucking cheerfully on the rusk that always came with the tea-tray, Rosa said, "Chloe, will you explain why you no longer wish to go to Almack's?"

Chloe suddenly felt herself back in the schoolroom, called to account by Miss Fancourt. She squared her shoulders and looked her former governess in the eye. "Cynthia and I have been friends since Papa's house party three years ago. Both the Glazebrooks and the Ransfords have been very good to me. Remember that Grandmamma and I stayed with the Ransfords while you were on your honeymoon, and Mrs Glazebrook was kind enough to invite me to Weymouth and then to France the next year." She paused and laid her hand on her mother's. "I will forever be grateful that I was in Nice when it was most important."

Her mother turned her hand to grip Chloe's but she said nothing.

"Then this year, we three—Cynthia, Ann, and I—have been together almost every day since the Drawing-Room. Cynthia and Martin made it easy for Ann and me to get to know the *ton*. Acquaintanceship grows quickly once you have made the first connections and they provided them for us. We now have a pleasant circle of friends. People are used to seeing us together. Calling us The Three Graces is foolish if flattering, but the fact is that we are linked in society's view." She took a deep breath. "If only Ann and I are seen at Almack's, Cynthia's absence will not be overlooked, as it might have been otherwise, and the whispering will start. I refuse to be made into a rod to beat my friend's back."

There was silence after Chloe finished speaking, then Mamma said, "Flora, you are most *au fait* with the *ton* and the *beau monde*. Is Chloe's assessment accurate, do you think?"

"I fear so," the duchess replied. "Scandalmongers love a new *on-dit*, and Miss Glazebrook's absence when the other two are there would give rise to a lot of petty speculation."

"What will happen if we do not go?" Rosa asked. "I assume we would have to return the voucher. What reason do we give?"

"None," the duchess said firmly. "You present your compliments and beg to withdraw your application for vouchers this year. Enclose the voucher with the note. It will put the cat among the pigeons, but that can't be helped."

"And when the girls' absence is noted?" Mamma asked.

"There will be whispering, of course. Some will assume that you have all been refused vouchers, and wonder why. You may lose some dancing partners, girls."

"If we do, they are well lost," Ann said.

"I don't care," Chloe said. "This will successfully separate the chaff from the wheat."

"A useful test of character," Cynthia agreed.

"And may receive fewer invitations, and acceptances to your ball, for example," the duchess continued.

"So be it," Chloe said.

"I must talk to Stephen, but we shall send our voucher back as well," Mamma said. "I only wanted to go because you would be going, Chloe."

"Well, it is certainly going to be an interesting Season," the duchess said.

"Thank you so much for your advice, ma'am," Chloe said. "I am most grateful."

"As am I, to all of you." Cynthia had tears in her eyes. "I cannot express what this means to me. I know Mamma will be most appreciative. She only applied this year because I thought it would look odd if you did and we did not."

"It was a very difficult situation," the duchess said sympathetically. "A final word of advice—offer no explanations, no excuses. I imagine the patronesses will not lower themselves to seek one, and if anyone else is so ill-bred as to comment, do not respond. If asked do you go to Almack's, simply say, 'no'. If asked why not, ignore the question."

"What if they press us?" Ann asked.

"Change the subject—ask if they have visited the new church of St Marylebone. It was consecrated at the beginning of February," Rosa suggested. "We'll visit it so that you can describe it if necessary."

"I believe there is a new organ there," Ann said. "I'll ask Mr Forbes if he can arrange for us to hear it played."

~~~

"I hope we did the right thing," Rosa said afterwards to her husband. "She was so insistent."

"She is very level-headed, and if she has considered it carefully, we must respect her decision. Will you mind if you are banished from Almack's for evermore? Remember, when I succeed my grandfather, we shall have to spend several months in Town each year."

"Not at all. Lady Ransford was able to procure a voucher for me two years ago, if you remember. It is a dull evening if you are not on the look-out for a husband. A terrible crush and dreadful refreshments."

~~~

"Where did you say we were going?" Hal Overton asked. He and his schoolfriend, Rosa's brother Robert, had arrived at Swanmere House the previous day for the Easter vacation.

"To visit a new church and hear the organ played," Ann said. "You must be on your best behaviour. The Duke and Duchess of Gracechurch are coming with their children. So are the Glazebrooks—you met them at Lady Ransford's when we went to Swanmere, remember? And Mr and Mrs Forbes and their children, Ambrose and Cecilia. I study music with him once a week. Chloe's mother will be there too, with her husband, Lord Stephen FitzCharles."

The two boys looked at one another. "Are you sure we should come?" Robert asked. "We are not used to dukes and lords and ladies."

"Nonsense. You go on very well with Cousin Swanmere," Ann said. "Perhaps Thomas Musgrave will be there too. He is tutor to the duke's son, Lord Jasper."

Hal's face brightened. "I should like to see Thomas again."

"I'm sure you will. He calls sometimes when he is free, but Rosa was going to invite him to bring Lord Jasper one day while you are here. And Julian has offered to take you up in his curricle today."

"Prime!" Hal cried. "We'll come, won't we, Rob?"

~~~

The plump beadle bowed deeply to the group gathered on the steps of St Marylebone Church. "Your Graces, my lords, my ladies and gentlemen. Pray enter."

The Husband Criteria

After the usual flurry of deferrals and cries of 'after you', they moved into the church, only to pause on the threshold, awed by the wave of sound pouring down from the organ above the altar.

"Go in, go in," Charles Forbes, who had arranged the visit, including organist, said from behind them.

They followed the beadle up the aisle between rows of box pews to where a bonneted and shawled woman busily unlocked doors and dipped curtsies as she encouraged them to take the proffered seats, pocketing the sixpences and shillings pressed into her expectantly curved hand with more curtsies.

A double gallery ran around both sides of the church, dimming the light from the windows. What would it be like on a dark winter morning, Chloe wondered. Would the few lamps manage to dissipate the gloom or would the congregation be lulled into a half-sleep? When she turned to Ann to comment, she saw that her friend sat with her eyes shut, carried away by the music.

Ann was completely engrossed in unravelling the intricate lines of harmony and melody that flowed from the massive pipes arrayed right and left of the man sitting in the centre of the great instrument, his back to the church. He lifted his hands and waited until the last reverberations had died away before starting again with a strident fanfare that buffeted the ears. In the pew in front, Tabitha put her head in her hands, overwhelmed by the torrent of sound.

Soon the tone moderated and more subtle harmonies were to be heard before the music rose again into a triumphant close. After some minutes a tall, long-limbed man nimbly skirted the base of the massive pulpit that dominated the front of the church and came down the aisle towards them. He was somewhat dishevelled; his fair hair needed a trim and his coat and trousers were sadly wrinkled. But none of this mattered when he smiled. His face lit up when he spied Mr Forbes. "Well, Charles? What do you think of her? Isn't she splendid? What a sound! I have not yet explored all the possibilities."

This was the musician who had so entranced her. Ann had to speak to him. Rising, she began to edge past Chloe, Rosa, and Julian.

"What did you make of the instrument, Miss Overton?" Mr Forbes said as soon as she reached them.

"It sounds truly splendid. I have never heard anything like it. Thank you, sir," she added to the organist.

"Allow me to introduce Mr Prescott. Prescott, this is Miss Overton, a fellow-musician."

"Very happy to meet you, Miss Overton. Would you like to see the organ? I was just about to invite Forbes here to step into the loft with me."

"Yes, please."

"What instruments do you play?" he asked as he led them to the hidden stairs.

"Pianoforte, harpsichord, spinet. Also guitar a little."

"Have you ever played the organ?"

"No, but I should love to." Ann looked at the array of keyboards, stops, and pedals. "There seems to be so much to remember."

"You quickly become accustomed to it." He grinned at her. "You still only have two hands and two feet." He sat on the bench. "You probably know this," he said as he began to play a familiar air by Handel, showing her how he could vary the sound by adjusting the stops. "Why don't you play, and I'll do the stops."

"Which keyboard should I use?"

"I'll guide you. You'll soon get the knack of it."

Ann couldn't resist. After a faltering start, she found the rhythm although she jumped when, without warning, trumpets suddenly blared from the pipes above her.

"That was wonderful," she said when she was finished. "Thank you, Mr Prescott."

"Now I suppose we should let Charles have a go," he said.

"May we come up?" Jasper called from below.

"If you promise not to touch anything," Mr Prescott replied.

Ann was inspecting the pipes. "They look like large wind instruments. How do they get air?"

"Through a bellows," Mr Prescott replied. "There are always boys who are happy to earn a few pence by pumping the bellows."

"May I try?" Jasper asked eagerly.

"And I?" Ambrose chimed in.

"Why not? Come around here and meet Ned. He'll show you what to do."

"I must make way for the others," Ann said when the organist reappeared. "Thank you again, Mr Prescott."

"Think nothing of it, Miss Overton. I hope we meet again, at one of Charles's musical evenings, perhaps."

Ann did not consider such a remark after some twenty minutes acquaintance too forward; between true musicians there could be nothing improper. She smiled and said, "I hope so, too."

She retreated to the pew, happy to sit and listen while Mr Forbes explored the possibilities of the organ, finishing with a rousing rendition of Handel's Hallelujah Chorus.

Chloe and her mother seemed more interested in the paintings that hung one over the other at the altar while others strolled around reading the memorial tablets.

"There is a tablet to the widow of the late John Dymoke, Esq. The 'Honourable the King's Champion'," Hal said, joining her in the pew. "What does the champion have to do?"

"Ride in at the coronation banquet and throw down the gauntlet, challenging anyone who disputes his Majesty's right to the throne," Julian said dryly.

"It sounds like a scene from an opera," Ann said, as Mr Forbes reappeared together with Mr Prescott.

"What does?" Mr Prescott asked.

His eyes gleamed when she explained, "There would have to be a pretender, who would take up the gauntlet, and a duel."

"A chorus of lords and ladies," Ann suggested.

"It couldn't happen in England, of course. Perhaps in some medieval country, where the king is actually the usurper."

"He stole the throne while the real king is away on crusade," Robert put in.

"An excellent suggestion. Now all we need is a poet to write the libretto," Mr Forbes said. "Are you ready to depart, ladies?"

"What do you say to continuing on to Gunter's for ices?" Julian asked when they had left the church.

A shout of acclaim, and the boys ran for the carriages. As Robert and Hal climbed into Julian's curricle, Ann heard Jasper say to his father, "Next time, we must take your high-perch phaeton."

"Mr Prescott excels at the organ," Ann said to Henrietta Forbes whom she had joined in the Forbes carriage while her husband and children strolled along the line of carriages.

"He is bred to it, one might say," Mrs Forbes replied. "His father is organist and master of the choristers at Wells Cathedral; he hopes to follow in his footsteps one day. But plenty of time for that. He came down from Oxford last year. This year, he is broadening his experience here in London; he talks of going abroad, to France or Germany next year."

"Or Italy," Ann said. "Think of all the *Missas* and *Requiems* and *Te Deums*. Chloe says there are still monasteries and convents where they observe the sung offices, just as in the middle ages. I would love to hear them."

"We went abroad on our wedding journey. We had to avoid France, of course, but it was before Bonaparte had started to rampage through Europe. We went to Munich and Vienna. Charles still raves about a concert where Beethoven himself played the pianoforte. We went to the theatre, the opera, and to court, and also explored the surrounding area—the Danube, the woods, and mountains." Mrs Forbes sighed. "It was wonderful—all so different, especially the food. The coffee and cakes, not to mention the hot chocolate…"

"Surely you could go again now," Ann said. "From what Chloe and Cynthia said last year, travelling on the Continent is quite manageable."

"Perhaps later, when Ambrose has finished at Oxford and Cecilia has come out," Mrs Forbes said. "Otherwise we would need a governess and tutor or we could not leave the children at all; we would have to occupy them the whole time."

"You would take them with you?" Ann was surprised, used as she was to being packed off to her grandmother whenever her mother had paid a visit elsewhere. That stay at Swanmere three years ago was the only time she and Hal had been included, presumably, she now realised, because Julian had invited them specifically to be company for Chloe.

"Yes, of course," Mrs Forbes said. "We would be away for at least six months—it is hardly worth going for less, and I should not like to leave them for so long. Ah, here are our ices."

As they took the glasses from the servant, Mr Prescott strolled up to them. "A splendid notion, this. Miss Overton, Charles tells me you are no mean composer and arranger. Have you written anything for the organ? I am always on the look-out for new voluntaries."

Chapter Seven

Rowland, Lord Stanton jumped down from the post-chaise and hurried up the steps of Gracechurch House. Nodding to the footman who opened the door for him, he swiftly crossed the spacious hall, his boot heels ringing on the black and white tiles. He would go straight to his mother's morning-room, see if he could surprise her. She would be waiting for him, he knew. She had written last week to inform him that they would remain in town over Easter and to come there, not to Stanton.

He slowed to a quieter pace as he neared the morning-room and stealthily turned the door knob before easing the door open. As a child, he used to tiptoe up behind his mother as she sat at her writing desk, hoping to surprise her. But today, no duchess sat planning her latest party; instead, a strange girl sat on the floor in the middle of the Turkish carpet, her back to the door. She was rolling a ball to a chubby infant who pitched it back before clambering to its feet and setting off unsteadily towards her.

The girl laughed and came up on her knees, her arms held out. "Come to Chloe, then."

"Chlo'," the child repeated and came into her embrace in a flutter of skirts.

Laughing, she lifted it above her, tilting her head back to look up.

"Chlo'," the child said again, and plunged both hands into her piled-up hair.

"Alexander! What are you doing? Stop. Ouch!"

But the child's grip was too tight to permit her to lower him to the floor, and with a crow of delight he tugged her hair loose so that it spilled down over her shoulders, in a seductive wave. *Like honey*, Stanton thought, wondering should he withdraw quietly.

The child suddenly released his hold on the girl's hair to point over her shoulder. "Man!"

She looked around and got hastily to her feet.

"I beg your pardon," Stanton said. "I was not expecting… I thought to find my mother here… I am Stanton, you know."

Her face cleared. "Lord Stanton. Good day, my lord. The duchess and my mother are upstairs. They should be down any moment. I am Chloe Loring and this is my brother, Alexander FitzCharles."

"FitzCharles? My Uncle Stephen's son?" He had met the infant a year ago, and there had been no mention of an elder sister.

"Yes. My mother married Lord Stephen last year."

As she spoke, she retrieved her hairpins from the boy's grasp, gathered the magnificent spill of hair together, twisted it quickly, and anchored it firmly on the top of her head. Stanton admired her composure. If he had been caught in similar circumstances—his neckcloth tugged loose, perhaps—he would have been mortified, but she behaved as if nothing untoward had happened.

"Why are you standing in the doorway," an impatient voice demanded behind him. Then, "Stanton! You are home!"

Stanton turned in time to catch Tabitha, as she threw herself into his arms.

The Husband Criteria

"I didn't know you were here. This is famous. You remember Alexander, don't you? And this is his sister, Chloe."

"That is not the way to make an introduction, Tabitha," he said gently. "What would my mother say? Now, do it properly."

The girl flushed. "I'm sorry." She took a breath. "Chloe, may I present my brother, Lord Stanton? Stanton, this is Miss Loring."

"Miss Loring." Stanton bowed.

Miss Loring curtsied solemnly. "My lord." Afterwards, she smiled at Tabitha. "You did that very well."

"I should have remembered. But, Stanton, we are agreed that Chloe is our cousin, just as Alexander is, because her mother is now our great-aunt."

He bowed again. "I should be honoured if she will agree to including me among her new cousins."

She looked surprised but said, "Indeed, if you wish."

"Thank you, Cousin."

"I think it is excellent that we have new cousins," Tabitha announced. "Just imagine, Chloe has a baby niece as well, she is six months younger than Alexander, her name is Kate."

He must have looked puzzled, for Chloe said, "It is confusing, I know. Kate's father is my brother Julian and he is as much older than I as I am older than Alexander."

Stanton shook his head. "It sounds like the old riddle 'brother and sister I have none…'"

She laughed. "It does, I suppose. The simple answer is that both of my parents married twice, and my brothers and I each share one parent. It's not that unusual."

"Mrs Fitzmaurice has a baby too, Stanton, but it is still very small. That is why they are not in town."

Ignoring Tabitha's interjection, he asked Chloe, "Are you and Lord and Lady Stephen staying with us?" It would be interesting to have a pretty girl of his own age at Gracechurch House.

"They are staying here but I am at Swanmere House with my brother and sister-in-law."

"But she calls often to play with Alexander," Tabitha assured him, "and sometimes I may go to play with Kate. And tomorrow, we are all going to Swanmere House for a family evening."

"A family evening?"

"Where we sit together, and talk and play games, perhaps listen to music," Chloe said. "My grandparents will be there—they are very old now but are looking forward to it, and other cousins and good friends. With Kate, we are four generations, but she will just be there for an hour or so."

"We have three generations," Tabitha said. "Grandmamma and Grandpapa came up yesterday, Stanton. They said that if you would not go home, then they must come to you."

~~~

Stanton wasn't sure whether such a family evening wasn't beneath his dignity as an Oxford student but he was prepared to take his chances, especially as the alternative was to remain behind on his own. He had been surprised when Jasper's tutor had joined them but his mother had explained that this Mr Musgrave was a friend of the Loring family. "Lady Swann-Loring also kindly invited Miss Barlow, but she decided to take the opportunity to see her grandparents who are passing through London."

The Husband Criteria

The large drawing-room at Swanmere House buzzed with activity. Miss Loring and two other young ladies were gathered around a pianoforte. At a side table, two schoolboys sat hunched over a board, while another played with a baby who crawled between him and a young girl. The remaining persons in the room ranged in age from Miss Loring's grandparents to a gentleman who, to Stanton's relief, was only a few years older than he.

Introductions made; he watched as Tabitha hurried to plump herself down beside the baby. Two of the boys—one was Lady Swann-Loring's brother and one Miss Overton's, he had learnt—dragged Mr Musgrave to one side and began to pepper him with questions. Jasper looked askance at this appropriation of his tutor; Musgrave must have noticed, for he soon drew him into the discussion. His grandparents, the dowager duchess and her husband Mr Harte, chatted with Lord Swanmere, Lady Loring, and Lord and Lady Ransford while Stanton's parents, uncle, and aunt had joined those he had mentally dubbed the other parents.

This was the most astounding thing of all. His father never participated in family occasions. It was only after Stanton had left Harrow aged seventeen that he sat down to dinner with him for the first time, just before he went up to Oxford. And here he was, talking and laughing like any other father. He had seemed more approachable at Christmas but Stanton had not realised how much he had changed. His mother seemed happier too.

Ambrose Forbes, who had been playing a game with Hal Overton, looked a little out of things. Stanton strolled over to see what the game was. A red fox and a flock of white geese faced one another across the board.

"Would you like to play, sir?"

When Stanton sat down opposite him, Ambrose took the fox and one of the geese and held them behind his back. "Choose."

When Stanton tapped his right arm, the boy opened his hand to reveal a goose which he handed over with, "I'm the fox. Just watch how I gobble up your geese."

"We'll chase you out of our farmyard," Stanton retorted as he set out his pieces.

Before they could begin, Chloe Loring came to look. "Are you playing Fox and Geese? Is it very complicated?"

"Do you not know it?" Stanton asked, surprised.

"Not to play. That is the drawback to having no brothers or sisters of your own age, I suppose."

"Why don't you try it? If you take the fox, I am sure Ambrose will advise you."

"Of course. Here, take my chair." Ambrose seated Chloe and brought over another chair for himself.

She listened intently to their explanations. "It sounds similar to draughts," she said finally.

"It is, a little, I suppose."

With Ambrose's assistance, she managed to conquer Stanton's geese although not without some narrow escapes. "That was most diverting. I must play with Hal and Robert while they are here," she said at the end.

"We could play another game; you can take the geese," Stanton suggested.

"Is it more complicated to manage a whole flock than a single fox?"

"Not really," Ambrose said. "As fox, you must watch each goose so that you are not penned in."

"I'm sure there is a moral there," Chloe said as she reached for the geese. "The Fox and the Geese—was it one of Aesop's fables?"

Stanton laughed. "If not, it should be, but perhaps you are thinking of the fox and the grapes."

"Probably. He decided they were very sour, as I recall. I have never understood why that was a comfort to him. Was he not a greater fool to desire them then?"

"Better just to accept he could not have them, you mean?"

"Or try something else instead of complaining. Perhaps the gardener had left a ladder lying about."

"That's what I would have done," Ambrose said. "Your turn, sir."

Stanton was fully absorbed in the game. Chloe watched as he turned the fox in his long fingers while he pondered his action.

She knew from the talkative Tabitha, who worshipped her elder brother, that he was eighteen, in his first year at Oxford, and home just for the Easter vacation. He was not precisely handsome, more striking-looking with sharp cheekbones and a firm jaw setting off a chiselled profile. Dark curls, disordered by his habit of thrusting one hand through them when concentrating, clustered above his forehead. Deep-set hazel eyes beneath winged eyebrows completed the picture.

Her eyes followed his as they scanned the board and identified an opening. Once decided, he moved quickly—tap, scoop, tap, allowing himself a small smile as he placed the unwary goose to one side.

When Kate's nurse came to remove her from the drawing-room, Tabitha came to stand at Stanton's side. "Two against one isn't fair."

"Ah," Stanton said as he captured another goose, "Chloe has never played before."

Tabitha stared at Chloe. "Never?"

"Never," Chloe confirmed solemnly. "Ambrose is my adviser."

"Then I shall advise Stanton."

Chloe liked the interplay between them. How many elder brothers would have patiently listened to his sister's whispers and then handed her the fox to make their move. Before long, the ranks of geese had thinned so much that it was clear that further resistance was hopeless, and Chloe cleared the board. Seeing Ann and Cynthia coming towards her, she said, "Pray excuse me. We have a little entertainment prepared…"

"What is it?" Tabitha asked excitedly.

Stanton put his arm around his sister. "Wait and see."

As Tabitha subsided, Chloe said, "Stanton and Ambrose, thank you for the games. They were most instructive."

Stanton rose with Ambrose as Chloe stood. "Not at all. It was our pleasure."

As she walked away, she heard Tabitha ask, "What shall we do now?" and his reply, "Try for a little patience, Miss." She minds her brother better than her governess, Chloe thought, amused, as she headed for the parlour that was to be the dressing-room for the performers.

Rosa moved into the middle of the drawing-room. "Dear friends, may I beg you to accompany me to the library, where we shall regale you with the *Dread Secret of Swanmere*, a tale that was only recently recorded and of which only three copies exist."

In the great library, the shutters were closed and the curtains drawn. Argand lamps, turned down low, gleamed right and left while candelabra illuminated four rows of small, straight-backed chairs set across the central width of the room. The book cases had been covered with painted drapes but it was impossible to make out the subjects of the paintings in the dim light.

Two black-wigged footmen clad in jet-black livery directed the curious guests to the chairs. One by one, the candles were snuffed; as the darkness grew, snatches of music could be heard, now suggesting wind or storm, now a hymnlike monotone. To the left, the light grew brighter, revealing a deep grotto at the base of a steep cliff. In the corner was a small table on which stood only a candle and a heavy tome. The music took on a martial note as a knight rushed in. A dark figure stirred in the corner of the grotto, and turned. It was dressed in a monk's habit, the cowl pulled low over its deathly white features.

"Hast thou decided, Sir Knight?"

"Aye. I must and will have Clara to wife. Her father has ridden out, leaving her with me and a squire. This is my chance. Come to the Castle tonight and be prepared to carry out the marriage ceremony."

"Art thou willing to pay the price?" The figure's voice was deep, yet horribly lifeless.

"I am."

"Willst thou serve my master for all eternity?"

"I will."

"Swear it. By bell, book, and candle, swear it!" As the voice rose demandingly the candle burst into flame and a muffled bell began to toll.

The knight laid his hand on the tome. "I swear!"

As he completed his oath, the music rose to a fury and the lamps flickered and died, plunging the room into darkness.

An uneasy moment later, a small flame lightened the gloom. One by one, the candles were re-lit and the guests blinked at one another.

"What happens next?"

"How Gothic."

"Worthy of Monk Lewis."

"Truly electrifying."

"Very well done indeed."

Rosa clapped her hands to silence the babble. "I beg that you will now turn your chairs the other way."

Amused and entertained, they complied. Now they faced the great hall of a castle. A damsel clad in blue and white, her guinea-gold hair flowing down her back beneath a light veil, sat at a writing desk, guarded by her squire. A harpist sat to one side.

"It is too tedious, now that my father and his men have left," the damsel sighed. "Pray play something for us, Rosalind."

"What wouldst thou hear, Lady Clara?"

"I don't care. Anything."

"The Minstrel Boy?" the squire suggested eagerly. Aside, he said to the audience, "It is tedious for me, too, left here with Sir Hugh to watch over milady. It is an honour, I suppose, but I had far rather gone hunting." He looked longingly out of the window and remained thus when Sir Hugh entered followed by the monk, only turning when Rosalind stopped playing.

The Husband Criteria

Both women were on their feet, looking from one man to the other.

"What a strange man, and how ill-bred not to lower his hood and show his face," Lady Clara said in an aside to Rosalind and her squire. "Indeed, I wonder at Sir Hugh, bringing him in here." Addressing the knight, she said, "Sir Hugh, will you not present our visitor?"

He bowed. "Indeed, my lady. May I present Brother Lawrence?"

The monk nodded briefly. "My lady." He held his white hand.

"My God! 'Tis like a dead man's hand. I cannot touch it," Clara whispered, drawing her own hand back in revulsion.

The monk came nearer.

"Take his hand, my lady," Sir Hugh urged her. "He will then unite us in wedlock."

"What! Have you lost your wits, Sir Hugh?"

"Aye. I am crazy for love of you."

He attempted to seize her, but the squire sprang between them, dagger in hand.

"You dare!"

A strange 'hound' bounded in, snarling and dragging at the monk's robes, toppling him to the floor. Rosalind abandoned her harp in favour of the poker and brought it down sharply on the knight's head while Clara snapped contemptuously, "You must be mad if you think I would ever marry you. Take his sword, Peregrine," she instructed the squire. "He has violated his knight's oath. Hark! The horns! My father returns."

~~~

"Pure Minerva Press," the guests agreed after Sir Hugh's vile plot had been foiled, he and the monk had received their just deserts and Clara, Rosalind, the squire, and the hound celebrated their triumph. The actors and musicians took their bows and everyone adjourned to the supper room.

"Who painted the scenery for you?" Jasper asked Hal as he addressed a large slice of apple pie.

"Rosa, Chloe, and Robert. They used old bed sheets. Chloe's mother advised them on working on such large scenes. They looked well, didn't they?

"Very. It was very clever to put the footmen into dark livery so that they could move around unnoticed," Thomas Musgrave said.

"That was my idea," Hal said proudly.

"We must think of something we can do, Mr Musgrave," Jasper said. "Of course, we do not have as many actors."

"If you do it before we go back to school, Rob and I will help," Hal said. "Are there any more macaroons?"

Chapter Eight

"You may have as many waltzes and quadrilles as you wish," Julian said, "but the ball will end with the finishing dance."

Chloe groaned. "Oh, Julian! Not Sir Roger de Coverley. It is so tedious."

"One country dance will not kill you," he said heartlessly. He turned to his wife. "I trust you will stand up with me, my love."

"I should be delighted to, sir."

"You and Rosa danced it at Papa's ball," Chloe remembered. "It was the first time you danced together."

"It was my first ball, too," Rosa said.

Ann looked from Julian to Rosa who stood smiling at each other, as if lost in the past. Just eight, when her father left for the Peninsula for the last time, she had very few memories of her own parents as man and wife.

"Be good," he had admonished her when he kissed her goodbye, then he had kissed her mother. "And you be good too." Now that Ann thought about it, it was a strange thing to say. Mamma had drawn a deep breath as if about to make a sharp retort but must have thought better of it. "Godspeed, and a safe return," she had said. "Come, children, we shall see your father off from the door."

That was the last time they had seen him. He had never come home. Before he left, he had arranged for them to move to the dower house at Overton Hall. Ann and Hal had had no objection to leaving London, but her mother had greatly resented the enforced move. Well, she would never discover the ins and outs of her parents' marriage. With a mental shrug, Ann turned her attention back to the discussion of the Swanmere ball.

"Must we have negus?" Rosa asked. "Perhaps it is reasonable to serve a hot drink in winter before the guests go out into the cold night, but generally after the finishing dance one is over-heated if anything. Some refreshment, yes, but not hot wine."

"Stephen's man, Piero, makes a delicious cool, creamy lemony sherbet called *ponch a la romaine*," Chloe said.

"I've heard of it," Julian said dryly. "It is a favourite of the Regent's."

"It is not as innocent as it sounds, then," Rosa said. "What else is in it besides lemons, Chloe?"

"Umm, rum and cognac. You can serve half ponch and fill the glasses up with champagne if you like."

"That sounds very strong. We don't want to send the girls home tipsy."

"What if you used soda water instead of champagne?" Julian asked. "Or some of each?"

"We could try," Rosa said. "Chloe, if you are going to Gracechurch House tomorrow, would you see if you can obtain the recipe?"

"Yes, of course. I was wondering whether we should send Stanton a card? He does not return to Oxford until the next day. He frequently comes here with Jasper and Tabitha, but they treat him more like another parent, and I think it would look odd if we did not include him, as if we thought him one of the children."

"You are quite right," Rosa said. "I'll have a word with Flora." A friendship had developed between the Gracechurches and the Swann-Lorings, and she and the duchess were now on Christian-name terms.

"An excellent notion," Flora said. "In fact, I was about to suggest it to you, for we could not miss the ball and I would not like to leave him to his own devices for his last night at home. What would you think of his leading Chloe out for the opening dance? It would be good experience for him, without raising any undue expectations, for he is far too young for that. But they have become good friends in such a short time."

"That was Tabitha, I understand. She introduced Chloe to him as their new cousin."

"She is so happy to see the family expand. It was only last year that I realised how bereft of relations she felt." She put her hand on her belly. "I wonder what she will say when she realises she is to have a little brother or sister."

"I am sure she will be delighted. She loves babies, and is quite envious of Chloe who can claim two, and her friend Miranda, who, I understand, has a new brother."

Flora laughed. "I fear you are right. I can just imagine her as elder sister, brooking no discussion and always knowing best."

"I'm sure she will become less peremptory as she grows older," Rosa said, with a smile. "But, to go back to the opening dance, if he is willing, it would be ideal. Neither of the girls has any particular favourites or, if they do, they are not admitting it. I have Martin Glazebrook for one of them, and if Stanton would stand up with Chloe, that would solve that problem."

"Splendid. I'll mention it to Stanton."

"And I to Chloe. Shall we see you at *Don Giovanni* on Saturday? Ann insisted we all go; she is more excited about its first London performance than about her ball, although she asked us to send cards to several young men; other musicians she has met at the Forbes's."

Flora raised her eyebrows. "Indeed? Are they all gentlemen?"

"Yes, although they may not be eligible *partis*, when it comes to fortune. Why should she not have her friends there? They are most amiable, when they surface from their music. And, I imagine, good dancers."

～～～

"There, Miss." Parker stepped back to check the set of the wreath of spring flowers that held Chloe's locks in place. "Perfect."

"It is the most beautiful thing," Chloe said. "How clever of my mother to find it. I love the way it just dips onto the centre of my forehead."

She stood to look in the long mirror. Her gown of rich white gauze over a satin slip, its bodice and skirts trimmed with blond lace and pink moss roses, shimmered with every movement. "My pearls," she said, turning back to the dressing-table. Papa had given them to her for her first ball. How everything had changed since then. And for the better, she had to admit, although she would do so only to herself; even the thought made her feel guilty. But none of it was her fault, she told herself, and Papa's illness

The Husband Criteria

could be set at nobody's feet. One heard every year of people dying from an inflammation of the lung.

Poor Papa. She laid a gentle finger on the pearls. The Nissards had always crossed themselves when a dead person was mentioned. It was a little prayer, Aunt Mary had explained. She had lit candles in every church they visited to pray for her dead husband and son. It must be comforting to be able to do that, to believe that it helped. Rest in peace, Papa, Chloe said to herself.

There was a tap on the door to her and Ann's sitting-room. "Are you ready, Chloe?"

"Yes. Come in."

Ann's white gown was trimmed with rosettes of cerise ribbon and clusters of cherry-blossom that matched those in her dark hair. A gold locket chased with forget-me-nots was suspended from a chain around her neck.

"Is that new?" Chloe asked. "It's beautiful."

"It is a present from my grandmother," Ann said, opening it. "She had this little portrait of my father painted from a miniature she had made when he got his pair of colours. He was younger then than I am now."

"You look like him," Chloe said. "Hal resembles your mother but you are more like your father. You have his smile."

Ann's lips quirked in just the same way as those of the young ensign. "Do I?"

"Yes, look." Chloe held up the hand-mirror. "See the way your lips turn down on one side and up at the other? And your eyes crinkle at the corners, just like his."

"I suppose they do. I had never thought about it. It is very good of Julian and Rosa to invite my uncle and aunt to receive the guests with them."

"It's your come-out, too," Chloe pointed out as she picked up her fan and reticule. "Now, stand straight, shoulders back, head up, and smile. Off we go."

~~~

"What if nobody comes?" Rosa said anxiously to Julian. "As far as the *ton* is concerned, I am a nobody."

"An exceptionally well-connected nobody," he pointed out.

She laughed. "Thanks to Delia. It is ironic, is it not?"

"I suppose it is."

"I'm glad you insisted on the finishing dance. I had no expectation of dancing at your father's ball, of course, but at the end you asked me to stand up with you. I fell a little bit in love with you that night."

"Only a little bit?"

She had to smile at his feigned outrage. "Even that was most imprudent. And then, when we rode to Lavenham, and you told me I might always turn to you if I was in need of assistance…"

"But you didn't, did you? I had to hunt you down."

"And here we are, about to welcome the guests to Chloe's come-out ball. We never would have thought it then."

He took her into his arms. "I have you now, and intend to keep you for the rest of my life."

She put her hands on his chest to hold him off. "Not now, sir, or we shall be late, and my gown sadly crushed."

"Later then?"

"Later."

He sealed the promise with a quick kiss. "My lady."

The Husband Criteria

Lady Swann-Loring placed her hand on her husband's arm and let him lead her from the room. With him by her side, she could face anything, even a *ton* ball.

~~~

"I think we can go in," Rosa said when there was no further sound on the stairs.

Gathering her flock, she led the way into the ballroom. The buzz of conversation died down when the debutantes appeared, everyone eager to see who would have the honour of leading them out for the opening dance. The Gracechurches and Glazebrooks stood together with Chloe's mother and Lord Stephen. After exchanging a few words, Stanton bowed to Chloe and Martin to Ann and all four walked onto the dance floor. After much discussion, they had decided on a German waltz, and a few practise hours had reassured the two couples of their compatibility. They had agreed that each couple was free to dance as they saw fit.

"Why, when one has all this freedom, agree to follow the same sequence?" Martin had said. "This way, one can make the best use of the space, and other couples can join in without turning the whole thing into a country dance."

Chloe stood with Stanton's arm about her shoulders and their outer hands clasped in front of them. He was immaculately dressed; his black coat and slim trousers were the very height of fashion; his snowy-white, crisp neckcloth was tied more elaborately than usual and his dark curls beautifully arranged. He was newly shaven, his cheeks looked smoother than usual, and a pleasantly astringent odour filled her nostrils. His kid-gloved hand held hers firmly. He was an excellent dancer, light on his feet and with a talent for leading his partner through the different figures, choosing them as the music and available space called for them.

The first notes sounded; wait for the introduction and catch the first phrase. They were off. After a couple of minutes, as agreed, Julian and Rosa took to the floor, together with Mamma and Lord Stephen. The Gracechurches followed, then more and more couples until the floor was full of swirling skirts and intent faces as the dancers came together and separated, now back-to-back, now side-by-side, fingers brushing, hands clasping and releasing, turning away and back again, at arms' length or caught close, but always aware of the exhilarating rhythm, that linked them in this mutual endeavour. Smiling eyes met as the dance ended with a bow and a curtsey. The couples reformed into groups and broke up again into new couples for the next dance. Who knew what the evening might bring, for that was the secret promise of a ball, that perhaps this time, this evening all might change; a stranger would walk onto the dance floor and into your heart.

~~~

Rafe Marfield always liked to take a turn about the ballroom, see who was there and who was not, before making his mental list of prospective partners. A bit daring to have a waltz as the first dance, perhaps, but it boded well for the success of the evening and Misses Loring and Overton danced it beautifully. Glazebrook partnered Miss Overton but who was the sprig of fashion dancing with Miss Loring? Very well turned-out; he must be new on the town. No doubt, he would find out later.

Miss Glazebrook was not yet dancing. She had come out last year, he remembered, pausing to bow to Lady Needham and exchange a word with his cousin Lallie, Lady Tamm. The young man, he learned, was Lord Stanton, heir to the Duke of Gracechurch.

"He is not yet on the town, just home from Oxford for the vacation, but this is almost a family occasion," Lallie said. "Men don't have come-out balls, do they?"

"Not as such. Generally, a twenty-first birthday is celebrated, especially that of the heir, but at home for the tenants, not in Town."

"And then they just slip into the *ton*?"

"Not if they are heirs to a dukedom," Lady Neary said acerbically. "It is wise of the duchess to have him try the waters on such an occasion as this."

"Very true," Rafe said, recalling his own first ventures into the *ton* ballrooms. His father had warned him that he would be subjected to intense interest from the *ton* matrons and their daughters and encouraged him to make friends among other noble bachelors as well as cultivating an impassive, off-putting demeanour towards the fairer sex. It was no wonder that young men tended to run in packs, each looking out for the other, he thought, as Mr and Mrs Forde came up to speak to Lallie—Mrs Forde was Tamm's sister. With a bow, Marfield wandered on.

"Three Graces? Not to my eyes." The little snigger identified the speaker as young Mr Norris. What did it say of a man that he would never shake off the qualifying epithet? "The Loring and the Overton are cosy armfuls, I suppose, but the Glazebrook is too skinny for my taste. What man wants a bag of bones in bed?"

Norris and his crony passed out of earshot, leaving Marfield desiring nothing more than to plough his fist into the coxcomb's face. How dare he dismiss her so? Could they not see how graceful she was, the elegant way her head was poised on her slender neck, the delicate collarbone and tender shoulder blades peeping above the low neckline of her gown like incipient wings? Glimpses of small round breasts tantalised, as did the outline of long legs beneath her skirts. Yes, she was slender, but not skinny. She rode well, he knew—he had admired her seat in the Row one morning when she was riding with her brother and the Nugents—and was an excellent dancing partner. He smiled to himself, remembering their discussion about ranking partners according to their ability. Those fools are blind, he thought, as he headed across the room to solicit her hand for the next dance.

Tonight, presumably because she did not wish to encroach on the other girls' début, she had not joined them but stood chatting to Miss Nugent and the Earl of Rastleigh. Marfield clapped the other man on the shoulder.

"Take heart, Rastleigh. With the appearance of Gracechurch's heir, you have forfeited your position as the *ton*'s most eligible bachelor."

"But only for tonight," Miss Nugent said. "I understand Lord Stanton returns to Oxford tomorrow."

"Still, the mere fact of his existence should help," the young earl said. "Miss Nugent, may I have the honour of dancing this next with you? Miss Glazebrook, will you grant me the following dance?"

"What economy of effort," Marfield said. "If the ladies permit, I shall follow suit."

"Why not?" Miss Nugent said, to which Miss Glazebrook replied, "Why not, indeed?"

~~~

There it was again, that little thrill that made her smile inside as she walked onto the dance floor with Lord Marfield. She had not allowed herself to hope that he would seek her out. Perhaps it was not I but Miss Nugent, Cynthia thought and, like at the Gracechurches, he felt obliged to ask me because I was there. The thought was quite lowering, but she would not let it spoil her pleasure. Rastleigh was also a most eligible partner. Dancing with him could only increase her standing among the *ton*. Almack's second ball was to be held tomorrow. To be absent one week might be explained away, but to miss two weeks would certainly cause talk.

Marfield raised an eyebrow as they took their positions. "You are very serious tonight."

She felt her cheeks grow hot. "Rather abstracted, I'm afraid. I beg your pardon, my lord."

"No need for that. It is not always easy to put our personal concerns aside, is it?"

"No, but you are right to challenge me. It was nothing important, not worth spoiling this evening for."

"'Sufficient unto the day?'"

"Exactly."

The music started and they glided into the waltz. There it was again, the perfect harmony of touch and step, of demand and compliance, becoming one with the music, swaying a moment too long in a turn only to be quickly gathered in on the beat. Their eyes met in a mutual smile. Cynthia felt she was floating while at the same time was safely anchored in his arms.

"What else do you enjoy, besides dancing?" Marfield asked as they strolled after the dance.

"Riding, but properly, not picking my way through the crush in the Park. Walking, especially in the country. I like to read, and to discuss what I have read. Then music—my harp, and singing. I enjoy it more with somebody else, particularly with Chloe and Ann. Ann takes us places we would never go on our own."

"How do you mean?"

"She is so talented. She can improvise an accompaniment, or add a voice to a song, just make it that little bit more."

"Do you play for others, or just for yourselves?"

"It depends. If a lady requests us to play after dinner, we frequently play together."

"Then I can hope to be fortunate enough to hear you on of these days."

She turned the table on him. "What else do you enjoy, sir?"

"I agree with you about riding and walking. Here in town, I fence. In the winter, I ride to hounds or take a gun out."

All outdoor pursuits, Cynthia noted. But then he asked, "What do you like to read?"

"All sorts of things, except the sickly sentimental—you know, dying children and death-bed repentances or stupidly moral, like self-sacrificing wives."

"Self-sacrificing wives?"

"Of neglectful husbands. Reduced to penury by his gambling, she spends too much in serving up a fine dinner when he invites his friends but barely orders enough to still her hunger when she dines alone, which is most of the time."

"What?" He stopped walking and turned to look at her. "You are not serious?"

She nodded. "I swear to you that I have read such a tale. Of course, in the end, he finds out and is so shamed that he instantly repents, gives up his clubs, cancels his orders with his tailor, and is happy to live in reduced circumstances, as long as he is with her. Whereupon, a distant relative dies and leaves him a fortune. But he continues to see the error of his ways, and they live happily ever after."

Marfield burst out laughing. "If you are ever in such straits, you could make a fortune telling such stories."

"Why is that?"

"It is so diverting, the way your expressions belie your words."

"Is my rejection of the moral so obvious?"

"And rightly so. It should be 'ladies, choose your husbands carefully' rather than 'submit meekly and suffer in silence'."

"I have never understood *Patient Griselda*," she said. "I would have refused to have anything more to do with him. How could you ever trust him again?"

"Trust is important to you?"

"Mutual trust is important in any relationship, but essential in marriage. Do you not agree?" She was on tenterhooks waiting for his response. She could not bear it if he pooh-poohed or made light of her comment.

"I do not see how one could have any hope of happiness without it," he said as they reached the other couple.

"Stanton is not the only new face among us," Miss Nugent said. "There are several gentlemen I have never seen before. There, talking to Miss Overton. They look—different."

"In what way?" Marfield asked.

"Less languid, I suppose. So many gentlemen cultivate a bored demeanour, as if the effort of getting dressed was too much for them. I blame Brummel."

"They are Miss Overton's fellow-musicians," Cynthia said.

"Musicians. Other than the orchestra. Is there to be an entertainment?" Rastleigh asked.

"You can never rule it out with them, but they have not been engaged as performers, if that is what you mean. They study music with Mr Forbes. They take it very seriously."

"Miss Overton too?" Miss Nugent asked.

"She goes to him once a week. He was most impressed by her talent."

"And the gentleman speaking to Miss Loring."

"That is Thomas Musgrave. His father is Rector at Swanmere. He is at present tutor to Lord Jasper FitzCharles."

"We shall not generally see him at balls, then," Miss Nugent observed.

"I imagine his duties would not permit it," Cynthia replied. Chloe had told her that Lady Tabitha's governess had agreed to supervise Lord Jasper that evening so that Mr Musgrave could come to the ball.

Chapter Nine

"Well, Miss," Ann's uncle said, when she joined them after dancing with Mr Nugent. "I have to hand it to Lady Swann-Loring, and Sir Julian, of course. Nothing's shabby—everything done to a cow's thumb."

"Pray mind your language, Sir Frederick," his wife hissed. "We may not come to Town so often, but we are no country bumpkins."

"What? No, my dear. I beg your pardon, ladies." To this last, he added a gallant bow. "I meant no ill. It is indeed a splendid occasion, Ann. Your aunt has been taking note of all your partners so that she can report to your grandmother. And inspecting all the gowns, too, I'll warrant."

"It would be foolish of me not to take advantage of such a parade of the latest styles," Lady Overton said. "I like that turban." She indicated Lady Neary with a discreet nod.

Ann smiled fondly at her uncle and aunt. He eschewed the more fashionable trousers in favour of his black silk knee-breeches and white stockings while she had seen no reason to swap her provincial mantua-maker for a London modiste. She also preferred the comfort of silver-framed spectacles to fiddling with a lorgnette and smiled benevolently on the world through her glasses. They reminded Ann of Sir Thomas and Lady Bertram in

Mansfield Park but of a more placid, contented disposition. Perhaps because they were childless—he had long since accepted he would be succeeded by his brother or his nephew—and they were spared the worries caused by a profligate heir or spoilt daughters.

"Shall I see if I can discover who her milliner is?" Ann offered. "You will not return home immediately, I trust. We could visit the shops one morning, perhaps find something my grandmother would like, too."

"An excellent notion, my love. Sir Julian has promised to take your uncle to Tattersalls, we might go then. But you are wanted, it seems." Lady Overton looked enquiringly at the gentleman bowing before them.

"Our dance, I believe, Miss Overton."

"Indeed, Mr Prescott." She tucked her hand into the crook of his arm. They were not usually so formal. At the Forbes's, the gentlemen simply used surnames without any honorific, and Ann had adopted this practice. They, in return, addressed her as Miss Ann, like a daughter of the house.

The minstrels, as Chloe and Cynthia referred to them, had apparently agreed to form a set for the quadrille, for Prescott led her to where three other couples waited, among them Miss Nugent and two other girls Ann did not know very well. Chloe and Cynthia were in the set beside them, she saw, Chloe dancing with Thomas Musgrave and Cynthia with Lord Stanton. Messrs Malvin and Nugent, with their partners, made up that set.

Mondays at the Forbes's frequently ended with dancing, and the quadrille was no novelty there, so Ann had no qualms about any of the gentlemen not knowing the steps, or being unable to hint their ladies in the right direction. She, Prescott, Miss Nugent,

The Husband Criteria

and Hayes were the first and second couples. Prescott was light on his feet, with an innate feeling for rhythm that made dancing with him a joy. He was not one of those men who were impelled to tug their partners almost off their feet, but allowed his lady the freedom of her own movements without ever losing her.

With each successive figure the groups of dancers became more united. A ripple of amusement and applause rewarded those gentlemen who, when called upon, danced a bravura solo rather than marking time with simple steps, but the dance swept everyone into the finale.

Their last bows and curtsies made, the dancers, as one, headed for the supper-room. Here, they remained in their quadrille sets, each settling at a table for eight where all manners of delicacies were set out.

"These smaller tables are an excellent notion," Miss Nugent said as she helped herself to a collop of salmon and some spears of asparagus. "Much better than squeezing in some twenty a side, as is frequently the case, with no elbow room."

Ann had not yet been to enough balls to comment, but the others nodded in agreement as they filled their plates.

Prescott raised his glass. "A splendid occasion, Miss Ann, and we are all most appreciative of being included, are we not, gentlemen?"

"Hear, hear!"

Hayes, Bradley, and Dennison rose, glasses in hand. Ann was used to the three men breaking into song at the slightest provocation. Now Bradley delighted in taking a second, an octave below Hayes, while Dennison provided a descant.

"Let charming beauty's health go round.
In whom celestial joys are found,
And may confusion still pursue
The senseless woman-hating crew;
And they that woman's health deny,
Down among the dead men,
Down among the dead men,
Down, down, down, down
Down among the dead men let them lie."

It was done so infectiously that the assembled gentlemen joined the chorus *con brio*, glasses raised, and with bows to their smiling ladies.

"Well sung," Miss Nugent said when all were seated again. "Do you sing regularly in a catch club?"

"Not formally," Hayes said. "We work together every Monday, but after dinner we play and sing for pleasure, you might say, and it usually includes a madrigal."

"Work? You too, Miss Overton? Like a music lesson?"

"You don't mean to say you still take lessons," Miss Gibbons, Bradley's partner, said. "I was so pleased to bid farewell to my music master."

"It is not a lesson as such, where you play a piece you have been set," Ann replied. "We share our latest work. If you are working on a quartet or a song, for example, it helps to have someone play or sing it for you. Mr Forbes is very helpful, too."

"Do you compose, Miss Overton?" Miss Hardy, Dennison's lady, asked. "How exciting! I love music, both listening to it and playing, but could not for the life of me think up something new."

The Husband Criteria

"Just as the author needs a reader, or the artist a viewer, we composers need our listeners and interpreters," Dennison said. "Without you, we would be poor creatures indeed."

"Have you seen *Don Giovanni*? What did you make of it?" Prescott asked the company in general.

"No. Mamma heard the subject was most unedifying," Miss Gibbons said.

"I suppose it is," Hayes said. "I certainly would not describe it as a *dramma giocosa*—a comedy."

"The music was sublime," Ann said, "especially Don Ottavio's two arias."

"Why, pray, did you not consider it a comedy?" Miss Gibbons asked.

"It began with Giovanni slaying Donna Anna's father, the Commendatore after he, the father, I mean, discovered Giovanni trying to seduce Anna," Miss Nugent said.

"But the Commendatore has his revenge," Miss Hardy pointed out. "He returns as his statue and drags Giovanni down to hell."

"So Giovanni is a rake," Miss Gibbons said.

The four men looked at one another. "I suppose you could say that," Hayes said finally. "His manservant kept a catalogue of all his conquests, listed by country."

Miss Gibbons drew herself up and sniffed. "Disgraceful!"

"Yes," Ann said. "You are left in no doubt of that, or that his end was just, but Mozart's genius is such that you cannot but have a certain sympathy for him."

The others smiled and nodded, recalling probably as Ann did, Giovanni's music.

"Nothing can condone vice," Miss Gibbons snapped.

"Of course not," Prescott said. "But one must admire the maestro's genius, ma'am."

"One could also say that Mozart reveals the duplicitousness of the seducer, how he is able to inveigle an unwitting female into believing he is sincere," Miss Nugent said. "It is a sad truth that too many girls fall victim to such men. I felt for Zerlina."

"Well put, Miss Nugent," Hayes said.

Miss Gibbons looked like thunder. Fortunately, she was distracted by a footman carrying a tray of tamarind ices which successfully cooled the fraught tempers enough that, when supper was over they, could return amicably to the ballroom before separating with their new partners. Ann did notice, though, that Miss Gibbons was not invited to dance by any other of the musicians, while she, Miss Nugent, and Miss Hardy by the end of the evening had danced with all four men.

~~~

When the finishing dance was announced with the first bars of Sir Roger, there was a murmur of surprise but couples soon began to line up behind Julian and Rosa. To Ann's pleased surprise, her uncle and aunt and other older pairs were among them.

"Miss Ann, may I have the pleasure?" Frank Prescott bowed before her.

It's not as though it were a second waltz, she told herself as they walked onto the floor. Chloe seemed to feel the same, for she was standing with Stanton while Cynthia was accepting Marfield's arm.

Chloe beckoned her. "Come, we'll start a second set here."

Cynthia and Marfield joined them. In the end, four sets of ten couple stood up for a vigorous, almost rowdy Sir Roger that left everyone laughing, breathless, and in high good humour.

The dancers revived with judiciously mixed *ponch a la romaine*, farewells were said, cloaks fetched, and carriages summoned. The dowager and Lord Swanmere had long since gone to bed but after the front door finally closed behind the last guests, Julian, Rosa, Ann, Chloe, and the Overtons gathered in the library, still elated by the success of the evening.

"Champagne, Morris," Rosa said to the butler.

"Brandy for me, if I may," Sir Frederick said.

"And for me," Julian said, going to the decanters and pouring two large measures. When the ladies had been served with champagne, he raised his glass to Rosa. "Congratulations, my dear. All went off splendidly."

"Yes," Lady Overton said. "And the girls did very well indeed. A ball is hard work for those giving it if they take their duty to their guests seriously as you all did, making sure that nobody was left without a partner. But you enjoyed yourselves too, I trust."

"Oh, yes," Chloe said, then yawned. "Excuse me. Now that I have sat down, I am suddenly exhausted." She finished her champagne. "I'll say goodnight, or rather good morning. Thank you so much, Rosa and Julian, for everything."

"I'll come up with you," Ann said. "Thank you, Rosa and Julian, and you too, Uncle and Aunt. I am so happy you were here."

Chloe linked her arm with Ann's as they carried their candles up the wide staircase. "I'm sure I'll be waltzing in my dreams."

"I too. I did enjoy tonight."

"I like your Mr Prescott."

Ann did not dispute Chloe's possessive adjective but simply said, "I'm glad."

So it was serious, then, Chloe thought, as they reached their sitting room.

"Good night. Sweet dreams," she added with a meaningful smile.

Ann flushed and laughed. "Good night."

Chapter Ten

"Will that be all, Miss?"

"Yes." Satisfied with her purchases, Cynthia paid for two new pairs of evening gloves and several yards of green ribbon shot with gold.

"It matches your eyes, Miss," her maid had said. "It's just the thing to refresh your Naples bonnet."

Cynthia loved to wander through the four departments of Messrs Harding Howell in Pall Mall where everything the female heart might desire could be found conveniently under one roof. She liked to slip out early in the morning when the air was fresh and the fashionable lounges not overly full. The walk back to Park Place for breakfast gave her time for reflection.

Despite, or perhaps because of Almack's rejection, she was enjoying this Season. She would never have dared hope that not only Chloe and Ann but all the Swann-Loring family would support her the way they did. And for the Gracechurches to side with them! So far, the consequences had been minimal. There had been a few pointed comments about not having seen her on Wednesday, but that was all.

Chloe's ball had been very well attended and none of the girls had lacked for partners. Stanton's presence had set the cat among the pigeons, Lord Stephen had remarked later, but the first appearance of a duke's heir could not go unnoticed. His disappearance from Town the next day lent the Swanmere House ball an undefinable lustre. Happy the girl who had stood up with him, and the young man with whom he had exchanged a few civil words, while mothers and daughters coming late to Town could only regret their tardiness.

He had danced every dance, including one with his mother. Instead of prowling the room as Marfield was wont to do, after each dance he had drifted back to the circle gathered about Chloe and Ann. He and Martin had swapped partners for the second dance. After that, he had led out first Cynthia and then Miss Nugent. Marfield and Rastleigh had closed ranks around him, introducing him to the less flirtatious girls while protecting him from the more brazen and their match-making mammas. Thank heavens Mamma had never attempted to force herself or Cynthia on a gentleman's notice.

'Apart from the fact that I would consider it beneath me,' she had said once. 'It can only lead to disaster. In my experience, a gentleman likes to think he has won his bride. It does no harm to be a little standoffish in the beginning; it is much better than being overly eager. But once he has made his intentions known, you should not trifle with him but let him down gently if you are not interested. Remember, you will still move in the same circles and you would like your previous suitors to continue to be well-disposed towards you.'

'And if you return his interest?' Cynthia had asked.

'Then you may encourage him gently. Follow your own instincts, my dear, and do not try to conceal who you are.'

That was important. You would have to be able to behave naturally with your husband, not always feel you had to be on your best behaviour, or perfectly dressed, if it came to that. Despite that prickly first encounter at Gunter's, she did not feel she had to watch her words with Marfield. They could talk about anything; he was able to follow her leaps from one topic to another—just look at his reaction to her sentimental tale. And there could be no doubt that his asking her to dance the finishing dance was sincere. When those first notes started, she saw him look around and then cross the room to come to her.

Sir Roger had been a truly delightful frolic. Chloe and Stanton had set the tone, leading with no lazy half-walk but a light, skipping dance step that had everyone moving lithely through the figures and left them breathless and laughing at the end.

'Iced punch,' Marfield had said as they savoured the delicious, cool sherbet. 'What an excellent notion—why did no one ever think of it before?'

'The idea of something other than negus was my sister-in-law's,' Chloe had said, 'but the recipe comes from my stepfather's man, Piero. Perhaps he brought it with him from Nice.'

'Hmm. I must have a word with him,' Stanton had said. 'See if he will share it with my man. It would be just the thing for a summer's evening.'

'I thought your nose would be held so hard to the grindstone at Oxford that you would have no time for such indulgence,' Chloe had said teasingly.

'Oh, they allow us one free evening each month,' Stanton had replied solemnly.

Marfield shook his head. 'Such dissipation! *O tempora, o mores*. Why, in my day we never lifted our heads from our books.'

'Judging by my brother's account of his time at Oxford, that was probably more from somnolence than diligence,' Cynthia had remarked and he had thrown up his hand. 'A hit! A very palpable hit.'

She smiled at the memory as, her maid at her heels, she quickly crossed St James's Street and turned into Dover Street. At this hour there were very few other people about; two housemaids flirted with a footman on the opposite side of the street, and an officer walked slowly and unsteadily ahead of her. She hoped he wasn't drunk. Perhaps it would be better to cross the road. She looked back at Cotter just as a curricle and pair whirled around the corner with a clatter of hooves and wheels, the horses plunging madly and the driver pulling frantically on the reins. A tiger chased after them on foot. He must have been cast from the dickey. One of the horses must have taken fright; as they watched, it reared up, kicking over the traces. The whole equipage veered sharply to the right. Cynthia and Cotter retreated up the steps of the nearest house as it hurtled past them.

"Watch where you are going, damn you!"

Cotter clutched Cynthia's arm. "He's knocked down that officer, Miss. I hope he don't run him over."

With a loud crack, the curricle lurched back into the street, rolled a little, and came to a stop. The groom ran up, gasping, and went at once to the distraught horses' heads. "The pole has snapped," they heard him call to the driver who continued to tug on the reins.

"Let us go on; we can do nothing," Cynthia said.

When the two women came abreast of the officer, they found him clinging to the railings. He was trying to stand, but seemed unable to put any weight on his left leg.

"Can we be of assistance, sir?" Cynthia asked. "Are you hurt?"

"I hesitate to ask, but if you could help me reach the steps so that I can sit and see if I can do anything with this deuced leg of mine…"

Cynthia glanced down, half-fearful of what she would see, but there was no sign of blood. "Is it broken?"

"I hope not. I only have it three weeks." He laughed. "I beg your pardon. It is an artificial limb, a very fancy one with working joints and the ankle seems to have been knocked out of kilter."

"I see." She looked doubtfully at him, wondering if she would be able to bear his weight. Cotter seemed to feel the same. She handed her mistress the parcels, saying, "Begging your pardon, Miss, but I think I'll manage better nor you. Now, sir, if you place your arm on my shoulder…"

The officer obeyed and, with Cotter's support, managed to hop to the steps where he sat with a relieved sigh. Cynthia, in the meantime, advanced to the front door and rapped sharply. When there was no response, she rapped again, preparing her plea for assistance, for the man could not be left sitting on the steps and the hapless curricle driver and his tiger were not yet in control of their horses.

The door opened and a sour-faced servant looked down his nose at her. "Deliveries are through the area," he said, indicating the steps down to the basement, and began to shut the door.

"Stop!" Cynthia put one foot on the hall threshold.

"That's enough, Missy! Off you go, now."

"Not before you go to the aid of this officer. He cannot stand or walk at present."

The manservant sniffed. "Over-indulged has he? Let him see how he gets home. What are we coming to, with bits of muslin knocking on gentlemen's doors. Be off, or I'll have you removed."

"How dare you! You should be ashamed of yourself, refusing to aid one who fought for England while you remained comfortably at home."

The man's face was beetroot red. His raised hand froze in the air.

"What the devil is all that noise, Bates?"

Marfield! It couldn't be. But there he was, coming to see what had disturbed his breakfast by the looks of it, stockinged feet shoved into backless slippers, and the skirts of a sumptuous ruby damask dressing-gown floating around him. Beneath it he wore shirt and trousers. His hair was tousled, as if he had recently risen from his bed. He advanced down the hall. Catching sight of her, he froze and then came forward.

"Cynthia! I mean, Miss Glazebrook! What—what may I do for you?" He stood back and gestured invitingly. "Pray, come in."

"Don't be ridiculous, Marfield. Of course I shan't come in. It would be most improper. What you may do for me is have your man here assist this officer who was knocked over by a curricle and needs help." She glanced over her shoulder. "And perhaps send a groom to the aid of that idiot who thinks he can drive a curricle and pair."

"You heard the lady, Bates. Help the officer into the house and then send to the stables."

"Thank you, my lord." Cynthia sketched a curtsey and retreated down the steps to where Cotter hovered protectively near the sufferer. "Good day, sir. I am sure you will receive all the attention you need."

He touched his shako in salute. "Thank you, ma'am. I am most grateful to both of you for your assistance."

She shook her head. "It was the least we could do."

The Husband Criteria

~~~

Marfield watched appreciatively as mistress and maid walked away. Did they realise how effectively those little spencers drew attention to their rears? Probably not, he decided. Judging by the agitated flutter of her muslin skirts, the lady was still up in the boughs. What had Bates said to her? Did he really want to know?

"Your pardon, my lord, but if you would assist me, we could get him on his feet without doing further damage. The curricle caught him in the ribs, and he also has an artificial leg."

Marfield obeyed. Between them, they soon had the officer—a lieutenant, about his own age, Marfield thought—upright. His arms about their shoulders, he managed to hop up the few steps and into the hall.

"The office, I think," Marfield said, and they manoeuvred him into the room reserved for business matters and eased him into an old-fashioned, deep-seated library armchair where he lay back, gasping. He was very pale and breathed unevenly as if every inhalation hurt.

"Your hat, sir?"

"What? Oh, yes." He removed the peaked shako and handed it to Bates, then ran a hand through his neatly trimmed black hair.

"Coffee and something to eat," Marfield said. "And send for a physician."

At this, their guest opened his eyes. "No need. Just need to catch my breath, that's all."

Marfield shook his head. "I shall have to answer to your advocate if I fail to take care of you."

"My advocate? Oh, the young lady. What a splendid girl."

"She is taken," Marfield snapped. "Bates."

"Yes, my lord."

Bates returned quickly with a tray of coffee, a decanter, and a plate of ham sandwiches. "I thought it simplest, my lord," he said apologetically.

"No, no. Excellent idea. Offer Lieutenant—"

"Simpson," their guest said. "Of the 52nd."

"I'm Marfield."

"I am in your debt, my lord."

"Nonsense, man." Marfield lifted the decanter invitingly. "A ball of fire in your coffee?"

The other man grinned. "Then I shall be doubly in your debt." He sighed. "What a cursed thing to happen. It took so long for my leg to heal completely so that they could fit the new limb and, of course, you must wait your turn with Potts—he is very much in demand. It is quite a thing, you know, for everything must be measured exactly. I hope the ankle is only knocked awry, and not permanently damaged." He accepted the coffee cup and drank deeply. "Ah. I feel much more the thing."

"The joints in your limb are functional, then?" Marfield asked.

"Yes. It's one of the new Anglesey limbs. Potts improved his design for the Marquess after he lost his leg at Waterloo. Now, the rest of us can benefit from his ingenuity."

"Were you also injured at Waterloo?" Marfield asked, passing the other man the plate of sandwiches.

"Thank you. Yes." The lieutenant volunteered no more and Marfield did not press the matter.

Just then the physician was shown in and Marfield withdrew, telling Bates to provide any assistance needed.

The Husband Criteria

"There is no lasting damage done, as far as the physician could ascertain, my lord," Bates reported later. "He cannot answer for the artificial limb, of course. The ribs are bruised rather than broken, he said. The lieutenant has requested that I procure a hack to take him back to his quarters."

"Send a footman—he is to make sure that it is not some broken-down nag or carriage but something more comfortable. He is to accompany the lieutenant in case he needs assistance."

Twenty minutes later, Marfield said goodbye to his uninvited guest, who wrung his hand as he thanked him for his assistance.

"And if you should speak to the young lady who came to my aid, my lord, pray convey my respectful compliments and heartfelt thanks." Taking the footman's arm, Lieutenant Simpson hopped down the few steps and pulled himself into the hack.

Bates shut the front door and cleared his throat. "Your breakfast, my lord? Your eggs are quite inedible. Should Mrs Paxton prepare more or fry a beefsteak or some mutton chops?"

"No," Marfield said curtly. He looked down his dressing-gown sleeve. "I must finish dressing."

He took the stairs two at a time, but his mind was elsewhere. *She is taken*. Where had that sprung from? Why had he felt it necessary to frustrate any further interest by Lieutenant Simpson? He knew nothing about the man, but could recognise his sincere admiration of Miss Glazebrook. And what of his own intentions? Up to now he had not gone out of his way to fix his interest with her. That must change.

Like an automaton, he allowed his valet to remove the dressing-gown, replace the simple neckcloth with a more elaborately tied one, and ease him into waistcoat and coat. He waited patiently while his hair was combed and brushed to sit just so, and a cloths brush was whisked over his shoulders to remove anything dust or stray hairs that might have lodged there.

"Boots or shoes, my lord?"

"Slippers for now."

He left Bates tidying the room and went down to the library where he sat at his desk and drew a sheet of paper to him.

Chapter Eleven

Cynthia brandished the latest copy of *The Ladies' Universal Register* as she came into her mother's dressing room.

"Listen to this, Mamma. From *Tonnish Topics and Society Secrets*. 'The most sought-after invitations this Season are not to balls, routs, or pick-nicks, but to the intimate evenings held in some of the best houses where multiple generations of family and close friends meet, mingle, and entertain one another. We understand that amateur theatricals are very popular, the more gothick and melodramatic the better, with each House hoping to contest the palm first won at Swanmere House.'"

"That is most gratifying," Mamma said. "I am glad that we have had our turn, for all the hostesses will now vie with each other to put on the most gruesome entertainment. Our Witches' Sabbath would seem very tame in comparison."

"It was just Macbeth and some Purcell," Cynthia said, "but between Ann's music and the boys' capering, it was quite effective. They also have something about Chloe's ball."

"Oh? What do they say?"

"'*Last week's ball at Swanmere House was marked by the first appearance in Society of Lord Stanton, heir to the Duke of Gracechurch, who took advantage of the Oxford vacation to lead out Miss Loring in the opening dance. He subsequently proved an amiable and personable dancing partner to several of our young ladies and we look forward to the day when he shall regularly grace our ballrooms. It was a most successful evening, we are told, with some forty couple standing up for the finishing dance in the early hours of the morning.'"*

"Is there anything about Almack's?"

Cynthia skimmed down the page. "Attendance at the April balls was less than expected, *'no doubt due to the further adjournment of Parliament and the postponement of the Queen's drawing-room. We are relieved to report that her Majesty continues to recover from her indisposition.'* Otherwise it is just the usual *on-dits* and hints at new crim cons. I'll leave it here for you."

"Thank you." Her mother looked up as her maid entered the room.

"A note for Miss Glazebrook, ma'am. The footman is to wait for a reply."

"It's probably from Chloe," Cynthia said, opening the note. "No—it's from Marfield. He invites me to drive in the Park with him later. He wishes to call for me at four o'clock."

"You have no other engagements this afternoon, have you?" Mamma asked.

"No." Cynthia went to her mother's little writing desk and penned a brief acceptance. She handed the note to the maid, striving to seem as if she received such invitations from earls' sons every day. As soon as the door closed, she sank into a chair. "Well, that is something I had not expected, especially after this morning."

"What do you mean, this morning?"

"I knocked on his front door at half-past nine, disturbed his breakfast by the looks of it."

"What!"

"I didn't know it was his door," Cynthia protested, and described the little encounter. "I couldn't leave the poor man just sitting there, could I? They were still wrestling with the horses, and he could not move of his own volition."

Mamma sighed. "No, if there was nobody else to go to his aid, you must have done so. Thank goodness it was Marfield, and not some rakehell."

Cynthia laughed. "You should have seen his face. I have never seen anybody so shocked in all my life."

"At least it shows that he is not used to females on his doorstep."

"That is true."

"What will you wear this afternoon?"

"My new pelisse over the muslin trimmed with cerise ribbons. It has no flounces or lace that might catch when I climb into the curricle."

"An excellent choice. Wear the bonnet with the turned-back brim so that he can see your face. I wonder sometimes what a gentleman thinks when a lady buries herself so deeply that he can either try to see her or tend to his horses. It's a wonder there are not more accidents."

"Perhaps that explains why so many gentlemen look so bored when driving a lady," Cynthia said as she carefully refolded Marfield's note. Normally she did not bother keeping such things, but this one was different. He had struck the perfect note between formal and personal, she thought.

Catherine Kullmann

My dear Miss Glazebrook,

I trust you have recovered from this morning's little contretemps and will do me the honour of driving in the Park with me in the afternoon. Should it suit you, I shall call for you in my curricle at four o'clock.
I have instructed the footman to wait for your reply.
Your obedient servant,
Marfield.

~~~

My dear Lord Marfield,

Thank you for your kind enquiry and invitation. I shall be happy to drive in the Park with you at four o'clock this afternoon.
Yours etc.
Cynthia Glazebrook

Marfield looked down at the little note and took a deep breath. He had never courted a woman before. His father had taken him aside before he went up to Oxford and, in a surprisingly frank discussion, had explained the various approaches a student could expect, from the professional ladies of pleasure to the so-called Oxford Toasts whose ambition it was to marry above their station by entangling a gentleman commoner or, even better, a nobleman.

"The first will lighten your purse and likely give you the clap."

"The clap?" Marfield had interrupted. He had heard the expression, of course, but was not sure exactly what it meant.

The Husband Criteria

"A disease that has you pissing pins and needles or gives you sores on your cock," Benton said bluntly, "and there's no real cure for it. What's more, you could infect your wife and your unborn children. It's not worth it, Rafe. Box the Jesuit if you need release, but avoid the Cyprians. You cannot always tell if one is a fire ship until it is too late. As for the others, such an unequal marriage must be unhappy. I hope I need not warn you against seducing the innocent, whether of your own rank or inferior to you, or taking advantage of any servant, no matter how willing she may appear to be."

"No, sir."

"The best thing to do is to marry young, as your mother and I did. But not everyone is so fortunate as to meet their future spouse at an early age. Our families saw to it that we were introduced, and we instantly took a liking to one another. That is important, Rafe. We still are very comfortable together, and I wish the same for you and your sister."

By the time he came on the town, Rafe had grown accustomed to being of a celibate disposition and had seen too much of fellows who treated venery as a sport or a hobby to wish to emulate them. He wanted more than a financial transaction or a quick coupling with a restless matron who had already borne her husband a couple of heirs. He had gained a reputation for being aloof and close-mouthed about his affairs. That there had been none was nobody's business but his own.

But things had changed. Strange that his father's offer of Ailesthorpe should come at the same time that his interest fixed on Miss Glazebrook—he glanced down at the note again. Cynthia. Or was it that he had reached a time in his life where he was ready, even eager to settle? It would be pleasant to take over Ailesthorpe with a wife at his side. But first he had to win her. He rang for his valet.

"I want the curricle brought round at ten minutes to four, Bates. Do we have a lap rug or similar that is suitable for a lady?"

"I'm not sure, my lord."

"Find out. If not, you are to procure one at once. The best quality, mind you, and for the curricle—not so large that it might get entangled in the wheels."

"Perhaps a cashmere shawl, my lord? It would be less bulky."

"Very well. Bring a selection."

"Very good, my lord."

Marfield drew up outside the Glazebrooks' home promptly at four o'clock. His tiger jumped down and went to the horses' heads while Marfield knocked on the front door. He was immediately shown into a parlour where Miss Glazebrook sat with her mother. Their eyes met and she smiled, a warm, welcoming smile of lips and eyes that revealed her true beauty. He felt himself smile in return, and for some brief seconds, the world stood still. Gathering himself, he crossed the room to bow over Mrs Glazebrook's hand.

"Good day, Marfield."

"Good day, ma'am."

"I shan't delay you—you will not want to keep your horses waiting."

"Thank you, ma'am." He turned to Cynthia who had risen from her seat. "Shall we, Miss Glazebrook?"

She looked ravishing in green trimmed with gold and an enchanting bonnet that framed her face without hiding it. She draped a shawl around her shoulders, picked up her reticule, and drew on her gloves. "Certainly, Lord Marfield."

All three were aware that by inviting her to drive with him, Marfield was signalling a more particular interest and that this signal would not go unnoticed by the polite world. Her acceptance signified her willingness to explore a possibly closer relationship. Today they set their feet on a new path. Who knew where it would lead?

Cynthia felt Mamma's eyes on her back as they left the parlour. Had she noticed that strange pause when he arrived, when their eyes met and it felt as if they had stepped out of time and place, into another world inhabited by just the two of them? It had only lasted a moment, and then they had snapped back to reality.

"What a handsome pair," she said of his matched bays. "Do you have them long?"

"Two years, now. Hold them steady, Tom," he added to his tiger then offered Cynthia his hand to assist her to step up into the carriage. She managed it neatly. When she was comfortably seated, he handed her a folded shawl.

"In case you feel the chill."

"Oh! Thank you. It is beautiful," she said, admiring the rich shades of red and orange that glowed against the green of her pelisse. She spread it over on her lap as he took his seat and gathered up the reins.

"Let them go!"

At the command, the tiger released his hold at the horses' heads and hurried to scramble into the dickey behind. Soon they had trotted up Park Place and turned into Piccadilly, joining the procession of carriages heading for the Park. Cynthia sat quietly;

Martin always preferred to reach this point before engaging in conversation. Apparently Marfield was the same.

Once this was safely negotiated, he smiled down at her and said, "Miss Glazebrook, do I need to apologise for anything my man said this morning? I did not hear all that passed between you."

"No. I imagine that his tasks include repelling boarders, or importunate ladies who knock on the door at half-past nine in the morning."

"Generally yes—not that it happens frequently, I assure you—but I wish he had shown more discretion this morning."

"You cannot really blame the man. I was carrying my purchases so that my maid could go to the officer's assistance. The way he was sitting, your man assumed that he was inebriated and that I was…" She hesitated, but it was too late to stop. "My maid and I were his companions in a night of revelry."

"Good God! Miss Glazebrook, I am appalled that you were so insulted, and at my door to boot. I am very sorry for it. Rest assured, I'll have a word with him."

"Pray do not, sir. Better to put it behind us, I think. Tell me, how did the lieutenant go on?"

"According to the physician I sent for, he has some bruises but no lasting damage was done. The foot is a mechanical problem that can be rectified, I understand. By the way, I am to convey his respectful compliments and heartfelt thanks."

"Thank you. I could not have left him there, you know."

"Many young ladies would have."

"Do you think so? My uncle was at Waterloo. We heard from him of the sufferings of the wounded. It took days for all to be brought from the battle-field, and you can imagine the state they were in then. But such sacrifices, whether of life or limb, are soon forgotten, are they not? My father has resolved that when hiring servants, or men to work on the estate, he will give preference to former soldiers."

"That is very laudable."

"Yes, but what can one man do? There are few positions that are suitable for the disabled, especially if they cannot read or write."

"Perhaps they could be taught," Marfield suggested. "A man who has difficulty standing can work sitting down. The wounded do receive a pension, I understand, but I don't know if it is enough to live on. Besides, it is not good for a man to be idle."

At this, Cynthia almost suffocated trying to repress her laughter.

He raised an eyebrow at her splutters. "What?"

"Do you really think it behoves us—the *ton*—to discuss the idleness of others, when our whole life is one of idle pleasure?"

"Idle pleasure or boredom?" he replied swiftly. "We are fortunate that we do not have to earn our bread, that is true, but a sensible man or woman will make good use of their time by improving their mind through reading or studious discussion, or practising their skills. And some pleasure must be allowed, for all work and no play makes for dull boys and girls, does it not?"

She cast a sidelong glance at him. He seemed focussed on his team, but there was a little twitch at the side of his mouth. He caught her eye and his smile broadened. She had to smile back. "You preach a very fine sermon, my lord."

"What of you, Miss Puritan?"

"Unfair!" she protested, then sighed. "I just wish my life had more purpose, that is all."

He transferred the reins to his whip hand and touched hers lightly with his left. "That will come," he said quietly. "This stage of our lives, where we have little or no responsibility for anyone other than ourselves will end soon enough. Let us enjoy it while we may."

She took a deep breath. "I hadn't looked on it that way."

They were turning into the Park, and already attracting curious glances. "Do you have brothers and sisters?" she asked.

"Just one sister, Anna. She is three years younger than I but, between school and Oxford, I never had the chance really to get to know her. She married at eighteen, at the end of her first Season and now lives in Northamptonshire. She has two children, and prefers not to travel at present."

"Have you visited her?"

"Twice. The year after she got married and last year. I was abroad in the interim."

"Where did you go? We went to France in September 1815. My uncle was stationed in Paris."

"Did you enjoy it?"

She shook her head. "It was too soon. The French were too wounded; the Prussian, Russian, and British armies swaggered about—I know they were the victors and had suffered huge losses, but it is governments who make war, not the people. We left after a month and went to Nice, but it was very thin of company. So many had left when Napoleon escaped from Elba. In the end we were home for Christmas. But I enjoyed seeing other countries; I would love to go back."

She paused to nod and smile at Miss Nugent who was, again, being driven by her brother.

Marfield raised his whip to salute the other couple. "You seem to be on better terms with your brother than I with my sister," he said when they had passed.

"Yes. Although it was similar with us, while he was away at school and Oxford. In recent years we have become good friends. Travelling together helped. Nothing encourages intimacy like sharing a carriage for days on end."

He laughed. "There is no truer test of character."

"Who did you travel with?"

"Some friends from Oxford. We went first to Brussels and then on to Paris. The Louvre was still full of Bonaparte's ill-gotten gains. It was the most fantastical collection you could imagine, sculptures from Greece and Rome, paintings by the greatest masters, all gathered together in one place."

She nodded. "We were just in time to see them. I think it was right that they were restored to their original owners, but I like the idea of a great collection that is open to all. Not everyone can afford to do a grand tour and if each country had such a collection…"

"But is it right to take unique treasures away from where they belong? What about Lord Elgin's marbles?"

"We had such discussions about them last year when Parliament was considering whether to purchase them for the Museum. My father could not decide how to vote. On the one hand, he felt that they belonged in Greece where they were originally erected, and could not countenance the despoiling of the temple where they were literally hacked from the walls. He also could not deny that his father, who made his fortune in India, had brought many beautiful pieces home. But they were all portable and, my grandfather says, acquired honestly. Lord Elgin says the same, of course, about his acquisition, although they were not at all portable."

"A nice conundrum. What did your father decide?"

"He voted in favour of buying them on the grounds that the damage was already done, and this way they would be appropriately cared for. If Parliament had been consulted while they were still in situ, he would have voted against the motion, but he could not turn back the clock and had to consider the situation as it was now."

"A Solomonic judgement." He broke off to return the greetings of two gentlemen riding past.

Cynthia had been intent on their discussion but now she saw that they were being subjected a great deal of covert glances from the assembled *ton*. She smiled at Chloe who sat in the barouche-landau with Rosa opposite old Lady Loring and Lord Swanmere. They had drawn up beside another carriage containing another old lady and Lady Benton. Chloe said something and all heads turned towards Marfield's curricle. The lady beside Lady Benton beckoned imperiously.

Marfield groaned. "My grandmother, the dowager Marchioness of Martinborough. She who will not be gainsaid. I cannot pull up beside them; would you object to our drawing in here at the side and walking the few steps back to them? Tom will stay with the horses."

"No, of course not." In fact, Cynthia would have preferred not to be presented in such a public manner, but she could not refuse. She sat quietly, admiring the skill with which he eased his equipage into what seemed a very tight space indeed. He jumped down and came round to assist her alight, then offered her his arm and led her through a gap in the rails that separated the lawn from the carriages and horses jostling on the ride.

"You know my mother, of course," he said as they walked back to the Martinborough carriage.

"I have had the pleasure of meeting Lady Benton several times," Cynthia agreed. She was relieved to see that the Swanmere carriage had moved on.

Marfield stopped beside the barouche and bowed. "Good day, Grandmother, Mother. Grandmother, may I have the honour of presenting Miss Glazebrook?"

"Good day, my ladies." Cynthia sketched a curtsey—anything more would be too extravagant here in the Park.

"Of course I know Miss Glazebrook," Lady Benton said with a friendly smile. "I am happy to see you again, my dear."

Her mother inclined her head a scant inch. She must be at least as old as Great-Grandmamma, Cynthia thought, noting the dowager's sharp eyes and wrinkled face surmounted by a pile of carefully-arranged silver curls protected by a green silk calash bonnet lined with pale pink and tied with green and pink ribbons. She clutched an ornate lorgnette, which was aimed balefully at the newcomers.

"Don't just stand there, giving me a crick in my neck," she snapped, gesturing to the seat opposite her. "Sit down. You too, Marfield."

Cynthia felt rather than heard him sigh.

"Just for five minutes," he said as he handed her up. "I cannot keep the horses standing for longer than that."

"You gentlemen—your horses are always more important to you than anyone else. Why have you not called on me?"

"I was not aware that you were in town, ma'am. When did you come up?"

"Yesterday," the dowager retorted.

Cynthia bit her lip to repress her smile.

Lady Martinborough turned her magnified gaze on Cynthia. "Glazebrook. Are you related to the Nabob Glazebrook?"

"He is my grandfather, ma'am."

"Hmm. And your mother? Who are her people?"

"She was Miss Raven."

"Raven? Ransford's daughter."

"Yes, ma'am."

The dowager snorted but before she could say anymore, Marfield intervened. "Enough, Grandmother. You will put me to the blush if you subject Miss Glazebrook to any further inquisition."

"It would take more than that to put you to the blush, you scapegrace. Don't you agree, Miss Glazebrook?"

"Now how am I to answer that?" Cynthia said. "Reluctant as I must be to contradict a lady of such advanced years and standing, you cannot expect me to agree with your characterisation of your grandson; I have always found him most gentleman-like."

"Well said, Miss Glazebrook," Lady Benton said. "I should like to talk more, but we mustn't keep the horses standing any longer." She held her hand out to Cynthia. "Goodbye, my dear. Pray come and call on me."

Cynthia touched the proffered fingers. "Thank you, ma'am."

Marfield rose. "We'll take our leave of you, ladies." He hopped down and held his hand out to Cynthia.

She placed hers in it, made a half-bow and with a polite "My ladies", gratefully stepped down onto the lawn.

The Husband Criteria

Another bow and a wave, and they were able to depart.

"Ooof!" Marfield let out a long breath. "I am so sorry; I had no idea she would go for you like that."

"I was beginning to wonder would she demand to see my teeth and run a hand down my calf," Cynthia said.

"You handled her very well. I liked your reference to her advanced years and standing. She couldn't really take umbrage at being called old in that manner."

"Thank you for drawing her fire. Still, there is one thing we may be grateful for."

"And that is?"

"You saw the carriage that was drawn up beside hers earlier? Lady Swan-Loring and Miss Loring were in it."

"Yes?"

"The old lady sitting opposite them was my great-grandmother, Lady Loring. Just imagine if they were still there when we reached your grandmother."

"Good heavens! It would have been lorgnettes at dawn, you think?"

"It is very likely."

He handed her up into the curricle, took his seat, and set the horses moving. At the top of the ride, he turned neatly and headed back towards the entrance. The interest in them had died down a little. Marfield slowed the horses, glanced over his shoulder as if to make sure his tiger was not paying them over much attention, and said quietly, "Miss Glazebrook?"

She looked up at him. He seemed very serious. "Yes?"

"Miss Glazebrook, Cynthia, I know it is too soon but, in light of our encounter with my grandmother, which will not have gone unnoticed, I feel I should assure you of the sincerity of my regard for you, and of my intentions."

"Oh!" She felt her cheeks grow hot, and that little, familiar thrill suddenly grew bigger and more exciting. "I am honoured, Lord Marfield," she began, "but…"

"But?" he encouraged her.

"As you say, it is too soon for such a discussion."

"There will be talk, I fear, more talk than such a drive would normally give rise to. I wondered if I should have a word with your father."

"No," she said at once. He seemed taken aback by her refusal; better to explain it. "I appreciate your consideration, Marfield, but that would put matters on too serious a footing. Why allow your grandmother to force your hand? If there is talk, let them talk. It is only tittle-tattle that will soon be ousted by something equally trivial."

"Perhaps, but not if I invite you to go with me to see the Elgin Marbles, say, or for an ice at Gunter's. I should like to do that. And dance with you at every ball possible. To court you, in other words."

"I still think it is too soon for you to speak to Papa. I too should like to see where this—whatever it is between us—takes us, provided we are both free to draw back without any rancour on either side. We must promise to be honest with each other, Marfield. If you discover we should not suit, you must tell me. I promise I would not hold it against you. Better to find out now than a year into marriage."

"You are a woman in a thousand! Are you happy to mention our agreement to your parents? I will not be able to avoid discussing it with mine," he added ruefully.

"Yes. I shall have to tell my mother that Lady Benton invited me to call. But they will be discreet, I know." She took a deep breath before going on. "I appreciate and value your frankness, Marfield. I think it only fair to tell you that I return your interest—and your regard."

"Cynthia!"

She felt his hand grip hers briefly before he turned his attention back to the mass of carriages and riders leaving the Park.

He smiled. "Excellent. Who knows, we may end thanking my grandmother."

There was certainly a new ease between them as they returned to Park Place.

"Will you let me know when you propose to call on my mother?" Marfield asked as he drew up outside the Glazebrook's house. "You know where I live, after all."

"Yes. What an eventful day it has been. Thank you for everything."

"No. I must thank you."

Marfield helped her down from the curricle and walked with her to the door, waiting until it had opened and she had vanished inside before returning to the carriage. An eventful day indeed, but it could not have gone better if he had planned it.

Chapter Twelve

In the Forbes's house, everything was subordinated to the requirements of music, so too the first-floor drawing-room that took up the whole front of the house and was connected to a smaller back room, forming an L. On Mondays, the musicians gathered in the front room, leaving the other room free for those who wished to consult Mr Forbes on a tricky piece or finish writing out a score.

Ann had completed copying the parts of the new piano trio that Bradley and Mr Forbes had promised to run through with her today. If she was satisfied, she would leave the parts with them so that they could practise more thoroughly during the coming week. As she opened the dividing door to the front room, she heard her name.

"Miss Ann is very devoted to her art. And, all things considered, her work is quite tolerable. But nothing can come of it, can it?" It was Bradley who spoke.

"Why not?" Dennison asked.

"She is a gentlewoman, and cannot perform in public. Once she marries, she will have no time for music."

"Don't say that," Prescott protested, to Ann's delight.

"Why, are you trying to fix your interest there?"

The Husband Criteria

"Why not? She would be the ideal wife, able to assist with my music, copy out parts for example. If I am appointed to a cathedral, she could make choral arrangements and write voluntaries for me."

"And iron your surplices?" Ann asked sarcastically as she stepped into the room, to the men's obvious dismay. "Such a tempting offer."

All three men frowned disapprovingly. Prescott reddened while Dennison said, "Here, Miss Ann, you can't refuse a man before he has proposed."

Ann was shaking inside but she refused to retreat. She stiffened her spine. "It is quite usual to hint a gentleman away if one does not intend to accept him."

"At least a musician would allow you to continue with your work. Many a husband would not countenance it."

"Indeed?" Ann spread out her sheets of music on top of the piano. "How liberal of him."

"With that attitude, you'll never marry," Bradley warned. "A man wants to be appreciated in his own home."

"And what contribution will he make to this establishment?"

"Contribution? He will provide it of course, and provide for you and your children."

"For his children, you mean."

"You will also enjoy all the advantages of marriage."

Dennison and Prescott looked at each other. "Here, steady on, old chap," Dennison said.

But Bradley was not to be deterred. "No girl wishes to remain an old maid."

This pronouncement, as final as if engraved on Moses's tablets of stone, was the last straw for Ann. "I would not be too sure of

143

that," she snapped. "A wise lady will be very sure of to whom and to what she is committing herself before she accepts an offer."

"Miss Ann! You shock me!" Bradley said, just as Mr Forbes, who had come in from the landing, intervened.

"That will be quite enough of that. Gentlemen, Miss Ann is here as a fellow-musician and is to be treated with respect and circumspection. Now, who goes first today? Dennison?"

"I am not so far advanced as I had hoped to be with my Lady of the Lake," Dennison apologised, "but if Miss Ann would essay the accompaniment, I shall give you the first verse of Ellen's Prayer to the Virgin. Very slowly and tranquilly, Miss Ann, if you please, like lake water slowly rippling."

"Let me play it through once on my own," Ann said, taking the music. He stood at her shoulder, humming the melody gently as she played, now and again glancing up at him as if to confirm her phrasing. "It's beautiful, Dennison," she said honestly at the end. "Let us hear you sing it."

"Bravo!" Mr Forbes said, when Dennison was finished. "How do you plan to continue?"

"I'm not sure yet. I have some ideas but they must ripen."

"Very well. Miss Ann, is your trio ready to be heard?"

"Yes." She handed Bradley and him their parts then sat again at the piano.

By the time Ann returned to Swanmere House that evening, she had put the earlier discussion behind her, and could confine her account of the day to its musical events before excusing herself to rest before dinner as they were going on to the Nugent's ball.

~~~

The Husband Criteria

"Come in, Rafe." Marfield's mother laid aside the novel she was reading and smiled at her son. "I hoped you would look in this evening."

"I thought it best after my grandmother's meddling." He dropped into his usual chair. "I would have ignored her if I didn't fear she would despatch a footman to command our presence. That would have caused even more talk."

"The *ton* does talk; you knew that when you invited Miss Glazebrook to drive with you," she pointed out. "Or did she somehow force the invitation—manoeuvre you into a corner where you felt obliged to issue it?"

"No, no. Nothing like that."

"I am glad of it; I would not have thought it of her. She always seemed very prettily-behaved to me."

"Yes." He smiled inwardly, recalling how Cynthia had confronted Bates, voice raised and eyes flashing.

"Then what is the problem?"

"It is not a problem, on the contrary—to be frank, ma'am, I would have preferred to do without my grandmother's notice. Afterwards, I wondered should I speak to Mr Glazebrook, assure him of my intentions."

"Rafe!" His mother swung her feet down from the day-bed where she was reclining and sat upright. "Are you serious?"

"Yes, but I would have preferred to take things more slowly. Cynthia, Miss Glazebrook agrees."

"You don't mean to say you discussed it with her?"

"Of course. You will agree that she is the person most directly concerned."

"I suppose she is. What did she say?"

145

"Speaking to her father would put matters on too serious a footing, and I should not let my grandmother force my hand. We agreed we would like to explore what is between us without any commitment on either side as yet."

"That is very sensible."

"She is not at all missish. I like that in her. She also said that I had been frank with her and, although it might not be usual for a young lady to do so, she assured me that she returned my interest—and regard."

His mother looked astounded. "That is direct indeed. So you are betrothed."

"Not yet."

"As good as, Rafe. You cannot withdraw now. It is a matter of honour."

He shook his head. "She made it clear that we are both free to draw back without any rancour or recriminations on either side."

"And you believe her?" She sounded incredulous.

"I do. There is something about her, Mother—she is pure gold; untarnished." He stopped, embarrassed by this spontaneous encomium. He was not usually given to such flowery speech. Better finish it. "We agreed to let our parents know, and should be grateful for your discretion and support."

"Yes, of course," his mother said. "You may rely on us. We need to contrive ways for you to meet without proclaiming it as yet to the world at large. The Ransfords are her grandparents, she said?"

"Yes. And Lady Loring—the old lady who was talking to my grandmother when we first saw you in the Park—is her great-grandmother."

"Is she indeed? She and my mother are cousins, through their mothers, so you and Miss Glazebrook must be cousins too." She must have noticed his shock, for she added, "Don't be alarmed; the connection is remote enough that there is no need to consult the tables of kindred and affinity. I could give a party, one of the family evenings that are all the rage, according to this."

He took the journal and read the little paragraph. "I have two objections, ma'am. I do not know how we would come up with a suitable entertainment. Also, if you call it a family party, you could hardly exclude my great-aunt and I would prefer not to have her near Cynthia. You know how malicious she can be, and especially towards young ladies, as if she resents them somehow. She was not kind to Anna during her Season."

"No. She is resentful of their opportunities, I think. When she was young, she would only consider a suitor who was her equal in rank or above. And he had to be presentable in every way; handsome, of impeccable morals, wealthy, of course…"

"Did such paragon exist?"

"One or two, I understand. She thought all she had to do was drop the handkerchief, but they were strangely reluctant to pick it up."

"I wonder why?"

"Why, indeed? But I agree. I can hardly give a family party and exclude her and Cousin Cassandra."

"Why not just invite the Glazebrooks to dinner without making a big fuss about it?"

"That would be simplest. But let us get the calls out of the way, first. If Miss Glazebrook calls, that is."

"She has every intention of doing so. I have asked her to let me know when."

"He is very taken by her," Lady Benton told her husband later that evening. "They are already on such familiar terms that they saw nothing improper in his requesting her to send him a note advising him when she would call here. I asked him to let me know in turn—I shall only be at home to the Glazebrooks that day. I am sure that Rafe means to put in an appearance too."

"Would it be too blatant for me to look in? I have to admit that I have no idea what she looks like, although I must have seen her on several occasions."

"It would, I'm afraid. If all goes well, I shall return the call and then we may invite them to a small dinner with the Tamms, perhaps, and the Ransfords. Tonight is Lady Nugent's ball. They will probably be there—I have seen Miss Nugent several times with The Three Graces."

"Three Graces?"

"So the *ton* has dubbed Miss Loring, Miss Overton, and Miss Glazebrook. Really, Benton, do you pay no attention to what goes on in society?"

"Very little," he admitted. "So we are to look in at the Nugents after dinner, are we, Lottie?"

"Yes." She tugged the bell-pull. "I must tell Wilson to put out a ball dress."

Would he be there? They hadn't discussed their plans for the evening—there had been so much more to talk about, but Cynthia hoped that Marfield would also be at the Nugents' ball. It took every ounce of self-control to suppress the internal bubble of excitement and anticipation and walk sedately up the grand staircase to greet the Nugents. The Swanmere House party arrived soon afterwards and it was natural for the two families to join forces.

"Did you enjoy your drive this afternoon?" Chloe asked with a meaningful glance.

"Yes." She had no wish to elaborate. Hitherto she had enjoyed the light-hearted discussions with Chloe and Ann about their various engagements and encounters but this, with Marfield, had suddenly become serious—and private. Rather than share them, she wanted to bask in her memories, recalling every word and expression. "I was delighted to see Great-Grandmamma with you. I am sure she enjoyed the little excursion."

"We encountered old Lady Martinborough," Rosa told the Glazebrooks. "Did you know that she and Lady Loring are cousins through their mothers. They had not seen one another for decades but instantly recognised each other. Lady Martinborough waved us down, but we could not block the Row for long. She is to take tea with us tomorrow. She never dines out, she informed us, but is partial to a dish of tea about four o'clock."

"You have your instructions." Cynthia's father was clearly amused.

"Indeed. Would you like to join us, Amelia?" Rosa asked.

To Cynthia's great relief, her mother shook her head. "I'm afraid I have another engagement. If you feel you need reinforcements, why not invite my mother? I don't know if she is aware of the connection—I never heard her mention it, but I imagine she would be glad to come."

As the ballroom filled, the usual coterie of men and girls assembled around the Graces. Chaperons were content to withdraw a little, secure in the knowledge that in that group no one would overstep the bounds. Out of the corner of her eye, Cynthia saw Lord and Lady Benton stop to speak to her parents and the Swann-Lorings. Strange to think that they were all related but, when she thought about it, it would be more unusual for there to be no connection between the families. If you went back three or four generations, all the *ton* would be linked by familial bonds, she supposed.

The sense of a tall figure behind her accompanied by a touch at her elbow had her turn a little away from the group to face Marfield.

"I trust I see you well, Miss Glazebrook."

"You do, my lord. And you?"

"Very well indeed."

The warmth in his eyes belied the trite exchange. "Are you free for the first dance?" he asked quietly.

"Yes."

"May I have it, and the supper dance?"

There was a challenge in his gaze. To make a point of asking her for the first dance was significant enough after their afternoon drive, but to dance twice with a lady was a public declaration of interest. She did not hesitate to meet his eyes. "Very well, my lord."

"Thank you."

By taking a step forward, he had them re-join the circle just as Matthew Malvin continued his account of a hot-headed young cub who had taken his elder brother's curricle without leave, let the spirited team get away from him and had come to grief that morning. "The prads escaped with a few cuts and bruises, but the pole of the curricle broke in two."

"What of the driver?" Marfield asked.

"Sore and very sorry for himself. He almost pulled his arms out of the sockets, trying to control the horses. His brother is furious, of course."

"I am surprised that the groom put the horses to for him," someone said. "He could well lose his place because of it."

"I suppose he didn't feel he had much choice," Cynthia said. "It was very wrong of the young man to put a servant in such a situation."

"Pray let us speak of something more interesting. This is no place for sermonising," a young man new to the group exclaimed impatiently.

Cynthia felt Marfield stiffen beside her. She placed a calming hand on his sleeve while Ann said, "And what do you consider to be an appropriate topic, sir? We are all ears."

He flushed at her arctic tone and turned on his heel with a muttered excuse.

"What a looby," someone said. "Who is he?"

"One Joseph Meredith. A connection of the Nugents, just down from Oxford. Thinks he is all the crack," Mr Malvin added to general laughter.

"There come the Nugents. The dancing will start soon," Miss Hardy said.

"Pray excuse me." Mr Malvin walked over to bow to Miss Nugent and lead her onto the dance floor at the first strains of a waltz.

"A waltz. Splendid." Marfield offered his arm to Cynthia while the other couples paired off. Mr Nugent and his partner

151

joined Mr Malvin and Miss Nugent, and the two couples danced a circuit of the ballroom alone before the other guests took to the floor.

"Did you speak to your parents?" Marfield asked as they waited.

"Yes. Did you?"

"Yes. My mother is already full of ideas."

"Ideas?"

"How we can spend time together without making it public."

"That would be good. I would like us to know each other better; it is difficult when there is always an audience."

He nodded. "She plans to use the newly-discovered relationship as an excuse to hold some small dinner parties and what-have-you."

"Family evenings?"

"Yes and no. There are some family members one would rather exclude. And I don't think we are able to put on High Melodrama either."

"We did a *ton* Witches Sabbath," she told him smugly.

"What? All silks and muslins and ostrich plumes."

"And lorgnettes and long gloves." She held an imaginary lorgnette to her eye and drawled, "'*Double, double, toil and trouble.*' Cook made marchpane miniatures for the spell."

He laughed. "What? Eye of newt and so on?"

"Mmm. We arranged them on a salver and offered them to the guests afterwards instead of rout cakes, together with a glass of baboon's blood."

"Baboon's blood," he repeated. "Burgundy?"

The Husband Criteria

She shook her head. "That would be too obvious, we thought. Champagne, coloured with a teaspoon of raspberry cordial. It tasted surprisingly good—and bubbled nicely."

"Very esoteric baboons, indeed. Who were the witches?"

"Ann, Chloe, and I. Martin was Wellesley, I mean Macbeth."

"Why Wellesley?"

"He is the most prominent soldier of his generation, is he not? And he made such a rapid ascent, from gentleman to baron to Duke in five years. What other man has presented patents as baron, viscount, earl, marquis, and duke on the same day in the House of Lords? Could it have been achieved without supernatural assistance?"

"When you put it like that... I would give much to see that performance."

"I doubt if it will be repeated." She looked around. "The others are dancing already. We are the last."

They were soon caught up in the exhilaration of the waltz. They danced in silence, as was their custom, a silence that bound rather than isolated.

When she rose from her curtsy, he placed her hand on his arm. "Come and greet my parents. They are over there, talking to the Tamms. My father will be pleased to see you. It was all my mother could do to dissuade him from joining her when you call."

Lord Benton was an affable gentleman of middle years with a full head of pepper-and-salt curls cut stylishly short. He was not as tall as Marfield, but broader of shoulder, as if someone had stretched the father to make the son. He immediately broke off his discussion with Lord Tamm to smile at Cynthia, and bowed very properly when Marfield presented her.

"I am delighted to make your acquaintance, my dear, and to learn of our connection through the Fromes. It is sad how quickly we can lose track of someone, is it not?"

"I fear my father was a dreadful tyrant," Lady Benton said. "He was very puffed up with his own consequence, and would not have encouraged my mother to maintain the contact with Lady Loring. He had no use for younger sons of younger sons, or their progeny, 'Let them dwindle into the ranks of the gentry, where they belonged,' he used to say, 'and not appropriate to themselves the standing of the nobility'."

"My sister and I were terrified of him," Marfield said. "He had a withering glance and could cut you down to nothing with a few words. Fortunately, we had very little to do with him."

"That wasn't fortune, that was by design," his mother said. "After I married, I never stayed at Martyn's Hall again. If we met, it was in town. My father-in-law could not avoid him at the Lords, of course, but they were not intimates, and he died before Benton came into the title."

"That generation was very much in the grand style," Benton said. "Even the way they dressed. I wonder did we change when we exchanged our periwigs, embroidered silks, and buckled shoes for what is essentially riding dress?"

"Step down from the pedestal, you mean?" Cynthia asked. "I think it very likely. Although last century's gentlemen's clothing was not as restrictive as our hoops, it seemed designed more for display than for activity."

"Impatience on a monument?" Lady Tamm asked. "That would be a fair description of old Lord Tamm when I knew him. He rarely left his rooms, and wore opulent banyans and a strange, squarish, velvet headdress that was called a *negligé* cap so that he had something of the oriental despot about him."

Lord Tamm did not dispute this description of his sire, but said, "I wonder what our grandchildren will say of us?"

"That will depend on us, will it not?" Cynthia said. "Both of my grandfathers are perfectly charming, as is Lord Swanmere who is considerably older."

"There is hope for us, so," Benton said just as Cynthia's partner for the next dance approached.

"Lady Benton spoke very frankly about her father," Cynthia said as they went home from the ball. "He seems to have been extremely difficult."

"What did she say?"

After hearing Cynthia's account of the conversation, her father said, "They already treat you as one of the family. Are they going too fast for you, Cynthia?"

"Nooo…" she said slowly, and then more definitely, "No. There is already such an, an ease between us that it is difficult to remember the need to be circumspect in public. His mother said she would try to arrange matters so that we could spend time together out of the public eye."

"Do you want that?"

"Very much. You know how the *ton* is, Papa. Everything is noted, and commented upon. Ideally, we could attend the same house party, but it will be months before that could be arranged."

"You cannot call on him, of course, but if he came here; you could stroll in the garden or sit unattended in the parlour for half an hour or so," her mother said. "But before we allow him to run tame here, he must speak to your father, Cynthia. His instinct about that was not wrong."

Cynthia sighed. "If you insist. But it must be clear that nothing is final between us and that we can both cry off at will, he as well as I."

"That is all very well, but unless you refuse his invitations to dance or drive, you will be unable to conceal his interest in you. If, in the end, nothing comes of it, the fault will be laid at your door; it will be assumed that he found you wanting in some respect, and that will affect your future prospects. Your reservations are understandable, but you should be aware of the consequences."

"Better that than enter into a marriage that you know from the outset will be miserable."

"We'll say no more then. Let us see what tomorrow brings."

Chapter Thirteen

At half-past three o'clock, Mrs Glazebrook's footman knocked on the imposing door of Benton House. After a moment, he returned to the carriage and opened the door for Mrs Glazebrook and her daughter to alight. They were bowed into the house by the butler and attendant footmen.

Cynthia swallowed a gasp at the opulent hall, which was a riot of colour compared with the austere black and white of Gracechurch House or the refined decoration of Swanmere House.

"This way, madam." The butler led them through a door at the back of the hall and down a wide passage. Opening a door at the end, he stood back to allow them enter a sunny parlour, then followed to announce, "Mrs Glazebrook, Miss Glazebrook, my lady."

The countess and Marfield came forward to greet them. "Do come and sit down," Lady Benton said. "I am not at home to anyone else today, so we have time to get to know one another." She smiled at Cynthia. "I must commend you and Marfield for being so frank with one another, and also with us. It is far better to be open about these things rather than beating about the bush."

"I agree," Cynthia's mother said. "For all that the Season is generally regarded as a marriage mart, I had never considered what it must be like to attempt to fix your interest with a lady with such avid spectators watching every movement. The Glazebrooks were neighbours of ours in Oxfordshire and I had known my husband forever."

"Benton and I met through our families," the countess said. "It was not exactly a made match, but we were given every opportunity to get to know one another."

"While we must make those opportunities," Marfield said. He looked at Cynthia's mother. "I hope you will allow me to take Miss Glazebrook to see the Elgin Marbles, for example."

"Alone?" Mamma said doubtfully. "It is too soon."

"What if Martin and Chloe—my brother and Miss Loring," Cynthia explained in an aside to the countess, "came, too. That must be unobjectionable, must it not?"

"It would be better," her mother acknowledged. "Marfield, I am aware that Cynthia was not in favour when you first suggested it, but I think you should call on my husband."

Marfield glanced at Cynthia. "I should be very happy to, ma'am, if Miss Glazebrook agrees."

Cynthia raised her hands and let them fall. "As long as you agree that we have as yet made no lasting pledge."

He stiffened, his features suddenly impassive, but nodded. "Very well."

Did he think she was reluctant to commit herself to him? It wasn't that. She hastened to explain. "A lady has the privilege of refusal; of changing her mind even, but a gentleman has not. I could not bear it if you offered for me against your better judgement, because you felt unable to withdraw."

The Husband Criteria

His stony gaze softened into a tender smile. "I promise you, I will not, and you must promise me that you will not accept me for such a reason."

"I promise," she said softly. It was as if they were alone in the room.

The arrival of a tea-tray broke the spell. Cynthia took in her surroundings while Lady Benton made the tea. This was a private room, she thought, looking at the comfortable padded bench built below the bay window with a work table beside it, the inviting armchairs and sofas by the hearth, and a round table surrounded by chairs, with an argon lamp ready to provide light for cards or other joint pastimes. Low shelves held a collection of books and journals. Over them hung a portrait of the Earl, Countess, a schoolboy Marfield, his younger sister, and another boy of about five. The family had gathered in a gazebo near a lake, the earl resting his arm on the back of his wife's chair. The younger children sat on the steps together with two beautiful spaniels while Marfield perched on the stone banister. He had made no mention of a younger brother.

"Sugar and milk, Miss Glazebrook?"

"Just milk, please, ma'am." She accepted the cup from Marfield who resumed his seat beside her.

"Miss Glazebrook, or may I say Cynthia?" the countess asked. "We are cousins, after all."

"Please do," Cynthia said quickly, as they heard voices in the hall.

Lady Benton frowned. "Who can that be? I said I was not at home."

The door was thrown open and a tired-looking lady in a crumpled carriage dress hurried into the room. She held the hand

159

of a small curly-haired boy clad in a nankeen skeleton suit and was followed by a tall, broad-shouldered gentleman of about thirty who had all the look of a country-squire, and a woman, a nursemaid probably, who carried an infant of about twelve months. The butler brought up the rear.

Lady Benton jumped to her feet. "Anna!"

"Mamma!"

The two women fell into one another's arms. Abandoned, the boy ran to the gentleman while the baby began to struggle to be put down.

Marfield held out his hand to his brother-in-law. "Welcome, Devenish. And Master Jack. Were we expecting you?"

"I'm afraid not. I had to come to town unexpectedly, and Anna decided to accompany me. It wasn't worthwhile writing ahead, she said. She wanted to surprise her mother as well."

"She certainly did that." Marfield looked to where the two women fluctuated between tears and laughter amid a torrent of words. "So this is your daughter?"

"Yes." Devenish set his son down and took the baby from the nursemaid. "Meet Charlotte, or Lottie, as she is known."

Master Jack, left to his own devices, edged nearer the tea table. Having scrutinised the offerings, he helped himself to a slice of plum cake and continued on towards Cynthia.

"I Jack," he announced. "Who're you?"

"Cynthia Glazebrook," she said promptly. She held a small plate out to him. "Would you like to put your cake on this, before you squish it. I hate squished cake, don't you?"

He took a big bite before depositing the remainder on the plate. He chewed vigorously, swallowed and said, "We have three carriages."

"Really? And how many horses?"

He paused to think, then held up four fingers.

"Four. For each carriage?"

He nodded.

"And that makes how many?"

He held up another four fingers.

"Shall we count them?"

Another nod.

Cynthia counted slowly to eight, touching each finger. "That's two carriages. There was one more. Shall we use my fingers?"

"Yes."

When she held them up, the boy solemnly touched each one as she completed the count. "Twelve horses. My goodness, that was a lot. Was it exciting?"

"At first it was, but then it was very bouncy and Lottie cried."

"Poor dear. I'm sure you are glad to be here."

"Yes. Mamma said I run around in the garden here, shake off the fidgets." He went over and tugged at his mother's skirts. "I go into the garden. You promised."

"First make your bow to your grandmother and uncle."

"And Cyntha."

"Cyntha?"

"That lady."

"Don't point," his mother said, and then, "I beg your pardon. I was so excited to see my mother that I did not notice her guests."

"That is very understandable." Mrs Glazebrook stood. "We shall leave you to your reunion."

"Go into the garden with Cyntha," Jack said.

"Cynthia must go home now," Lady Benton said. "Will you go with your uncle Marfield?"

"And Cyntha," the boy said stubbornly.

"Why don't we all go?" Marfield said. He turned to Mrs Glazebrook. "If you permit, ma'am, I'll see Miss Glazebrook home later."

"That might be best."

There was a flurry of introductions, Mrs Glazebrook took a brief farewell of her 'dear cousin', who apologised for the disturbance and bade her son to show their visitor out. Lady Anna's eyes rounded at this consideration but she was distracted by her own son's demand for the pot. He was dispatched with the nursemaid who was to bring him back to the parlour and then take the baby. Lady Benton excused herself to confer with her butler about bedrooms for the visitors and Cynthia was left alone with Marfield's sister and her husband.

Lady Anna sat, baby Lottie in her lap. "I beg your pardon, Miss Glazebrook, but did I understand correctly that we are cousins?"

"You did, Lady Anna. We discovered yesterday that my great-grandmother, Lady Loring and your grandmother, Lady Martinborough, are cousins through the Fromes. Apparently they were great friends before their marriages, but lost contact over the years. My great-grandmother rarely came to town," she added, "but she is here now for my cousin Chloe's come out, and the paths of the two ladies crossed in the Park; amazingly, they recognised one another at once."

As she hoped, this convoluted explanation succeeded in distracting her ladyship until Marfield returned, carrying a shawl which he handed to Cynthia.

"Your mother thought you might need this later."

"Thank you." Cynthia put it with her gloves.

"Where is Jack?"

"He'll be back in a couple of minutes," Lady Anna said. "Oh, it is good to be here again. I positively yearned for fashionable society. I told Sir John that we should take a house next year, but when he said that he had to come up on business, I decided we would all come. I knew Mamma would not object."

Jack rushed into the room. "I ready. Come, Cyntha, come, Uncle." He grabbed Cynthia's hand and attempted to tug her up from the sofa.

"Not that way," Marfield admonished him. "This is how you assist a lady to rise." With a bow, he offered his hand. Cynthia placed hers on it and rose gracefully.

"Now me. Sit down again, Cynthia."

Cynthia let herself be pushed back onto the sofa, the child made a creditable bow and held out his hand.

"What next?" he demanded when she stood beside him.

"You offer her your arm." Marfield demonstrated how to crook his elbow and Cynthia tucked her hand into it. "I fear, Jack, you are not yet tall enough. Perhaps she will agree to take your hand."

"But of course." Cynthia held her free hand out to the boy. He seized it and towed them away triumphantly.

Chapter Fourteen

The rear of Benton House gave onto a wide terrace from which a short flight of steps led down to the neatly laid-out walled garden where beds of flowers and shrubs were divided by a framework of gravelled paths; Jack immediately raced off to explore these, zig-zagging between the beds while every so often returning to Marfield and Cynthia, before darting off again.

"He's good for half an hour at least," Marfield said. "Let us stroll down to the end; there is a little arbour where we can sit out of sight of the house and still keep an eye on the boy. We should be grateful to him, for I doubt that we would otherwise have been able to escape so neatly."

She sighed. "They all mean well, I know, but I do wish they would not cluck."

"Cluck?"

"Like mother hens."

"Nicely put. I should have said 'interfere', Cynthia. If I may?"

"If you are to call me Cynthia, I refuse to address you as Marfield. What is your Christian name?"

"Rafe."

"Rafe."

The Husband Criteria

She said it contemplatively, as if tasting it. He was surprised at how much he liked hearing it on her lips. He tucked the hand on his arm closer to his side.

"I hope your mother did not think me utterly brazen in saying what I did," she said abruptly.

"What do you mean?"

"About not wanting you to offer for me out of a sense of obligation."

"I think she admired your frankness, Cynthia. I certainly did."

"I was forever being scolded for being too frank, too direct. 'You need not always speak your mind, Cynthia', my father used say, and 'nobody is interested in a girl's opinions,' my governess said. Mamma warned I should keep my views to myself if I wanted to find a husband. This did not incline me towards matrimony," she added dryly. "And today, I wanted to explain, and wondered whether I should, and then I thought if I hesitate already, it bodes ill for us. And so I put it to the test. Mamma gasped. I was waiting for her to say, 'Cynthia!', but your answer was perfect."

"I think it was very brave of you, for when we speak our mind, we also reveal something of ourselves, do we not? It was evident that you were thinking of me, me as Rafe and not as Marfield, and were concerned as to whether we would suit rather than simply wanting to bag a future earl."

"If anything, that would put me off," she admitted.

"I hope it will be many years before I come into the title. But my father has offered me an estate of my own—an estate in Lincolnshire, so that I—we—would be independent and could lead our own lives. So you could think of me as simply being a country squire if that would help?"

165

"It might. Are you happy at the idea?"

"Yes. Being a man about town palls, you know. I look forward to seeing what I can make of the estate, try out some of the recent innovations in agriculture. What about you? Should you like to live in the country?"

"I think so. I should certainly like to manage my own household. Being a young lady is very tedious."

"How old are you?"

"Twenty-one. Why?"

"Will you be offended if I say you are not the usual sort of young lady?"

"Because I say what I think? How can you say that? How many of us have you engaged in a serious conversation?"

"None. And you know very well why."

"Because the conventions make it more or less impossible."

"Precisely. But I still think you are unique; since that first day at Gunter's, when you put me so neatly in my place."

"You need not have been so unkind to Chloe."

"No. I did not recognise her—for want of a better word, lack of flirtatiousness. You don't flirt either."

She laughed. "I don't know how to. When I see other girls simper and flutter their eyelashes, I want to smack them. And, as for gentlemen who pay effusive, ridiculous compliments…"

He raised her hand and kissed it fleetingly. "*Mea culpa.* But I have not done it since, you must admit."

When his lips touched her hand she gave a little gasp. "N-No." Her voice steadied. "Was it very hard to stop doing so?"

"Not with you. One does it when one doesn't know what else to say. With you, that is never a problem."

Her smile dazzled him. "That is a true compliment, sir. I thank you."

Jack galloped past them, his right arm flailing. "I ride horse!"

"A splendid one," Cynthia called back. "He is apparently both horse and rider."

"Ingenious, you must admit."

"Your sister says she wishes to engage a governess while she is here. It is probably the right time, but I cannot but feel that a certain natural spontaneity will be lost."

"You would miss his 'native woodnotes wild'?"

"That is prettily put. Is it Shakespeare?"

"No, but said of Shakespeare by Milton in *L'Allegro*."

"I don't know it. I must seek it out."

They had reached the stone bench. "Shall we sit? It will not be too cold for you?"

"Not at all."

She settled beside him, her shoulder touching his. Both their bodies relaxed. Acting on instinct, Rafe raised his arm so that she could snuggle against him. She did so, as his arm came around her. Sometimes there was no need for words, he thought. She must have felt the same, for they sat in mute accord until, all too soon, a small figure hurtled towards them.

"Uncle! Cyntha! I sit too." Jack put a purposeful knee onto the bench, wriggled his way between them and heaved a great sigh. "I sleepyhead!" His head flopped against Cynthia's side as he closed his eyes.

Over his head, Cynthia's rueful eyes met Rafe's. They both struggled to repress their laughter. Rafe's arm tightened and, after a quick glance down, he leaned over his nephew to kiss her, a soft kiss that was accepted and returned as swiftly.

"Will I see you at Almack's?" he murmured.

"No." She squared her shoulders. "Mamma and I were refused vouchers."

"What? Why?"

"I don't know. It was the same last year. We would not have applied again but for Chloe and Ann. Theirs were approved, but they returned them. They did not give the reason, but the truth is that they insisted they would not go without us. It would be too marked, they said."

"They are good friends indeed," Rafe said, impressed.

"Yes. I begged them to consult Lady Swann-Loring and Lady Stephen FitzCharles, for such a decision can have delayed repercussions and I didn't want them to burn their boats, as far as Almack's was concerned. But Lady Stephen said she would return her vouchers too."

Rafe wondered whether the patronesses would regret refusing the future Lady Marfield—if he succeeded in bringing the thing off, he thought. Better not get too complacent, but he could not but be pleased with today's progress.

"You need not stay away on my account," she said. "Indeed, there is no reason why you should not go."

He smoothed her eyebrow with a gentle finger. "There is one excellent reason—you will not be there."

Cynthia's heart melted. Could there be a simpler admission of devotion? To the world he might be aloof, but for her, he dropped all his shields. When she raised her hand, he turned his cheek into her touch, then pressed a kiss into her palm.

"How shall you spend Wednesday evenings?" he asked.

The Husband Criteria

She shrugged. "There are no big balls, of course, but there are frequently smaller, more interesting *soirées*. If I am to be honest, I prefer them—they are more personal, like our family evenings. We like to spend one evening a week with my great-grandmother and Lord Swanmere. It is less tiring for them if we go to Swanmere House than if they go out. Sometimes my Ransford grandparents come, or Chloe's mother and Lord Stephen."

"What do you do?"

"Make music, read aloud—we are reading *The Antiquary*; play games, talk about what we have done recently, crack jokes… nothing in particular as you see, just enjoying one another's company."

"It sounds delightful—much more so that the usual *ton* entertainments."

She eyed him; he seemed sincere. "Does your family not get together?"

He shook his head. "There are not enough of us, I suppose. I call to see my parents regularly, of course, and we meet at different events."

"Tonight, at least, you'll have your sister and her husband," Cynthia pointed out.

"True. We had better take Master Jack back." The child's breathing had assumed a steady rhythm. He did not stir when Rafe picked him up and carried him to the house.

"I'll take him up the back stairs; it is the most direct way to the old nursery. Will you wait in the parlour for me?"

He took her back to the room they had been in previously and gestured to the bookcase. "I'm sure you'll find something to read there. I'll be as quick as I can."

169

"There is no need to hurry. I imagine the nursery is at the top of the house as usual."

"The third floor," he confirmed, shifting the child to one shoulder as he spoke. "Up we go."

She smiled to herself as he strode out of the room, moving easily and appearing to have no qualms about carrying Jack up five or six long flights of stairs, although the boy must weigh between two and three stone. Still, he need not race up and down on her account. She could occupy herself quite happily, she thought, as she drifted towards the books.

"And who might you be, Miss? This is a family parlour. What are we coming to, when a green girl feels she can intrude as she likes, instead of waiting in the hall as you were doubtless told to do."

Shocked by the blatant rudeness and strident voice, Cynthia turned slowly. A well-corseted, elderly woman stood in the open door brandishing an elaborate lorgnette that was more weapon than an aid to sight. Judging by her cheeks, rouged in the style of the last century, and modish dress, she was a member of the family, not an overly-zealous housekeeper.

"Well?"

Cynthia raised her chin at the renewed challenge. "I am Miss Glazebrook."

She was not about to add any further clarification. The circumstances were too odd; if she and Mamma had called on Lady Benton, why was she now here alone? To say she was waiting for Marfield could sound both presumptuous and scandalous. When the new-comer continued to stare at her, she said, "You have the advantage of me, ma'am."

The Husband Criteria

The lady inhaled so deeply that Cynthia feared her bosom, perched as it was above the high waist of her gown, was in danger of exploding. She bit the inside of her lip so as not to smile.

"Hoity-toity, are we? Rather than defy me, you will kindly explain yourself, Miss."

"Aunt! What brings you here?"

On hearing Lord Benton, the lady immediately stepped back. As he came into the parlour, Cynthia could see her retreating down the hall.

"My dear Miss Glazebrook! Has everyone abandoned you?"

"No, my lord. While my mother and I were with Lady Benton, your daughter and her family arrived—quite unexpectedly, I gathered."

"Anna is here? And the children? Good God!"

"And her husband. My mother and I took our leave, of course, but your grandson insisted I go into the garden with him. There was no reasoning with him so Lord Marfield suggested he and I take him out and let him run around. He, Marfield, I mean, would then see me home. Jack eventually tired himself out and fell asleep. Marfield carried him in and is now taking him up to the nursery. He suggested I wait here for him."

"And I imagine my wife and daughter are also in the nursery," Benton said.

"Very probably. That first hour after a long journey…"

"Especially when one is travelling with children. Pray sit down, Miss Glazebrook."

He flipped up his coattails and took a seat opposite her. "I must apologise for my aunt. She is the worst sort of maiden-aunt, petty and begrudging, a would-be tyrant."

"I didn't know what to say to her," Cynthia admitted.

171

"Best to say as little as possible," he agreed. "She does not live with us year-round, you know, but does come to us every year for part of the Season. I tend to let my mother deal with her. I hope you won't let her put you off, my dear. You would really have very little to do with her."

Cynthia felt her cheeks grow hot at this reassurance. He did not appear to notice, but said, "This is not your first Season, Miss Glazebrook?"

"No, I came out last year."

"What do you make of the whole gallimaufry?"

She had to laugh. "What an absurd description, but fitting somehow. I enjoy some of it, but not all."

When Rafe returned, clad in a driving coat and carrying his hat and gloves, she and his father were agreeing on the preposterousness of hostesses who refused to recognise the capacity of their houses, cramming so many people in to their parties that it was possible to transverse the rooms without ever taking a full step, being carried on by the inexorable press of one's fellow guests.

"And then they pride themselves that it was a sad crush," Benton said. "The only higher accolade would be if someone were asphyxiated. There you are, Marfield. Ready to take Miss Glazebrook home?"

"I am at her command," Rafe said. "And, more to the point, my curricle is outside."

"You don't want to keep your horses waiting," Benton said. He rose and held out his hand. "Goodbye, Miss Glazebrook. I have enjoyed our talk."

"As have I, my lord." Cynthia dipped into a slight curtsey as she lightly clasped his fingers. "Goodbye. Please give her ladyship my compliments."

"My mother sends you hers," Rafe put in. "She hopes that it will be less eventful the next time you come."

Chapter Fifteen

"Miss Loring requests that you be so good as to ascend to her sitting-room, Miss Glazebrook."

"Yes, of course." Leaving her parents and Martin to go on into the drawing-room at Swanmere House, Cynthia continued up to the second floor.

Chloe jumped up when she saw her. "There you are. I told Rosa we must have half-an-hour in private for a comfortable coze. It has been an age since we had one. If you only knew the inquisition we suffered on your behalf."

Cynthia's heart sank. "Old Lady Martinborough?"

"Yes. What precisely happened in the Park? She kept on talking about her grandson, but never said who he was and we did not like to expose our ignorance."

"That was Marfield—his mother is her younger daughter; she is considerably younger than the current marquess, which is why the dowager is his grandmother and not his great-grandmother. She beckoned to him, but he couldn't pull up beside her because your carriage was in the way, so he drew up and we walked back."

"Marfield! That explains it," Ann said. "We didn't have time to look up Debrett. It was all 'my grandson and your great-granddaughter, Chloe', and Lady Loring replying, 'You evidently know more about it than I do, Louisa'."

Chloe laughed. "At first we were confused because nobody ever calls Grandmother, 'Chloe', and Rosa said, 'You are mistaken, ma'am, Chloe is Lady Loring's granddaughter'. I think she had forgotten I was called after Grandmamma, but then Julian whispered it to her. Then the marchioness said, 'I don't mean these two', gesturing at Ann and me, 'I mean Miss Glazebrook', and Aunt Ransford said, 'Miss Glazebrook is my granddaughter, ma'am, but I know nothing to connect her and your grandson'."

"It was as good as a farce, Cynthia. And all done so politely. I had never realised how sweetly cutting a Christian name could sound. We were trying not to go into whoops. Then Swanmere said that he could only claim to be an honorary grandfather to any of us girls—was that not sweet of him?—but that you were a very prettily-behaved young lady any grandfather could be proud of, and did not deserve to be the subject of such a conversation. If there were something between you and her ladyship's grandson, he had no doubt that the young man would approach your father in the proper way, and until then there was no more to be said."

"How wonderful," Cynthia gasped. "How did the dowager respond to such a set-down?"

"She drew herself up and glared through her lorgnette but before she could say anything, Morris came in with the tea-tray and Grandmamma began to reminisce about something that happened aeons ago, around the time of the King's coronation, and it all blew over. But now, tell us about Marfield."

Cynthia looked at her friends. "Pray keep this to yourselves. He is courting me; in fact, we have a tentative understanding but do not want to make it public yet. I, we need a little more time to be sure."

"He cannot keep his attentions secret," Ann objected. "On Tuesday, he drove you in the Park, introduced you to his grandmother and danced twice with you in the evening. Short of putting a notice of his intentions in *The Gazette*, he has made his interest very clear."

"That with his grandmother was not his fault," Cynthia said. "I hope we can arrange some joint excursions with you and Martin, say, and that the gossips will turn their attention elsewhere."

"Do you like him, Cynthia?" Chloe asked.

"Very much. The more I know of him, the better I like him. But I want to be sure. And I want him to be sure, too. I have told him he can withdraw at any time. Better that than to be rushed into a betrothal. Remember, we swore we would approach marriage sensibly, not let ourselves be carried away by our feelings."

"As long as the feelings are there, too," Chloe said. She got to her feet. "We had better go down."

"Wait. What about the two of you? What have you been doing?"

"Nothing as significant," Chloe said, "at least as far as gentlemen are concerned. Isn't that right, Ann?"

"Yes."

"Has none of the musicians taken your fancy?" Cynthia asked. "I thought they were quite personable, and very entertaining."

"True, but I don't want to marry any of them," Ann said. "None of us is what you could call practically-minded, and the gentlemen would expect their wives to manage their homes. I would get annoyed if he were at his music all day while I was ordering meals and checking the weekly accounts."

The Husband Criteria

Chloe laughed. "In that case, you are more in need of a wife than a husband."

"Or a husband who can afford to maintain a large household—housekeeper, nursemaid, governess, and does not object to his wife devoting herself to her music," Cynthia suggested. "You must add that to your husband criteria."

"I'm sure they are as rare as hens' teeth," Ann said. "I think I'm destined to be an old maid."

"What of you, Chloe? Do you not feel even the slightest *tendre*? Is there no gentleman who makes your pulse race?"

Chloe turned slightly pink but shook her head. "The gentlemen of the *ton* are too much of a muchness for my liking."

"Is Thomas Musgrave coming tonight?" Ann asked as they left the room.

"Yes," Chloe said, "at least he said on Monday he would. He is not obliged to when the duke and duchess bring the children, but he would like to, he said."

"I imagine it reminds him of home. I like him; he is most entertaining."

"Yes."

Ann looked oddly at Chloe's curt reply but they had reached the bottom of the stairs and Cynthia did not pursue it.

~~~

"Well, Miss," Lady Loring said, "you have made a conquest, I hear."

Cynthia frowned. "I would not describe it so, ma'am. Marfield honours me with his attentions. But, I beg you, do not make a fuss, or bruit it further abroad."

"Hmph. I'm no chatter-box."

"I did not mean to imply you were, ma'am. Indeed, I hear you managed to silence Lady Martinborough yesterday."

"For that you may thank Swanmere. But when am I to meet him?"

"When the opportunity presents itself," Cynthia said firmly. "Just don't summons us to your carriage in the Park, like Lady Martinborough."

"Is that what she did? I had not thought her so foolish."

"When you feel the time is right, why not invite him to one of our family evenings?" Rosa suggested.

"Thank you. I think he would like that."

The arrival of the party from Gracechurch House put an end to the discussion. Apart from the Gracechurches and their children, and Lord and Lady Stephen, Thomas Musgrave appeared with a lady Cynthia did not know. She was dressed neatly but not in the first stare of fashion, and looked around a little shyly as Mr Musgrave said, "I have convinced Miss Barlow to come with us this evening."

"It is very kind of you to invite me, my lady," Miss Barlow said to Rosa. "Indeed, I did not need to be convinced; family constraints made it necessary for me to be elsewhere on previous occasions."

"I am delighted to see you, Miss Barlow," Rosa said.

"Ann, I have brought you a new singer, a fine alto indeed," Thomas said as he made the further introductions.

Cynthia was struck by his proprietary air. She glanced at Chloe who had turned very pale. "That is splendid," Ann said. "You must sing with us, Miss Barlow, but Miss Loring and I must try this change first."

The Husband Criteria

Thomas Musgrave chuckled. "What did I tell you?" he said to Miss Barlow, as Chloe obediently followed Ann to the pianoforte. "Miss Overton lives for music."

~~~

Ann played a few phrases while Chloe looked intently at the music spread out before her; looked but did not see, for a film of tears obscured her sight.

"Slip out through the music-room," Ann murmured, as Thomas approached with Miss Barlow. "I'll deflect them."

Heart-sick, Chloe dropped onto a chair in the music room. He had never looked at her with that mixture of pride and affection, possession, even. That must be Miss Barlow singing: She did have a beautiful voice, rich and full, unlike Chloe's light soprano.

Alas my love you do me wrong
To cast me off discourteously;
And I have loved you oh so long
Delighting in your company.

Greensleeves! How appropriate. But it should be 'thoughtlessly', not 'discourteously.' He never thought of her in that way.

He had attracted her from the beginning, that very first day at Swanmere, but by the end of the summer, she had convinced herself that it had been merely a young girl's first fancy, and in the succeeding years she had been able to meet him civilly when he was visiting his parents. But this year, when he came into the drawing-room at Gracechurch House, her heart leaped and she thought, 'there you are'. She had made no secret of her pleasure in seeing him, but as they all felt it, no one had realised that her feelings ran deeper. In and out of Gracechurch House, as she was to see her mother and Alexander, their paths crossed frequently despite the fact that he usually was not invited to *ton* events. Once or twice, he and Jasper had joined Lord Stephen's excursions, and he had come to her ball where he had danced with her but as he had danced every dance, she could not claim that he had singled her out in any way. The supper dance had been her choice, when he sought a dance, but even if he had recognised this as a hint, he had not followed up on it.

Their circumstances were unequal of course, but if Julian could marry his sister's governess, why should she not marry the rector's son? If he could get a good living, together with her fortune they would do very well. She was not hanging out for a splendid match; she liked the Musgraves; his sister was a good friend and she could imagine being one of their family. Now Thomas's voice rose:

> *Drink to me only with thine eyes,*
> *And I will pledge with mine;*
> *Or leave a kiss but in the cup,*
> *And I'll not look for wine.*

Suppressing a sob, Chloe left the music-room by the other door and went up to her sitting-room. Her maid looked up, surprised, when she came in.

"I have a sudden headache, Parker. Make me a cool compress, and I'll sit here quietly for ten minutes. Perhaps it will pass off as quickly as it came on."

She lay back on the chaise longue, the cool, damp linen redolent of lavender covering her forehead and eyes. She felt

Parker drape a shawl over her. Ten minutes, she promised herself, and then she would go down again. Ten minutes to shield herself against him, against that crooked smile and affable manner, of pleasure in his company. She could not ignore him; he was in no way at fault in the matter; she could not claim he had encouraged her. It was her own fault for reading more into his behaviour than was there, for building castles in Spain.

~~~

"How could you encourage them to sing those songs," Cynthia hissed to Ann as they played a piano duet together. "I hope Chloe didn't hear them."

"They weren't my choice. Thomas said they had found a book of old songs in the schoolroom at Gracechurch House."

"Did you know Chloe saw him that way?"

"I had wondered. She was always very pleased to see him and, of course, she is at Gracechurch House more often than we are."

"But she doesn't live there, or share a schoolroom."

"No. Ssh. There she comes."

By the time Cynthia and Ann had finished playing and Julian had read the next chapter of *The Antiquary*, Chloe had recovered her composure and was able to chat to her grandmother and Miss Barlow. The governess was a rector's daughter, whose late father had not left her enough to support herself.

"My brother said my mother and I could come and live with him, his wife and their three children, and I went there initially."

Lady Loring snorted. "And found you were at your sister-in-law's beck and call, I have no doubt."

Miss Barlow nodded. "I was running from morning to night. Then my mother became ill, and I nursed her to the end. In the meantime, there were two new babies. My mother had one hundred pounds a year, which she left to me. When my brother learnt this, he decided he should receive half of it for my bed and board."

"But you would still have been expected to assist your sister-in-law," Chloe said.

"Naturally. I decided I would prefer to be reimbursed for my exertions rather than pay for the privilege. I had received a good education and my godmother arranged for me to meet her Grace." She smiled. "It is such a good position that my brother could not take umbrage at my accepting it."

Chloe had to smile back. "Well done, indeed. Tabitha is a delightful girl; I am sure you enjoy instructing her."

"I do, although when she is convinced she is right, there is no talking to her. When it gets too much, I tell her to make her case in an essay which has the advantage both of silencing her and requiring her to consider the points she wishes to make. We then practise putting them in a less confrontational manner."

"That is well-done," Lady Loring said. "She should be able to stand her ground, in a genteel manner, of course."

"Of course," Chloe agreed.

Tabitha then came up and challenged her to a game of fox and geese. "Rosa said there is time before supper."

"That was thoughtful of you, to ask her," Chloe said as they headed towards the table where Jasper had just defeated Lord Stephen.

"It is most frustrating, to have to stop at the most exciting part. You can resume afterwards, I know, but it is never the same."

The Husband Criteria

"It is like adding more hot water to a cup of tea that has gone cold," Cynthia agreed. "It is never the same as freshly made."

~~~

"Miss Barlow was surprisingly open about her circumstances," Ann said when the visitors had left and the family was discussing the evening.

"She was probably grateful somebody showed an interest in her," Rosa said quietly. "Frequently, a governess is ignored or overlooked, you know; certainly she is not considered to be a person with her own history and wants and needs."

"I suppose not," Chloe said.

"She had nobody to speak for her, and so she must do it herself," Lady Loring said. "Swanmere is Thomas's father's patron, and the castle is on calling terms with the rectory."

"Do you think it is that serious between them?" Julian asked. "He certainly seemed very protective of her."

"He is considering seeking ordination when he is twenty-five," Swanmere said. "A wife who is a daughter of the rectory would only be to his advantage when he is seeking a living."

More advantageous than a baronet's daughter, Chloe thought sadly. She must put all thought of him behind her now. "I think they would be a good match; she knows what is expected of a Rector's wife—and they look well together."

"What do you mean?" Julian asked.

"Some couples fit together; I don't mean in their appearance, but in their demeanour, how they behave towards one another. You and Rosa do," she added.

"Chloe is right," her grandmother said. "Well, between Gracechurch and you, Swanmere, as patrons, he should have no difficulty in getting a good living."

Chapter Sixteen

*H**ow quickly quondam Graces must quit their pedestals. De-Graded, one might say, or even Dis-Graced. Only weeks ago we would have expected our Wednesdays to be gratified by the presence of our three latest Incomparables, but their brief reign seems over, for there is no sight of them in our innermost sanctum. As the Swan of Avon reminds us, 'All that glisters is not gold'; even the brightest Diamond may turn out to be paste or purest marble a plaster-cast.*

Mrs Glazebrook frowned as she read this effusion from *Tonnish Topics and Society Secrets*. "What impertinence! It is fortunate that they do not mention any names."

Cynthia sighed. "They do not have to, Mamma. Martin brought this. He felt it was better we saw it. It was in the window of a print shop. It is called, *'In the Sculptor's Studio'*."

The print depicted three gentlemen viewing a classical group entitled *The Three Graces*.

'*I can make you a very good price, gentlemen,*' the artist said.

'*We are not interested in damaged goods.*'

'*Not damaged, I assure you, sirs. A little shop-worn, perhaps, but that is all.*'

"Disgraceful." Mamma folded her spectacles. "You had better show them to your father."

Cynthia stopped on the threshold of the study. Marfield. Now of all times. Her father caught sight of her before she could retreat.

"Come in, my dear. I think we understand each other, do we not?" he added to Marfield.

"Indeed, sir."

"What have you there, Cynthia?" Papa asked.

She handed him the print and the journal. "My mother wishes you to see these, sir." Squaring her shoulders, she turned to a smiling Rafe. "You should look at them too, my lord."

He raised an eyebrow. "My lord? I thought we were past that, Cynthia."

She felt herself flush. "Things have changed."

"In what way?"

She gestured to her father who looked like thunder as he scrutinised the papers.

"May I?" Rafe took them from her father's grasp. "What claptrap! You do it too much credit by taking it seriously." He dropped the pages on her father's desk and came and took her hands. "Cynthia! You will not let such nonsense affect you?"

"How can I not?" she said desperately. "You know what wicked tongues the *ton* has. This will be only the beginning. Heaven alone knows what will be laid at our door. You would do well to keep your distance."

His hands slid up her arms to grip her shoulders and he shook her slightly. "What sort of man do you think I am?" he asked savagely. "One who'll refuse at the first fence?"

"No," she gasped, "but your parents…"

"My parents will support me—and you. They know better than to give credence to such scandal-mongers."

"So we should pretend nothing has happened? Brazen it out?"

"Why pour oil on the flames? If we are fortunate, they will be quickly extinguished. The secret is not to give them the satisfaction of seeing they have singed you."

"I suppose you are right."

She was barely aware that her father had left the study. Rafe's arms closed around her in a firm embrace, an embrace she returned instinctively so that her breasts pressed against his chest. She raised her head and his lips met hers, gentle at first, then more demanding. She shivered as he deepened the kiss, his hands slipping down to curve around her bottom—another new sensation—and hold her to him.

At last he lifted his head. "Well? Do you continue to shy at taking the fence with me or shall we press forward, side by side?"

Together—as companions? "Partners in life?" she asked hesitantly.

"Precisely."

"But…" It was only now that the real, the essential difficulty became clear to her.

"But what? What troubles you, my heart?"

"I do not think that I can honestly promise to obey you unconditionally—or indeed anyone," she hastened to add. "It is not personal, Rafe, I promise you, it is the thought of swearing to subordinate my will and-and my person, my very self to another."

"Cross your fingers, then. I don't want or expect unconditional obedience from my wife. Where is the fun in that?"

Cynthia glared at him. "Firstly, I think the parson might object to crossed fingers. Secondly, I shall take my marriage vows seriously, my lord, and I expect you to do so too."

187

His grin faded. "I'm sorry. I should not have responded so frivolously. It was partly because I could not imagine myself as an overbearing or tyrannical husband."

"I am glad to hear it, but that does not change anything. We cannot simply rewrite the vows to suit ourselves."

"Not rewrite them, no. But tell me, to whom do we make them?"

"To each other—and to the Almighty or, at least, before Him."

"Not to the parson or our parents, or anyone else present?"

"No. They are merely witnesses."

"Therefore we can agree on what those vows mean, can we not?"

"I suppose so." Puzzled, she dropped into one of the deep armchairs beside the fire. "In what way, though?"

He came to kneel beside her. "If I were to promise I would never demand or expect your obedience, or constrain you to do something against your will, would that ease your mind?"

"Would you really do that?"

"Why not? I don't want a submissive little mouse of a wife but a companion who is not afraid to contradict or even oppose me."

"I could promise to consider your opinion," she offered. "I would do that anyway, if I loved and respected you."

"As I would consider yours. That is part of what honouring and cherishing each other means, is it not?" He sat back on his heels and smiled at her. "You are not the only one who has been considering the marriage vows. And, I assure you, I shall be very much in earnest when I make them. In the end, it all comes down to trust, doesn't it? Do you trust me not to abuse my position as your husband? Do I trust you not to abuse your position as my wife?"

"How could I do that?" Cynthia asked. This was something she had not thought of.

"Some men feel unwelcome in their homes because their wives are termagants who constantly belittle them. Other women take lovers or run up enormous debts for which their husbands are liable."

"And you think I might…?"

He hugged her. "Of course not. You are the most honourable and virtuous of women. The mere fact that we are having this discussion proves it."

She framed his face with her hands. "I never thought I would find a man like you, one with whom I wished to spend the rest of my life, be his life's companion, as he would be mine."

"Cynthia! Is that a yes? Will you indeed be my wife?"

"Yes, Rafe." With a sigh, she released the burden of doubt that had plagued her and raised her face for his kiss.

"Shall we give the tabbies something else to talk about?" Rafe asked Cynthia who had gone to the over-mantel mirror where she tried to tidy her hair. "If I might send a footman to tell my tiger to bring my curricle here, we could drive to Gunter's."

"Yes, let's. An ice would be just the thing." She pulled the bell beside the fireplace and went to sit on the sofa. "I'll have to put on a bonnet before we go out. Is there an ice house at Ailesthorpe?"

"I hope so. If not, we'll see if we can build one." He broke off to give the footman who answered the bell his instructions, then went to sit beside her.

"The lease is up at midsummer. It is a repairing lease, and before it ends, a schedule of dilapidations must be drawn up. Only then will we know what repairs are necessary and changes we wish to make. That will decide when we can move in. The steward and the architect will do the inspection, of course, but my father and I intend to be there as well." He turned towards her and took her hand. "Would you come too if my mother accompanies us? I would like you to see it before any decisions are made. And if we make them before the wedding, they can get on with the work while we are on our wedding journey."

Cynthia was touched by how eager he was but also dizzy with this talk of their wedding and wedding journey, of their first visit to the estate that would be their future home. She was leaving familiar shores to embark on an exciting new voyage. Pray God that she—no, they would come to a safe harbour. She glanced at the man sitting by her side. Together, they would do it. Of that she was convinced. All she had to do was set sail.

"I should be delighted to come if Lady Benton is agreeable."

"I'm sure she will be."

"Before we leave, let us tell my parents that we have come to an agreement."

"Yes, dear."

Her face must have shown her surprise at this meek reply, for he grinned at her.

"I must practise being a husband. In every way," he added and drew her into his arms for a long kiss.

When she was able to breathe again, she took his hand. "Come." Her parents rose when they appeared in the parlour door.

"It is all agreed between you, I see," Mamma said, coming to embrace her. "I wish you every happiness, my love. And you too, Marfield," she added. "I think the two of you will suit very well."

The Husband Criteria

"Thank you, ma'am." Rafe bent to kiss her mother's cheek. "I promise you I will do my best to make Cynthia happy."

"And to support her in unhappy times," Mamma said gently. "That is as important, for they will come and it is best to face them together. That goes for you, too, Cynthia."

"Yes, Mamma."

Did Papa notice how Mamma's admonishment stung? Perhaps, for he said jovially, "Do not fear, Marfield, Cynthia was never one to take to the bed with the vapours. You may rely on her to be a true helpmeet."

"I have never doubted it, sir," Rafe said. "I count myself most fortunate in having gained her consent."

~~~

"There!"

"Well-spotted." Rafe guided his team into the space just vacated by another carriage in Berkely Square. The trees were now in fresh, yellowish-green leaf, creating a sun-dappled shade where girls and their beaux could stroll, watched by sharp-eyed chaperons, or sit in their carriages as they enjoyed an ice. Cynthia noticed many sidelong glances cast their way as they waited for their order, but she was too happy to care about what might be said about her.

He broke off to take an orange ice from the waiter's tray and hand it to Cynthia.

"Thank you." She let the delicious coolness trickle down her throat. "Mmm. Delicious." She looked about her. There was no sign of Chloe and Ann. Perhaps they were in the Park.

191

"Could you take me to Swanmere House afterwards? I must talk to Chloe and Ann about that wretched item in *Tonnish Topics*. They should at least be warned."

"Yes of course. Should I come in with you?"

"No. You may leave me there. Julian will make sure I return home safely."

~~~

Chloe was aware of sidelong glances as Rosa's barouche progressed slowly through the Park, glances that were frequently accompanied by muttered comments, concealed by a raised hand, and punctuated by laughter trilling from a passing carriage. Something was amiss. She scrutinised her companions. Both Rosa and Ann were smartly dressed, with modish bonnets and pelisses. There was nothing in their appearances to warrant such ill-bred comment.

"Do I look acceptable?" she asked. "Is my bonnet straight? Do I have a smut on my face?"

"Yes, yes, and no, you don't have a smut," Ann said just as Rosa replied, "Everything is just as it should be. Why do you ask?"

"We seem to be attracting an unusual amount of attention, but it strikes me like ridicule than admiration. Don't be too obvious, but look how Mr Norris and his companions are sniggering."

"Who cares about them?" Ann said. "Someone is always the butt of their jokes."

"That is true, but it is not only them. And while no one has cut us, fewer have gone out of their way to acknowledge us. It's as if we are being weighed in the balance."

"You are very perceptive," Rosa said. "I had not noticed anything different."

"Perhaps because you are facing forward," Chloe said. "But I like to watch people, I admit."

As Lady Benton's carriage neared, her ladyship bowed and smiled, then said something to the elegant young lady sitting beside her.

"Do you see the difference?" Chloe said once her ladyship had passed. "That must be her daughter, Lady Anna, with her. Cynthia said she was in town. I imagine Lady Benton was explaining our newly-discovered connection to her." As she spoke, she smiled at Miss Nugent who sat in her brother's curricle.

"I'm looking forward to Lady Nugent's archery fête," Rosa said. "It will be something different."

"Are you tiring of the *ton*," Chloe asked.

"More of the Season. I would prefer it if we had fewer engagements. I seem to be tired all the time."

Chloe looked at her sister-in-law more closely. She did look a little strained, especially around the eyes.

"At home, you and Julian always have your private time between five and seven. I'll ask Mamma if she is willing to chaperon Ann and me some evenings so that you need not go out every night."

"We don't have to go out every night," Ann said hopefully.

Rosa frowned. "If you start picking and choosing among the invitations, you may find that you receive fewer."

"We should be able to skip some of the routs at least. Half the time you never get to speak to your hostess as it is."

"That is true," Chloe agreed. "We need to know which are the more select invitations. I must ask Mamma."

Chapter Seventeen

"No," Cynthia said flatly.

She had arrived at Swanmere House at the same time as Rosa and the girls, taken a brief farewell of her betrothed, and joined the others. Now she, Chloe and Ann had gathered in the girls' sitting-room.

"What do you mean, no?" asked Chloe who had just explained their intention to reduce their attendance at *ton* parties.

"Because it will be misinterpreted. Have you seen the latest *Tonnish Topics and Society Secrets?*"

"No."

"They refer to our not having been at Almack's and wonder why. Have we been degraded or disgraced? It is a pun on the Graces, of course. There is also an unpleasant print in the print shop windows. Martin saw it."

"What sort of print?" Ann asked.

"Gentlemen are viewing The Three Graces in a sculptor's studio. They complain they are too damaged but the sculptor says no, only a little shop-worn."

Ann looked shocked but Chloe was fuming. "What impertinence! They should be horse-whipped."

"I agree, but we must ignore it all. You had to be aware of it, but it is vital, Marfield says, that we pay no attention to any of it and simply continue as usual. If you start staying at home, people will say it is because you are embarrassed, or even ashamed to face the *ton*."

"I can see that." Chloe looked back on the events of the afternoon. "But I am concerned about Rosa. She told us that she thinks she is with child again. She needs to rest."

"Between your mother and mine, we shall be able to arrange enough chaperons, and to make sure you are seen at the right parties," Cynthia said. "Tell her not to worry."

"'Marfield says'," Ann quoted. "Is it agreed between you?"

Chloe had never seen Cynthia look so smitten. She smiled as she said, "Yes."

"He does not expect you to distance yourself from us, from the scandal?"

Cynthia was horrified at the suggestion. "Of course not. He knows I would never leave you in the lurch. You might have gone to Almack's and abandoned me, after all. I shall never forget the way you stood up for me."

"I wonder what the patronesses will think when they realise they have snubbed the future Countess Benton," Ann said.

"I don't really care," Cynthia said. "They are so two-faced; in public each lady smiles and nods but in private delights in refusing applicants as the humour takes her. Anyway, I hope Marfield's father lives for many decades to come. We are to have our own estate in Lincolnshire. I can't wait to see it."

"When is the wedding?"

"We haven't really discussed it, but the way he is talking, it will be before the end of the Season. But please keep the news of our betrothal to yourselves for the moment. You may tell Rosa and Julian, of course, and the grandparents, but that is all."

Marfield bent to kiss his mother's cheek. "You look happy, Mamma."

"Yes. I enjoy having Anna and the children here."

"They bring some life to the place, especially Jack. He knows what he wants, doesn't he? I wonder how he will respond to a governess."

Lady Benton nodded. "It is vital that she wins his affection. He can be led, but not driven. She will need to be firm but not harsh."

"I agree. He must be tamed but I would hate to see his spirit broken."

"Yours wasn't."

"Was I so headstrong?"

"A little stubborn, perhaps. I suppose we spoilt you a little, but you were very good, especially after poor Ned became ill."

"How did you get on with Mr Glazebrook?" his mother asked after a moment's silence during which their thoughts had gone to the son and brother who had succumbed to illness before he had been breeched.

"Very well. He is happy to accept me as a suitor and relies on me to make his daughter happy. The fact that I was not thrown by her hesitation but understood her qualms boded well for us, he said. We did not go into any particulars about settlements, but agreed to leave that to the men of business once she had overcome her reservations, as he had no doubt she would."

"Will she? Are you as sure?"

"I am. In fact, she has. You may congratulate me, Mamma."

She jumped up and threw her arms around him. "I do, with all my heart, Rafe. I wish you both every happiness and a long life together."

"Thank you. I wish to bring her to Ailesthorpe as soon as possible so that we can discuss what changes we would like made. You will accompany us, won't you?"

"Yes, of course, but why the rush?"

"I would like to be married by the end of the Season. Some repairs and renovations will be necessary at the end of the lease, and if we decide on them in advance, they can be done while we take our wedding trip."

"Cynthia has agreed to all this?"

He smiled at his mother's obvious astonishment. "Yes."

They both frowned as Lady Georgina strode into the parlour and thrust an open journal at his mother. *Tonnish topics*, Rafe saw resignedly.

"There you are, Charlotte. You will forgive me for interrupting, I know. I thought it essential that you know what is being said about visitors to this house. I knew I was right about that Glazebrook female. An encroaching miss, if ever I saw one."

"I have made enquiries," Lady Georgina continued magisterially. "Miss Glazebrook is accounted one of the so-called three Graces, together with a Miss Loring and a Miss Overton. The fact that Almack's refused to admit them says it all. You should be as particular, Charlotte. I, myself, discovered Miss Glazebrook alone in this very room."

"Indeed?" Rafe's mother said coldly. "May I remind you that you do not decide who is admitted to our private apartments? As a guest in this house, it behoves you to treat our other guests with courtesy, does it not?" She opened her fingers and let the journal fall. "Furthermore, I am surprised that you pay such attention to this ill-bred tittle-tattle. Benton would be most displeased to hear you speak so disrespectfully of anybody you met under his roof."

This last was said with what Rafe later described to his betrothed as they waited for the performance to begin at Lady Needham's *soirée musicale* as "a steely smile. My aunt turned as red as a turkey-cock and began to gobble incoherently. I picked up the journal and handed it to her; she took the hint and departed."

"Did you tell Lady Benton about the print?"

He began to laugh. "Yes. That just made her take the bit between her teeth. Be warned. She is planning an exclusive rout in our honour. At first she talked of holding it on a Wednesday, but then she decided on another day so that she could invite the patronesses of Almack's."

"Good heavens."

"She is over there, conferring with your mother. Our fathers have wisely left them to it. And here comes my sister."

This must be what it was like to be trapped in a run-away carriage, Cynthia thought as she turned to greet Lady Anna who, eyes sparkling, leaned in to murmur, "I am so pleased I decided to come to town. Just think, I would have missed all the excitement. We shall stay for the wedding, of course. Baby is too small but Jack can strew rose petals for you."

Cynthia caught the eye of her betrothed who struggled to conceal his amusement at a prospect that promised both delight and disaster. "What a kind offer," she said, "but we have made no plans as yet. I must consult with my mother."

"Yes, indeed." Lady Anna did not take offence at this reminder that others were more nearly concerned with the approaching nuptials. She was further distracted by Rafe's offer to introduce her to Lady Tamm. "You have not yet met our cousin, the granddaughter of our mother's sister, for whom you were named."

"Oh, yes! I always found the first Lady Anna's story so romantic. She eloped with her brother's tutor," she confided to Cynthia before turning to greet her newfound cousin.

Lady Tamm and Cynthia were, as Rafe's sister soon explained, also cousins through old Lady Martinborough. Cynthia must have looked as dazed as she felt, for Lady Tamm said, "It is confusing, is it not? For weeks after I met the dowager marchioness, I was being presented to new relatives. And that was only on the Martinborough side. You will become used to it, I assure you. I knew very few of my relatives while I was growing up, and am always delighted to meet more."

"That is fortunate, for here is another one." Cynthia smiled at Chloe who had just joined them.

"Of course I know Miss Loring," Lady Tamm said, "but I did not know we were related. And the third in your coterie, Miss Overton, is also your cousin is she not?"

"If we are to be precise, she is my brother's cousin," Chloe said. "It is through their mothers, but I am not one to split hairs and glad to account her mine too. More than that, she is a very dear friend, as is Cynthia."

"That is excellent. It is difficult to make friends within the *ton*," Lady Tamm said. "The Season does not lend itself to those moments of quiet intimacy that promote friendship. Perhaps that is why we tend to find our friends within our families."

"Is Ann not with you?" Cynthia asked Chloe.

"She is, but she went off somewhere with Lady Elizabeth Hope."

Chapter Eighteen

Lady Needham's large drawing-room was crammed full of the cream of the *ton*. Most of those present had found seats but there was no sign of the performance beginning. A restive hum arose as people began to wonder what caused the delay. The absence of their hostess and her daughter were also remarked upon.

Ann had not reappeared, Cynthia noticed. Had there been some sort of mishap? But then Rosa must have been informed, and she sat composedly across the room as if nothing were amiss. At last the double doors to the music room were folded back and those still standing moved forward to the gilt chairs that had been set along the sides, leaving the centre free for the pianoforte.

Lady Needham entered from another door, and raised her hand for silence. An imposing woman, beautifully gowned and turbaned, she had no problem in making her well-bred tones heard at the back of the room.

"My dear friends, I apologise for keeping you waiting. Tonight I have the honour of presenting to you the renowned soprano Frau Marianne Albrecht who is a great favourite at the Munich court. Unfortunately, Herr Albrecht, her husband and *pianiste*, has badly scalded his hand so that it is impossible for him to play tonight. I am immeasurably grateful to Miss Overton who has kindly agreed to step into the breach. Please welcome her, and Frau Albrecht, who will first sing two arias by Mr Handel. These will be followed by some of Herr van Beethoven's settings of Irish songs. After a short break, during which Miss Overton will play a piano solo, Frau Albrecht will return to sing Herr Mozart's *Exsultate Jubilate*."

She withdrew to the side of the room. A tall, full-bosomed lady of about Ann's mother's age, swept onto the space that had suddenly become a stage. She was clad in a gown of deep amethyst silk, cut with a lower waist than was fashionable, the modest bodice trimmed with cream gauze. Ideal for a singer, with no risk of a deep breath revealing more than was seemly, Cynthia noted. Her fair hair was piled on her head and secured with a headdress of violets and pearls—no feathers that might shed irritatingly during a performance. Amethyst and pearl drop earrings completed the magnificent ensemble.

Ann followed a couple of paces behind. She had removed her long gloves and her bare hands and arms set her apart from every other lady in the room. She could not match Frau Albrecht's splendour, but her white gauze gown trimmed with pink rosebuds and worn over a pale rose silk slip was perfect for a girl in her first Season. She was followed by Lady Elizabeth carrying music which she placed in the piano note-stand before taking a seat beside the *pianiste*, ready to turn the pages for her.

Cynthia was nervous for her friend; this was completely different to playing in Rosa's drawing-room for the family and a few guests. Ann looked paler than usual but as soon as she sat at the piano and ran her fingers over the keys, any anxiety disappeared. She smiled at Frau Albrecht who nodded back. She was ready.

"She is really first-rate," Marfield said in the brief interval between the Handel and Beethoven.

"Frau Albrecht?" Cynthia asked.

"Yes, a glorious voice, but I meant Miss Overton. She is her equal."

"That is true. I have often played and sung with her, but had never realised how we must hold her back. It is like harnessing a prime bit of blood with a hack. You can see how she responds to another true musician, how they instinctively support each other. You would never think they were playing together for the first time."

~~~

Ann had escaped to another world. She had initially been nervous when Lady Needham asked her to step in, saying that Mr Forbes had said that, "your playing is superior to his, and you excel as an accompanist." In the end she had agreed to meet Frau Albrecht and went with Lady Elizabeth to a smaller drawing-room where there was also a good piano.

"We use it for music lessons and practising, as well as family evenings," Lady Elizabeth explained. "It is useful, too, for the musicians to make their final preparations, which they can hardly do upstairs—it would quite spoil the effect if our guests had to listen to their scales, arpeggios and other exercises."

"Or one phrase repeated twenty times," Ann agreed.

"So this is your young miss," Frau Albrecht said when Lady Elizabeth introduced Ann. "It is vorth trying, I suppose. So, Miss Owerton"—her English was excellent, but she was inclined to

203

confuse her Ws and Vs—"let me hear you play. There is a selection of my *répertoire* on the piano. Do you know any of it?"

Ann looked through the sheets of music, laying several to one side. Beethoven's Irish airs were familiar to her, although she preferred Mr Moore's more heartfelt melodies. Several Handel arias, and Mozart's Exsultate Jubilate joined the pile.

Frau Albrecht looked over her shoulder. "That will suffice. Play some of the Mozart, if you please."

"Shall I turn the pages for you?" Lady Elizabeth asked.

"If you would, my lady," Ann replied gratefully. Seating herself, she played a couple of scales to get the feel of the instrument and then began properly.

After some minutes, Frau Albrecht said, "Start again, please. This time, with me."

Yes. This would work. The two women smiled at one another and hastily reviewed the chosen works, Frau Albrecht explaining how she phrased particular passages. Her husband, nursing a bandaged right hand, joined in with his insights. Ann would have been too shy to suggest it, but she was extremely grateful when Lady Needham summoned a maid and directed her to take Miss Overton to a bedroom where she might make herself comfortable before the performance. After she had straightened her gown and tucked in some stray strands of hair, the maid directed her to the water closet before taking her back to the little drawing-room.

"Are we ready?" Lady Needham asked. "I shall lead the way."

The Handel and Beethoven had been received with enthusiastic applause. When the performers left the drawing-room, Mr Forbes was waiting to compliment Ann and say she was doing splendidly, while Frau Albrecht embraced her, exclaiming, "*Meine Liebe*, that was *wunderbar*."

Now she sat alone at the piano, poised to play *Summer at Swanmere*, her musical evocation of that summer when she had taken the first tentative steps beyond her self-centred mother's restricting orbit. She might never have the opportunity to play it before so many people again. Once, at least, she would introduce her heart's darling to a greater audience. She looked out at the assembly where Rosa and Julien smiled expectantly and Mr Forbes nodded encouragingly. She soon sank into the music, rapt but completely in control of the melodies and harmonies, of the rhythms, tempi, and changes of mood. At first the listeners seemed puzzled by this unknown work that was not in any common style, but gradually they settled into an unusual stillness.

When she stopped playing, there was a long moment's silence. Her heart sank. They hadn't liked it. Gathering all her composure, she began to rise. The first hand-clap broke the spell and the room was filled with thunderous applause. Ann stood and curtsied.

"That was magnificent, Miss Overton," Lady Needham exclaimed. "So very different. Do tell us what it is called."

"It is called *Summer at Swanmere*," Ann said, with a smile for Julian and Rosa.

"Swanmere. Who is the composer?"

"I am," Ann said.

Lady Needham stared at her. "You? I am rarely dumbfounded, Miss Overton, but you have taken my breath away. Well done. Very well done indeed."

"*Brava*, Miss Overton." Herr Albrecht, who had been sitting to one side, stood as she passed him. "Did I understand correctly that it is your own composition?"

"Thank you. Yes, it is mine."

"I will not delay you, but should like to speak to you about it later."

"Yes, of course," Ann said, and continued into an ante-room where Frau Albrecht lay on a chaise longue. She opened her eyes when Ann came in.

"Excellent, Miss Owerton. I had them leave the door open so that I could listen. You have a rare talent."

"Thank you," Ann said again, overwhelmed by all these compliments. She would have liked to sit quietly for a quarter-of-an-hour, to be able to come to herself, but Mozart waited.

"Some refreshment before you go back, Miss Overton?" Lady Elizabeth asked. "We have lemonade, orgeat, and ratafia?"

"Lemonade, please, just a small glass." It was both tart and sweet, and Ann sipped it gratefully, trying to compose herself. She put down the glass and smiled at Frau Albrecht. "Shall we?"

The buzz of conversation in the drawing-room hushed as soon as the three ladies reappeared. Frau Albrecht gave the nod and Ann began the introduction. *Exsultate Jubilate* was one of her favourite pieces. She had often played it for Chloe but this was completely different, she thought. Frau Albrecht's glorious, golden soprano traversed the runs and trills effortlessly, soaring and swooping like a bird riding the currents of the air. The final Alleluia was so exhilarating that at the end Ann just sat beaming at the singer as she acknowledged the applause. Frau Albrecht had to take her hand and draw her to her feet to face the audience.

The Husband Criteria

Lady Needham came to thank the performers, with a special word for Ann, "Who stepped so wonderfully into the breach for us tonight. And now I am happy to say that supper is being served downstairs."

Lady Elizabeth murmured to Ann, "The Albrechts will have supper up here, but you must come downstairs."

"May I not say goodbye to them?"

"Of course."

"You vill take a glass of champagne with us, *meine Liebe*," Frau Albrecht said as soon as she saw Ann. "Come, Hartmuth, pour a glass for Miss Owerton."

"Gladly. Please forgive my English. *Parlez vous Français?*" At her nod, he continued smoothly in French. "Let us drink to our saviour. We cannot thank you enough for coming to the rescue this evening, Miss Overton. May I also say how pleased I am to have heard such a fine artist and interesting new composer?"

"Thank you. You are very kind. It was such a pleasure and an honour for me to play for Frau Albrecht. How long do you remain in London?"

"Three weeks. I am to sing in *Cosi fan Tutte* in ten days' time," Frau Albrecht told her.

"Oh! I must be sure to go and see it."

"I shall send you tickets. It will be a small thank you for tonight."

"That is not necessary," Ann protested. "I so enjoyed playing for you."

"You are very kind, Miss Owerton."

"Miss Overton." Lady Needham's son, Lord Hope, had come into the room. "My mother has sent me to escort you to the supper room."

Ann quickly made her farewells and placed her hand on his lordship's arm.

"You are not only talented but very brave, Miss Overton," he said as they left the room. "My mother was in despair—she quite thought we would have no music tonight. She prides herself on presenting celebrated performers to her guests, especially since the war ended and they are able to travel from the continent again. Were you not at all daunted?"

"A little in the beginning, but once I began to play, all fear fled. It was a joy to play for Frau Albrecht."

"I suppose it must be like riding a first-rate bit of blood instead of an old nag."

She laughed. "I would not be so impolite. Many ladies have good voices and are well-trained, but it is not the same, I grant you. A better comparison would be with a steady goer, reliable but never among the winners."

"Missing that extraordinary turn of speed?"

"Or fine response to the jockey."

"Is that how you see the accompanist—steering and supporting the singer, encouraging her to greater efforts?"

"It is not a very good analogy, but if we are talking of horses…"

"That is fair," he acknowledged.

The hum of conversation increased when they walked into the supper room and several people stopped them to compliment Ann on her playing. Not all comments were favourable,

"You are quite the professional, Miss Overton," one matron remarked acidly. "We shall see you on the stage next."

"My mother is most grateful to Miss Overton for saving the day for us."

The lady flushed at Hope's interjection and stammered, "Yes of course, as are we all."

~~~

"What a nasty woman Lady Prior is," Lady Loring said the next day when they were discussing the evening. "It is fortunate that Hope was with you. His mother showed great foresight in sending him to collect you, but I would not have expected anything less."

"What do you mean, Grandma?" Chloe asked.

"She was emphasising that Ann is a lady, and her guest, not a paid performer like Frau Albrecht. Last night was a private affair, but in general anybody who can afford a ticket can go to hear her." Lady Loring looked at Ann. "You may receive some invitations to perform at other houses. I suggest you restrict your acceptance to occasions where the other musicians play for love of music and not to earn their living. You may be all the rage this Season, but next year any stepping away from your own circle could be held against you."

~~~

"Lady Loring is right," Henrietta Forbes said some days later. "If you become a professional musician, you will no longer be regarded as one of the *ton*."

"As I have only had that honour for the past few months, I would not be unduly concerned," Ann replied.

Henrietta put her hand on Ann's. "The thing is that, as a young single lady, almost a girl, you would find it impossible to find a home within the musical community. Only consider, Ann. Unless your private means are sufficient, you would have to earn enough to support yourself, a chaperon and a maid. That means you would have to find enough engagements. You would be exposed to all sorts of men, many of whom would have no hesitation in taking advantage of you in every possible way. There are some women within the community, but they are the daughters and wives of musicians. They have grown up within it and have the protection of their families. They do not claim to belong to the *beau monde* but, just like it, the community consists of a web of connections and relationships. You would stand outside it and very few people would invite you in. And you would have to be wary of the motives of those who did."

"So I should forget my music?"

"You should forget any idea of performing publicly. You can continue to compose and see if you can find a publisher. Charles would help you there."

"Did you know they have circulating libraries for music on the continent? Herr Albrecht asked for a copy of the score of *Summer at Swanmere*. He said he would show it to some publishers. He would also play it himself so as to make it known. He would act as my agent, he said."

"That's an excellent beginning. Just show Charles any agreement before you sign it."

Chapter Nineteen

Cynthia's eyes widened as she stepped into the entrance hall of the Royal Academy at Somerset House. Although they had come early, they were not the first visitors to this year's Exhibition, which had opened some days previously, however it was not the fashionable society moving purposefully towards the sinuous staircase that held her attention but the two larger than life marble statues of male nudes. On her left a lithe, exquisite figure recalled an Apollo she had seen in Paris some years previously and facing her was a gigantic sculpture of a man with broad, overly muscular shoulders and torso who stooped as if too tall for the space allotted to him.

While Rafe and Sir John Devenish procured catalogues, Lady Anna gestured to the two statues, murmuring to Cynthia, "Are they not my brother and my husband to the life? Just think of Rafe's unstudied elegance and John's vigour and strength."

To Cynthia's eye, Apollo combined elegance, intelligence, vigour, and strength, while the other had something of the brute to him, but she felt it would be unwise to say so. Each to her own, she thought, contenting herself with saying. "They are both fine figures of men."

"Who are?" Rafe had come up behind her.

"Apollo, and is it Hercules? Just very different."

"And whom would you prefer?"

She glanced over her shoulder. "Oh, Apollo. I think he would appreciate the Graces more, don't you?"

A smile glimmered deep in his eyes. "I do."

Sir John looked up from his catalogue. "The numbering starts in the Great Exhibition Room at the top of the house. Do we begin there or take in each room as we go?"

"It is probably best to follow the correct order," Anna answered. "If it gets very full, it will be easier if everyone is moving in the same direction."

"Very true. Shall we go up, then?"

"This way." Rafe stood back to let the ladies enter the stairwell, where they stood transfixed by the sight of the steep stairs that wound their semi-circular way up to the very top of the building; so narrow that the visitors went in single file, those ascending hugging the wall and those descending clinging to the iron handrail.

"I'll lead the way," Rafe said, "then Cynthia, Anna, and you bring up the rear, John."

Bulk has its uses, Cynthia reflected, grateful that Sir John's stalwart presence would prevent a press of impatient climbers from behind. Despite the slow, steady pace Rafe set, she was out of breath by the time they reached the very top floor but there was no room to stop and recover; the press of people carried them inexorably into the Exhibition Room.

She had never experienced such a shock to the senses. The immense room was lit from on high by wide arched windows that stretched from the ceiling to a high stucco frieze. Between this frieze and the floor, a depth of some thirty feet, she estimated, the walls were completely covered by gilt-framed paintings of

The Husband Criteria

various shapes and sizes, all so cunningly fitted together that no space was left free. Dazed, she found a seat on one of the benches in the centre of the room and looked more closely. But look as she may, she could not detect a rationale behind the juxtaposition of pictures—large and small portraits, delicate flower studies, vibrant landscapes, re-enactments of old battles, and classical allegories mostly illustrated by scantily-clad female figures, all claimed their place on the walls.

"However did they piece it together? It must have been like making a mad, dissected puzzle."

A gentleman standing near her laughed. "You are not far wrong, ma'am, but there is some method to their madness."

"Indeed? Pray enlighten us, sir." Rafe put his hand on Cynthia's shoulder as he spoke, and the gentleman shifted his stance so that he addressed both of them.

"D'you see that fine line of stucco along the walls, just at door height? You can just glimpse it between the frames. We call that the line, and we all want to have our works hung on it. The nearer, the more prestigious the placement. Now look more closely. Just beneath it are smaller paintings; there they can easily be viewed even when the place is full. To see the ones below them, you must stoop, or fight your way to the front. Above the line, you will find larger works—full-length portraits, allegories, or landscapes, for example. But you are correct, ma'am, in assuming that it is then partly a question of filling the gaps. As you see, the higher pictures are tilted forward to make it easier to see them. Did you bring opera-glasses?"

"No, I did not think of it," Cynthia admitted.

"I did or, to be exact, my mother did." Rafe took a pretty ivory and gold pair from his pocket and handed it to her.

213

"That is so kind of her. Thank you." She turned back to their interlocutor. "If it is so important to be on the line, what of those paintings that are displayed in the other rooms?"

He smiled. "If you are a young tyro, exhibiting for the first time, you are exalted to be included. If you are a veteran, you are not so pleased."

"I can understand that. Thank you for your explanations, sir."

"Not at all, ma'am. Happy to be of service. If you will take my advice, don't try and inspect each painting, but let them come to you—what catches your eye."

"Thank you."

"May I ask your name, sir?" Rafe asked.

"Oh, indeed, allow me to give you my card. Josiah Richardson, Associate of the Royal Academy, at your service, sir."

"Thank you. I am Marfield."

Mr Richardson bowed. "Much obliged, my lord. Thank you."

After Mr Richardson had taken his leave, Cynthia asked Rafe, "Why did you want his card?"

He shrugged. "I assumed he was an artist, and we shall have a house of our own, shall we not? It would be worth looking at what he produces."

It was real, she thought. By the end of the Season, they would be man and wife, with their own home. She would have a say in how to furnish it. She gave a little wriggle of excitement. "I shall look at the exhibits with quite a different eye. No dreary allegories, for a start."

"What do you like?"

"I don't really know—I have never thought about it, at least not with the idea of a painting hanging on my walls. Let us just wander around and see what appeals to us."

He flicked through the catalogue. "Here is a list of exhibitors, and the numbers of their paintings. Shall we start with Richardson if he is in this room?"

"Yes."

"Here we are. *A portrait of three children playing at Beat my Neighbour*. Number one hundred and eleven."

"I like it," Cynthia declared when they had found the painting not too far from the line. "I prefer it to ones like that." She pointed to the portrait of a boy and a girl with their parents, all dressed in their best finery and as stiff as posts. "These children are real; just look at their expressions as the girl puts down a winning card. I wonder how he captured them."

"He probably did many quick sketches and from them did the painting in his studio," Anna said. "This was most likely a commission. I wonder if he could do the sketches for one of Jack and Lottie before we leave town. He is over there, John; do go and ask him."

Their inspection of the pictures was driven largely by the movements of the crowd; it was simpler to take advantage of a gap than to force one's way through. But the visitors were as fascinating as the exhibits. Generally the *beau monde* kept itself to itself, but anyone who was respectably dressed and could afford a shilling for the catalogue might visit the Royal Academy's Exhibition of Pictures. Here true art-lovers, the *connoisseurs, cognoscenti,* and *dilettanti,* remarked on the finest details, pronounced judgement on newcomers, noted the progress of younger exhibitors since the previous year, and applauded any bravura innovation by the established masters. Fashionable impures vied with society matrons in scrutinising the latest portraits, commenting freely on the success or otherwise of the artists in capturing the likenesses of their subjects. Apart from these knowing observations, there was a constant susurration of polite greetings as the gyrations of the assembly brought acquaintances within speaking distance only to separate them again.

"Good day, Miss Glazebrook."

At the sound of the boy's voice, Cynthia paused just inside the door on the Inner Room. Lord Jasper FitzCharles bowed to her, as did his father, the duke.

"I am happy to see someone I know," the boy declared. "I have never before been in such a mass of people."

"It is a little overwhelming," Cynthia acknowledged, "but I hope you have managed to see some of the paintings. One cannot take them all in at once; it is simply too much."

"Yes. I mean to come back several times if Mr Musgrave or my painting instructor will take me. Have you seen these?" He took Cynthia's hand in a manner strongly reminiscent of Jack and towed her to look at two landscapes. "Aren't they beautiful? One is a landscape, painted from the sea, and the other a seascape painted from on land."

Cynthia took the catalogue from Rafe and flicked through the pages until she came to the relevant numbers. *"View of Nice from the* Baie des Anges *and View of the* Baie des Anges *from the* Villa della Torre. That's Lady Mary Arkell's place. We visited there some years ago. These are very good. I love the way the artist captures the light."

"Yes." Jasper jiggled with excitement. "Look at who it is."

"Lady S. F. Chloe's mother?"

"Yes. Isn't it splendid."

"What does the H after her name stand for?"

"She is an honorary exhibitor, not a professional artist as most of them are. But I intend to be a proper artist, a professional. In a year or so, I shall be old enough to start studying here," he added with a defiant look at his father.

"We'll see," the duke said mildly. "First you must apply yourself to your other studies."

Cynthia looked over the narrow handrail down into the vertiginous depths of the semi-circular staircase. She swallowed hard and closed her eyes.

"Cynthia?"

She swallowed again and looked up into Rafe's concerned face. "It's a long way down, isn't it? If someone slipped, everyone ahead of them would fall like a row of dominoes."

"It will not seem as bad once you have set foot on it," he said reassuringly. "Hold on to the handrail and fix your eyes on me. We'll go slowly, and you need only call 'stop' if you feel unsteady. John will prevent anyone smashing into us."

He broke off as a group of young men, who had been among the loudest commentators in the exhibition rooms, brushed past with a perfunctory, "Your pardon, sir," and clattered on down the steps, paying little heed to those coming against them.

"They are out of the way, at least. Ready?" Rafe asked and at Cynthia's nod went down a couple of steps, then waited until he saw her grasp the rail.

She obediently fixed her eyes on him, admiring the little curls that just brushed his collar, the set of his coat at his shoulders and the way his firm thighs flexed beneath the tails of his coat. Indeed, she was quite sorry when they left the stairs at the first-floor landing.

"The Council Room has the works presented by the Academicians on their election," Lady Anna said. "Shall we go in there first? It might be less crowded."

Less crowded it was, though the centre was occupied by the same unruly fellows who had pushed past them on the landing. Their gaze was fixed on the ceiling above them and as Cynthia's group came in, one drawled, "*'The Graces Unveiling Nature'*. I suppose the one with rows of titties is Nature. How very unnatural, more sow-like than human."

"The Graces are very appealing. Nothing unwomanly about them, as you can see from their erm *lack* of costume. I approve, don't you, chaps?"

"Indeed. There is quite a resemblance to our own Graces, is there not? Here, Smith, give me your glasses for a moment." The speaker took the opera glass and focussed it on the ceiling where the three clustered together, completely naked but for a narrow drape of apricot gauze framing their bodies that were so turned towards the figure of Nature that only their backs were displayed from below the waist.

When Rafe stiffened, Cynthia turned away from the speakers and frantically clutched his arm. *Say nothing*, she implored him silently. *Pretend you did not hear it, or understand the allusion.*

The Husband Criteria

He looked down at her and she tilted her head towards the door, afraid of drawing the boors' attention if she spoke. Better to leave quietly. He nodded.

"Enough, sirs! There are ladies present." Heads swivelled towards the weather-beaten elderly gentleman whose stentorian voice commanded the attention of everyone in the room. He had the look of the quarterdeck, Cynthia thought. "If you are unable to conduct yourselves in polite society, you may withdraw until you have found someone to lick you into shape."

The four so admonished puffed out their chests like so many cockerels, but soon deflated as they realised that the consensus was against them. Red-faced, they slunk away. A communal exhalation expressed the relief of the onlookers as, without further comment, they returned their attention to the works of art on display.

Cynthia was shaking inside, grateful for the comfort of Rafe's hand covering hers where it remained on his arm.

"Come, sit for a moment."

Lady Anna looked curiously from one to the other as he found a chair, but only said, "Have you seen Miss Kauffman's paintings? I am a great admirer of her work."

They gradually made their way down through the building. The exhibition of sculpture in the Model Academy was like a breath of fresh air; the purity of the white marble providing a welcome respite from the whirligig of colours and motifs in the rooms devoted to paintings. The greatest press of people was around one exhibit; when they worked their way through to the front of the crowd, they faced the most lifelike representation of two young girls sleeping, the younger cradled by the elder, their curls mingling as if, exhausted from play, they had just lain down for an instant. But the two sisters slept the sleep of death. Impossible not to be moved by their monument, or to be desperately sorry for the unfortunate parents who had endured such a loss. Cynthia was not the only person who brushed away a tear.

Chapter Twenty

Martin Glazebrook put down his coffee cup. "Listen to this, Cynthia. It's from the latest issue of *The Sportsman in Town*, '*S*portsmen visiting the Exhibition must remember that the vulgar tongue of the Fancy is out of place at Somerset House. Only yesterday, we hear, was it necessary for Captain F——r to remonstrate with some unlicked cubs in no less a place than the Council Room, and to remind them of the presence of ladies. Shame on those concerned.' You were there yesterday; did you notice anything?"

"Notice? We were in the Council Room at the time. There were four of them commenting loudly on the ceiling painting of The Three Graces and Nature; they commended the Graces' lack of costume and were about to compare them with what they had the temerity to describe as 'our own Graces'. I didn't know where to look, and I thought Marfield about to explode, when fortunately this captain intervened. Thank goodness there is no mention here of what they said."

Martin's face darkened. "Do you know who they were?"

"Two of them looked vaguely familiar, of the *ton*, but not of our set. I have never danced with them, for instance."

"I'll drop into Whites' later; see what's what."

"Whatever you do, don't create a stir. They left with their tails between their legs, and it is best to let the whole thing die down."

"If it does."

Cynthia was not too happy at this but there was no point in arguing with her brother. Lady Benton's rout was tomorrow night. After breakfast she would bathe and have Cotter wash her hair in preparation for the hairdresser's visit tomorrow. The modiste was to send her new gown this morning; then they would review everything she needed for such an occasion. There was nothing worse than finding a loose button or a burst seam in a glove just when you were dressing for a party.

~~~

Cynthia stretched luxuriously before curling up on the parlour window seat with Mrs Fay's *Letters from India*. She rarely was alone at home, but today her mother was paying calls and her father and Martin were also out. After her bath, she had put on a morning-gown sprigged with soft green and yellow, over the lightest of short stays. Once her hair was dry, Cotter had dressed it simply, saying, "We'll leave it settle for a couple of hours, Miss, and I'll do it properly before you go out."

Later they were invited to Gracechurch House for a family evening. The Glazebrooks had been surprised to be included. The duchess was very kind, Cynthia thought, remembering how helpful she had been about the Almack's disaster. Well, it could not be said to have harmed her. Chloe and Ann were not yet ready to consider marriage but it was their first Season—just look how she herself had changed between one year and the next.

"Lord Marfield has called, Miss."

Oh. The butler would have denied her to any other callers save Chloe and Ann, obviously he knew what way the wind was blowing. "Show him in here."

Rafe was pleased to be led to a family parlour and even more delighted to find his betrothed alone. She was wearing one of his favourite gowns, but usually she wore a matching green spencer over it. Today he could see that it covered her to her throat, the collar decorated with a little lace frill that would stand proud above the neck of the spencer. Odd that a primly buttoned-up bodice was almost more alluring than the fashionable, low-cut evening gowns. Her hair was piled loosely on her head, caught by a green ribbon. His fingers itched to remove it, see her hair tumble down. A husband's privilege.

She came to him, ungloved hands out-stretched. "I had not thought to see you today."

"I am not unwelcome, I hope?"

"Of course not."

He slid his hands up her arms to her shoulders and, his eyes on hers, bent to kiss her.

There was no resistance; indeed, instead of offering her cheek she raised her chin invitingly. When his lips touched hers, her bare hands rose first to his shoulders and then, as he deepened the kiss, to clasp behind his neck. Skin upon skin. They both shuddered when she gently rubbed the fine hairs at his nape against the grain. When he lifted his head, she smiled at him, the tip of her pink tongue peeping out to touch her reddened lips.

Unsure how long they would be private, he took a jeweller's case from his pocket. "This is for you. To mark our betrothal."

"Rafe!" Cynthia's jaw dropped when she opened the flat case to reveal a necklace composed of small gold bows with green enamel centres interspersed with pink stones culminating in an elaborate central pendant of the same materials, ending with a pink teardrop.

"Oh, it is wonderful. So beautiful, and so different, so cunningly made. Thank you so much, Rafe." She put it down carefully and threw her arms around his neck.

He let her take the lead this time, relishing her sweet kiss.

"In the parlour?" It was Martin's voice. "I'll join them. Bring some ale."

Rafe and Cynthia separated quickly. She snatched up the jewel case. "Look what Rafe has brought me," she said when Martin came in. "Isn't it beautiful?"

He stared at her. "I must get used to the idea that you are betrothed and may be alone with him. For a moment there, I was going to throw him out."

~~~

With a peculiar mixture of trepidation, anticipation, and excitement, Cynthia alighted from the carriage at Benton House. Over the course of her two Seasons, she had attended many parties in London's great houses but never before at a house where she, in the fullness of time, would become its mistress. She touched Rafe's necklace, the outward sign of her changed status. She was not dreaming.

To mark her son's engagement, Lady Benton had invited forty relatives to dine, including several from the Glazebrook side. Cards had also been sent to a further hundred guests for dancing from 10 p.m. As requested by Lady Benton, Cynthia and her family were arriving a half an hour before the other dinner guests who would then be received not only by the earl and countess but also by their heir and his newly affianced bride.

Entering the hall, they found Lord and Lady Benton, Marfield, and Lady Anna with her husband, Sir John Devenish. To Cynthia's surprise, Jack stood some paces back, his hand held firmly by his nurse. Once the flurry of greetings and embraces had subsided, the boy looked at Sir John.

"Now, Papa. May I?"

"You may."

Released, he darted towards Cynthia, then apparently recollected himself, slowed down and, when he reached her, bowed. "My felicitations on your betrothal, Cyn-thi-a."

Touched by this carefully rehearsed phrase and pronunciation of her name, Cynthia curtsied, as solemnly. "Thank you, Jack," she said, before crouching down and holding out her arms. "Do you have a kiss for me?"

He threw his arms around her and pressed a smacker onto her cheek, then said, "Mamma says when you are married to Uncle Marfield, you will be Aunt Marfield."

"I suppose I will. Shall you like that?"

"Yes. Aunt Eliza gives me comfits."

"Ah. So that will be my duty?"

"Yes, and to read me stories."

"I see. That does not seem too arduous."

"That's enough, Jack," Sir John intervened. "You promised you would not tarry once you had spoken to Cynthia. Off you go, now."

"Goodbye, Cyntha." Jack withdrew from her embrace, bowed to the company with a general "Good night," and retreated to his waiting nurse.

"We go upstairs," he informed her and disappeared down the hall, although not without turning to bestow a valedictory wave on the assembly.

"Shall we go up?" Lord Benton offered Cynthia's mother his arm, his wife accepted that of Mr Glazebrook, and they began the ascent of the grand staircase.

Rafe murmured to Cynthia as they followed. "I don't know which pair is prouder, or more excited. You would think they had made the match themselves. Just watch them preen themselves later."

Cynthia cast him a sideways glance. "Are they simply happy for us, or had they given up hope of ever marrying us off, do you think? Of course, it cannot be denied that you are a tremendous catch, a nonpareil one might say."

"Might one indeed? In that case, I trust you will treat me with the appropriate reverence."

"You may rely on that," she said in such honeyed tones that he first looked askance, then held her back at the return of the stairs to snatch a kiss. "Vixen!"

"Do you mean to say, Sis, that Marfield here meets all of your husband criteria?" Martin demanded.

"Husband criteria? What do you mean, Mr Glazebrook," Lady Anna asked.

"It must be two years ago now that my sister and her friends began to develop a list of the qualities they looked for in a husband," he said carelessly. "Not the obvious things like birth and wealth, but whether he was kind, a good listener, generous or mean-spirited, or a fortune-hunter. They said the artificiality of the Season makes it difficult to assess a fellow's character and to weed out those who might ignore or mistreat their wives."

"That is true. And you passed this test, Rafe? Well done."

"I must assume I did," Rafe replied. "This is the first I have heard of it."

Martin began to laugh. "My father asked her if she intended to subject prospective suitors to a *viva voce* but she said she would have more *finesse*."

"Martin!" Cynthia felt her cheeks grow warm.

"What did you do?" Lady Anna asked as they emerged onto the landing where the others waited.

"No more than what any sensible lady should do; I paid attention to what they said and did, and how they made me feel—respected or talked down to, for example."

"So there is a list," the other woman persisted.

"There is not," Cynthia said in desperation. "My friends and I discussed what we wished for in a husband, of course; I think all girls do, and if they do not, they should—but there is no list that we went through item by item after a ball, marking each gentleman's score."

"Like a hand of piquet?" Rafe asked, a slow smile growing in his eyes. "I suppose I should be grateful I was unaware of this."

"You made a bad start at Gunter's, but afterwards passed with flying colours," Cynthia assured him.

They crossed the wide landing, following the older couples into the ante-room where three elderly ladies rose from their seats, a significant honour, Cynthia recognised, as she was presented first to Marfield's grandmother, the dowager countess, then his great-aunt Lady Georgina, and his cousin Cassandra. Miss Benton was a timid-looking lady who was in danger of being overwhelmed by a deep purple gown and turban that looked as if they had been made for someone else.

"I am delighted to make your acquaintance, Miss Glazebrook," the dowager said, "and wish you and my grandson every happiness."

"Thank you, my lady."

"It is always heartening to see the line continue," she added.

Lady Georgina sniffed audibly. "Not yet, I hope, Sarah. Let us have the wedding first."

"You forget yourself, Aunt." The earl did not wait to see the effect of his cold rebuke but turned to Miss Benton with a gentle smile. "I trust you have recovered from your megrim, Cousin."

Miss Benton flushed at this mark of attention and stammered, "Yes, I thank you, Benton. So considerate."

"The first carriages have drawn up, my lady."

~~~

Flanked by his parents, Cynthia and Rafe accepted the good wishes of their relatives. On her side came the Ransfords and the party from Swanmere House; both Lady Loring and Swanmere had struggled up the stairs. They would not stay for the ball but were insistent they must celebrate Cynthia's happiness.

A plethora of Martyns, from the dowager marchioness to Lady Tamm, was followed by the Fromes who included the earl, countess, and Lord and Lady Franklin. A handful of untitled sons and daughters of all houses made up the numbers. Cynthia knew almost all of the guests, but none of them apart from Chloe, Ann, and the Nugents were among her intimates.

The Husband Criteria

Dinner consisted of just one lavish course, albeit with several removes, followed by dessert. In an unusual departure, the earl joined his wife at the head of the table, yielding his place at the foot to the betrothed couple who sat side by side. At first Cynthia had felt uneasy at this distinction but, once she had served the soup and Rafe had apportioned a fine salmon, she realised it gave them more of an opportunity to talk privately than they would have had if they had been placed among the guests along one of the sides.

The array of dishes was repeated twice on the long table so that each guest might have a good selection of the delicacies offered. She could not but admire the proficiency of a household that could serve such a meal and would, some few hours later, provide a ball supper that she did not doubt would be of equal excellence.

"I shall have to take lessons from your Mamma," she said to Rafe as she helped herself to some spears of tender asparagus.

"In what subject?"

"How to manage this sort of occasion."

"I believe it all comes down to having good servants."

"Managing them is an art in itself," said Cynthia who had counted upwards of fifteen footmen waiting on the company under the stern eye of the butler. "I suppose Lady Benton has superior servants who instruct upper servants who in turn direct lower servants…"

"You make it sound like Dr Swift's fleas."

"Dr Swift who wrote *Gulliver's Travels*? Did he suffer from fleas? What have they to do with your mother's servants?"

229

He grinned and quoted,

> *So, Nat'ralists observe, a Flea*
> *Hath smaller Fleas that on him prey,*
> *And these have smaller yet to bite 'em,*
> *And so proceed* ad infinitum

She had to laugh. "I suppose it is something like that, but reversed."

When the tablecloth was removed and the dessert set out on the gleaming mahogany, footmen went around the table with glasses of champagne. Earl Benton stood.

"My lords, ladies and gentlemen, it is with the greatest of pleasure that we celebrate the betrothal of our son Marfield to Miss Cynthia Glazebrook and welcome her to our family. Pray join me in rising to drink their health, wishing them a long life together in health and happiness."

Amid the clink of glasses and murmured toasts, Cynthia felt submerged in a wave of good will as smiling faces turned towards her and Rafe. When the guests had reseated themselves, Rafe stood.

"Thank you, sir, and thank you all for your good wishes. In particular, I wish to express my gratitude to Mr and Mrs Glazebrook, for in my gaining a wife, they will lose the presence of a beloved daughter in their home. May this be the first of many occasions our two families celebrate together."

When he raised his glass, Cynthia joined the company in drinking with him, amid cries of 'hear, hear'.

The Husband Criteria

Her father rose to respond. "The pain of parting with our daughter is lessened by your heartfelt welcome of her, my lord"—he bowed towards Lord Benton—"and our knowledge that we are entrusting her to one who will always have a care for her happiness. To the happy couple!"

To Cynthia's relief, that was the final toast and the guests settled to addressing the creams, jellies, and fruits of the dessert.

"What may I give you?" Rafe asked. "The apricot custards are my favourite."

"I must try them then. It is very early for apricots. Does your cook preserve them, or are they from your succession houses?"

"I have no idea."

"It doesn't matter. Mmm. This is very good. Perhaps I might speak to him one day, ask for the recipes for your favourite dishes."

He raised his glass in a silent toast. "That sounds charmingly domestic. I am going to enjoy being married to you, Cynthia."

Lady Benton glanced around the table, then rose slowly, the assembly rising with her. The gentlemen remaining standing as the ladies filed out, Lord Swanmere escorting Lady Loring. Lady Anna caught up with her future sister-in-law at the door. "Come upstairs with me, Cynthia. You may refresh yourself in my bedchamber before you face the next onslaught of guests. It will be many more this time."

"Just let me say goodnight to my great-grandmother and Lord Swanmere who go home now—the ball would be too much for them. Their carriage should be waiting."

"Goodnight, child," Lady Loring said, with a fond kiss. "Although now that you are an affianced lady, I should call you that no longer, I suppose."

"Goodnight, ma'am, and you too, sir." Cynthia turned to Swanmere. "Thank you for being part of our celebrations."

Swanmere harrumphed. "Honoured to be here. Goodnight, my dear."

As soon as the door closed behind the elderly couple, Anna said, "We must hurry. My mother firmly instructed my father not to linger over the port—fifteen minutes at most, so that the dinner guests may be in the ballroom before the ball guests start to arrive."

As she spoke, she led Cynthia up to the second floor and into a pretty bedroom where a maid waited.

"Sit here, at the dressing-table. Your hair has come a little loose at the back—all those embraces. Jillson will fix it for you."

"Thank you. You are most thoughtful, Anna."

"Pooh! Are we not to be sisters? I always wished for one."

"Did you? So did I."

"You and Rafe are going to settle in Lincolnshire. That is not so far from us that we cannot visit you regularly. And you must come to us. Jack will insist."

~~~

The dinner guests were still taking tea and coffee in the music-room, the third in the great enfilade of state rooms on the first floor of Benton House, when Lady Benton put down her cup. "It is time."

At her sign, the footmen opened the doors to the great drawing-room, a magnificent space decorated in shades of cream, gold, and a soft, muted green. Tonight, it was empty of furnishings apart from the settees and sofas set along the walls. Two overmantel mirrors, one at either end of the long room and a dozen pier glasses reflected the light of hundreds of candles from three immense, crystal chandeliers. The carpets had been taken up and the floorboards gleamed where a wide margin had been left round the edge of the room but in the centre a splendid multi-hued design had been chalked on the floor; garlands of flowers surrounded two centre medallions depicting the Benton coat of arms and the new one that had been granted to the nabob on his return from India, linked by two interlocked gold rings. The chalked pattern served two purposes, to emphasise the splendour of the occasion and to prevent the dancers from slipping on the highly-polished oak.

Her hand on Rafe's arm, Cynthia followed his parents along the unchalked side aisle to the ante-room where they would await the ball guests. She had never seen anything so elaborate as that floor—or so ephemeral—one dance would see the pattern irretrievably smudged and by morning it would only be so much coloured dust that had clung to the ladies' satin slippers and puffed around the dancers' ankles, leaving its traces on skirts, silk stockings, and gentlemen's inexpressibles—a curse for lady's maids and valets.

'*Golden lads and girls all must/As chimneysweepers, come to dust*', she thought. *Don't be so maudlin*, she admonished herself, while resolving never to have chalked floors at her future balls.

Cynthia found she already knew most of the ball guests filing past with quick smiles and congratulatory murmurs. But who was the vivacious lady whose dark hair curled onto her high forehead over speaking brown eyes? She was about thirty, Cynthia thought, and walked with all the assurance of one who was not only a recognised beauty but a personage.

Lady Benton inclined her head slightly. "Countess Lieven. We are happy to see you."

"As I am to come." The lady's slight bow mirrored that of her hostess. She smiled at Lord Benton, then paused before Cynthia, one beautifully arched eyebrow raised slightly. "I do not know this young lady."

"Allow me to present Marfield's betrothed, Miss Glazebrook. Miss Glazebrook, the Countess Lieven."

So this was Almack's haughtiest patroness. Cynthia dipped into a curtsey. "My lady."

"Miss Glazebrook." The countess extended the first and middle finger of her right hand and Cynthia briefly touched them with her own. "My felicitations, Miss Glazebrook, and to you, Marfield."

Rafe bowed. "Thank you, my lady."

The countess passed on, followed by her husband, the Russian ambassador. Cynthia took a deep breath. At least one of the patronesses had come.

The Nugents were next. Their good wishes were sincere, as were those of Lord Rastleigh. The Needhams, the Nearys, the Gracechurches, Chloe's mother with Lord Stephen, Lady Jersey, another patroness, who smiled rather ruefully as she gracefully expressed her felicitations, but no mention was made of vouchers denied. Gradually the line of newcomers thinned until, at last, Lady Benton said, "We can go in now."

The musicians waited as Cynthia and Rafe walked onto the empty dance floor, stopping at the linked gold rings. "Ready?" he whispered.

"Yes."

When the leader raised his violin, Rafe put his arm around Cynthia's shoulder. She mirrored his gesture and their outer hands joined in front of them as the seductive strains of the introduction to the waltz crept through the hushed room. Their eyes met in mutual anticipation as they glided into the opening steps. No one else existed; their parents, their friends, and the one hundred and more onlookers vanished as they gave themselves up to this silent union, no longer two but one. Every sense was heightened; she responded to his lead as if she read his thoughts. Once she laid her head dreamily on his shoulder, and he held the step a fraction longer before spinning her away, catching both her hands and raising them high so that they revolved under them, never letting go. The leader was following them, he realised, stretching a note where necessary and making up the time on the next.

He was dimly aware of their parents joining them, together with Anna and Martin. Soon the dancefloor was full of waltzing couples. When the music stopped, she sank into a curtsey. He raised her and kissed her hand, then they were surrounded by smiling well-wishers.

~~~

Rafe waved a final farewell as the Glazebrook carriage drew away from Benton House.

"Thank God that is over," he said to his parents when he returned to the hall.

"Why? Did you not enjoy the evening?" his mother asked.

"I should have enjoyed it more if I had been allowed to spend even a quiet quarter of an hour with Cynthia. People were so busy congratulating us, or wishing to dance with the bride-to-be, or wanting to know had we set the date." He smiled ruefully. "I had never thought about it, but generally at a ball one is left in peace when strolling after a dance—it is recognised that that is one of the few opportunities to exchange some private words, but apparently once you are betrothed, it is assumed that there is no further need for such consideration. Still, it was a splendid occasion and I am most grateful to you, Mamma."

"It went off well, I thought. We were not left with only a few couple rattling round for the last hour. It was inspired of you to invite Countess Lieven to stand up with you, Rafe."

His father nodded. "She could hardly refuse the bridegroom. Of course you had to ask Lady Jersey too, but she loves to dance."

"Miss Loring and Miss Overton did not want for partners; that Three Graces nonsense seems to have blown over," Lady Benton said.

"Let us hope so," Rafe said. "Cynthia is concerned that it might be revived next week when we are out of town."

"Surely not? The *ton* will have moved on to the next *on-dit* by then." Lord Benton yawned. "It is half-past four o'clock. I'm for my bed. Come, my dear. Good night, Marfield."

Chapter Twenty-One

Unlike most *ton* mammas, Amelia Glazebrook had never indulged in secret daydreams wherein her daughter carried off the matrimonial prize of the Season. Her Cynthia was of too captious a disposition to attract and sustain the interest of one who need only throw the handkerchief to assure himself of the lady of his choice. No one had been more surprised when Marfield had not merely tolerated but accepted Cynthia's vacillations, and Amelia had watched in amazement and with no little satisfaction as he gentled her without crushing her spirit. Her daughter had found her wings but was no longer determined to fly solo.

At Lady Benton's party she had been the recipient of many congratulations on the engagement together with good wishes for the bride-to-be and in the days afterwards, a steady flow of ladies with marriageable daughters called at Park Place, many for the first time. But all of them, and especially the latter, were only interested in one thing. Once the obligatory courtesies had been exchanged, the mother would say confidentially, "I wonder, dear Mrs Glazebrook, now that you no longer have need of it, would you be willing to share the list with us?"

"List—I'm afraid I don't understand."

"I have it on the best authority that Miss Glazebrook used a list of the qualities or criteria, I believe she called them, she sought in a husband to assess her suitors."

Amelia smiled. "I am sure she gave prudent and prayerful thought to the matter, as any sensible young lady would. Matrimony is a most serious step, you will agree. However, I am not aware of any list."

"Prudent and prayerful!" Martin snorted when she repeated this exchange that evening. "How could you, Mamma? They will be calling her Saint Cynthia next."

"I had to say something," his mother pointed out. "But really, the idea of a list is ludicrous."

"It's your fault, Martin," Cynthia said. "If you had not made that remark at the Bentons'—I suppose Lady Anna or Sir John must have repeated it—or one of the servants, for that matter—there would be no talk of a list."

"Do you mean there is a list?" her mother asked.

"Not as such. As you said, we—that is Chloe, Ann, and I—prudently and prayerfully considered what we looked for in a husband."

"Established criteria, in other words. Well, I shall continue to claim ignorance."

~~~

Other mothers tried more indirect approaches. Little lunches, where ten or twelve young ladies were invited without chaperons were suddenly all the crack. Between three and five o'clock, they chattered over tea, sandwiches, cakes, and other delicacies before

The Husband Criteria

being collected to drive in the Park. While Cynthia, Chloe, and Ann continued to deny the existence of a husband list, the conversation frequently turned to what were now referred to as husband criteria.

"Some qualities are universally sought," Chloe said one day, "but there will be others that are particular to each individual—a common taste in reading, perhaps, or does he like music."

"Does he insist on letting dogs roam around the house?" one girl said suddenly. "Dogs make me cough and sneeze."

"That would be difficult to manage," Ann said.

"My father's spaniels are only allowed in the library, and I never go in there. I suppose we could agree on something like that."

"Hmm," another girl said, "that may be all very well for a daughter, but not for the mistress of the house."

"I'm afraid of dogs," a third said quietly. "I was badly bitten by a stray when I was a child."

"If you truly trusted him, he might be able to help you overcome your fear—of his dogs at least, provided they were properly trained," Cynthia said. "The real question is, can you tell him of your fears or concerns and will he listen and try to help you resolve them?"

"You mean, talk seriously to him? As if he were a woman?"

Chloe bit the inside of her mouth to stop herself laughing out loud at the girl's shocked face. "As if he were a person. Have you no brothers?"

"Two younger ones. They tease me all the time, threatening to set one of the dogs on me. Fortunately, my mother will not allow them in the house while the boys are at school and the keepers have them well trained. Indeed, I heard one of them tell my brother that if he heard he had mistreated a dog that way, he would forbid him the kennels."

"Mistreat the dog! What about his treatment of you?"

"I suppose he does not feel it is his place to comment on that."

"I never know what to say to a gentleman, especially an older one," another girl who was in her first Season said. "When I look around at a ball, everyone seems to be having an interesting conversation except me. All I can manage is, 'Yes' and 'No'."

"That is not very pleasant for the gentleman," remarked Miss Nugent, who was probably the oldest there and in her fifth Season. "When I came out, my brother told me to make an effort to talk to my dancing partners. He said, 'Imagine if you had to walk across the ballroom floor to address a lady, especially when you are new on the town—you think every eye is on you. If you later have to struggle to get a word out of her, you feel everyone assumes you are a dead bore.' Some of them are, of course," she added candidly, "but the time will pass quicker if you make the effort to smile and converse a little."

"My brother said much the same." Cynthia passed her cup for more tea. "You don't have to flirt, just be polite. You don't have to wait for him to start—say something, even a comment about the weather."

Ann started to laugh. "And if he doesn't respond, remember how Elizabeth decides it is a greater punishment to oblige Mr Darcy to talk while they dance."

"Oh, *Pride and Prejudice*," the lady who could not tolerate dogs said. "Which of the four gentlemen—Bingley, Collins, Darcy, or Wickham do you think would best meet the husband criteria?"

"It goes to show that there is no unique set of criteria," Miss Nugent said after an animated discussion. "For all that Lydia may have dreamt of a great match, Darcy and she would have been totally unsuited. She will be happiest with Wickham."

"For a while at least," Chloe said. "He is too unsteady to remain faithful."

A young lady who had listened quietly to the previous conversation put down her cup and saucer. "Supposing you have met a gentleman who meets all your criteria but your family is opposed to the match—what then?"

The others looked at each other. She was just seventeen, Cynthia recalled, one of the youngest debutantes that year. A quiet girl, not a hoyden. The sort of girl who might be taken in by a charming scapegrace.

After a moment, Miss Nugent said, "I suppose it depends on why they consider him unsuitable. Plenty of girls have fancied themselves in love with their music or drawing master, for instance."

"Or a handsome young groom," someone added to general laughter.

The quiet girl flushed. "No, I mean a gentleman—one who moves in our circles."

"I think you would have to ask your parents what they have against him—beg them to be honest with you," Cynthia said gently. "They may consider he is too old for you, or that you are too young to seriously consider marriage. My grandparents insisted my mother have two full Seasons before they would agree to a betrothal."

"Or they may wish for a better match for you. All you can do there is wait until you are of age and, if all of you are still of the same mind, marry against their will," Chloe put in. "But, whatever you do, do not agree to an elopement or to marrying without a settlement. If your parents won't act for you, perhaps another relative will. If necessary, engage your own man of business."

"Why is that necessary?"

"Because once you marry all you have becomes your husband's," Chloe said bluntly. "He may squander your fortune or gamble it all away and you will have no recourse. Without a settlement, you will have nothing of your own. A man who tries to convince you otherwise or cajole or coerce you into an elopement is not worthy of your consideration."

~~~

"The cat is properly among the pigeons now, and I understand we have you to thank for it," Francis Nugent remarked to Marfield at the Chess Club.

"In what way?"

Mr Nugent tossed the latest issue of *The Sportsman in Town* across the table. "Read the first paragraph. I don't agree; I would prefer a lady who has given some thought to the matter to a tender Parnell who is fearful of everything but agrees to the match because 'Mamma knows best'." This last was said in such mincing tones that Marfield had to laugh.

"I danced with such a one last night," Mr Nugent continued gloomily. "A pretty little thing, whose mother waylaid me—you know the way they do—and I thought why not trot her out, but she hardly raised her eyes to me, let alone her voice. I returned her to Mamma as soon as I could. It's all very well for you to laugh," he continued, "you have made an excellent choice; she is kind and thoughtful—seemed to realise that my sister was a bit at a loss this Season. She misses Arabella Malvin, you know. They were like sisters, have been from the beginning. Your lady made a point of welcoming her to their set. It made a difference. I wish you both happy, Marfield, 'pon my soul, I do."

"Thank you. Does your gratitude extend to standing with me as groomsman?"

"I should be honoured. When and where is the wedding?"

"When—by the end of the Season; where has not yet been decided. I'll let you know as soon as we do." Marfield picked up the little bulletin.

Many sportsmen are alarmed to find themselves in the sights of husband-hunters who select their prey according to strict criteria and do not hesitate to put their victims to the question. True Corinthians will decline to accommodate such female inquisitors. As the poet writes in his Remedia Amoris, *'princiipis obsta', or 'resist beginnings'—before it is too late to avoid the hen house.*

"Hmph! 'True Corinthians.' Niffy-naffy fellows or nincompoops, they mean. As if mothers and daughters have not been assessing suitors from the dawn of time."

"Very true. Are we to have a game? I owe you for last week's defeat."

~~~

"We suddenly have two distinct varieties of gentlemen," Caro Nugent observed. "Those who make more of an effort to engage in conversation and those who show us inquisitors, as they call us, the cold shoulder."

243

"The sheep and the goats?" Matthew Malvin asked as he deftly negotiated the turn into the Park. "Have you had any surprises?"

"Surprises?"

"Men you expected to be sheep who turned out to be goats."

She laughed. "Frequently, over the years, but in this case, who would you put into which category?"

"According to the bible, sheep are good and goats are bad."

"But was that meant to apply for all time? It's like comparing apples and oranges—a distinction between similar objects rather than an assessment of their qualities."

"That is true. There is something very docile about sheep; they are given to following their leader. And their fleece is probably worth more than a goat's hair."

She raised an eyebrow. "Useful attributes in a husband, you mean? A goat is more independent-minded, thinks for him or herself. I had rather wed a goat than a sheep."

Matthew grinned. "When you put it that way, I must agree with you."

"Thank you for agreeing to take me driving, Matthew. Francis is at the Chess Club and there is no other gentleman I could ask without embarrassment. You would not take it wrongly, I know." She sighed. "I do miss Arabella. The Season is not the same without her."

"Or maybe we're getting too old for it, Caro."

"But what is the alternative? Even marriage will not help us escape it. Otherwise, ladies can opt to be ape-leaders or bluestockings, or a combination of the two, and gentlemen, dilettantes or roués."

"And end up like Danlow?"

She shuddered. "Lord Henry, you mean? That was the most dreadful thing."

"Yes. I went to his trial last year."

"Did you? Why?"

Matthew was silent for a moment. "I don't really know. I never particularly liked him, but if Bella had set her heart on him—"

"You would have accepted him?"

"Made an effort to, at any rate. But after what happened, I needed to see him again, I suppose, see if he seemed any different, if there was something I should have recognised."

"And was there?"

"He was diminished, of course, standing alone in the dock, but his lip curled in just the same way—you remember—and he never said a word, not even after he was found guilty and they draped the black cloth over the judge's wig."

"They said he took poison."

"Yes, after the sentence was pronounced. It all happened so fast. He dropped to the floor. At first, they thought he had fainted, but they soon spoke of poison."

"Dreadful," she said again. "One must be sorry for his family."

"His elder brother was there. Not Rickersby, another one— Lord Frederick, not long returned from abroad, someone said."

"Poor man. What a homecoming."

"He seemed shattered. They wouldn't let him take the body— the judge said that although Lord Henry had cheated the hangman, he should not avoid dissection."

Caro covered her mouth with a gloved hand.

"I'm sorry," Matthew said. "It is not a fit subject for a lady."

"I haven't seen either the Marquis or his wife this Season. It's understandable, I suppose. Their children are still quite young. We must hope it will all be forgotten by the time they come on the town."

Chapter Twenty-Two

A little bird tells us that one of the ton's *most eligible bachelors, Lord M——d is soon to lead his Graceful bride, Miss C. G. to Hymen's altar. The happy couple will make their home in Lincolnshire.*

Chloe looked up from *Tonnish Topics and Society Secrets.* "How quickly they change their tune," she said to Rosa. "I wonder who feeds them this information."

"Servants, perhaps, or a clerk in some solicitor's office. There are settlements to be drawn up, you know, especially where an earldom is concerned."

"And a nabob's granddaughter. Rosa, I remember Julian saying that my father had made ample provision for me, but he never told me exactly what it was. Ann does not know either what her father left her. Why are girls left so in ignorance?"

"Partly because gentlemen tend to think that business matters are their concern, but also sometimes a girl is very young when her father dies. Ann was, for instance. And you were only sixteen. Why don't you ask Julian? I am sure he will be happy to explain it to you."

"Explain what?" Julian asked from the door of the parlour.

"The provision Papa made for me," Chloe said. "What is it? What happens if I don't marry? Do I not get anything then?"

"Of course you do. He left ten thousand pounds in trust for you. It is invested in Consols and brings in five hundred pounds a year. It has not been touched since Father died, so another thousand pounds has accrued to the capital which means an additional fifty pounds in your annual income."

"Wait. I never thought—you must think I am very silly indeed—where does my pin money come from? Who pays for my gowns? When I think of what the Season must cost…"

Julian put his arm around her. "I have been more than happy to meet your expenses, Pet. Indeed, I had quite an argument with your mother, who was determined to support you. It was all I could do to reassure her that I did not refuse her offer of assistance out of resentment towards her, but because of my affection for you."

Chloe smiled. "But you could not stop her giving me things. She always has something—a fan, or a shawl or a reticule—"

"She is very generous," Rosa said, "but she always was. You never wanted for anything."

Chloe nodded. "I took it for granted, I suppose."

"As a child should. I do not mean that a child should be spoiled but she should not have to worry about financial matters. It is for its parents to manage them, and to give their children the best they can afford."

"Now that I am an adult, I need to understand such things. Ten thousand pounds sounds like a great amount of money."

"It is a very good dowry," Rosa said. "Any husband would be pleased if his bride has such a fortune."

"Do I not keep it?"

"Only if it is arranged before the marriage when the settlements are drawn up," Julian explained. "Otherwise, your husband could dispose of it as he liked."

"And if I didn't marry? Could I live on five hundred pounds a year?"

Rosa and Julian looked at one another. "For a start, you will always have a home with us," Rosa said, "but yes, you could. A single lady could live quite comfortably on such an income but a gentleman who had to support his wife and children would need to practise some economy. He could keep a horse, but not a carriage, for example, and there would be no question of his daughter having a Season. Also, comfort is relative," she added. "Our single lady might have a small house or rent part of a larger one in a town like Weymouth but it would not be like living at Loring Place or Swanmere."

"And if a lady had only, say one hundred pounds, or one hundred and fifty a year?"

"She would have meaner lodgings, and perhaps only one maid-servant. She might supplement her income by teaching, as I intended to do before the Chidlows offered me a home. Or she might seek a residential post as a governess or companion, as I did with your family. That way she can save her income until she is ready to set up her own establishment."

"It is quite lowering," Ann said, when Chloe reported this conversation to her. "I wonder what was in my father's will. He was a younger son, so will not have been as well-off as your father. I'll write to my uncle at once."

~~~

Sir Frederick Overton replied by return of post. Major Overton had left his daughter two and a half thousand pounds, some of the income on which had been paid to her mother to cover Ann's expenses and pin money. Her grandmother had insisted on defraying the expense of her Season, Sir Frederick hoped that she had not outrun the constable, but included a draft for twenty pounds in case she was in need of additional funds.

"How kind of him," Ann said, then, "Two and a half thousand; at five per cent, that is one hundred and twenty-five pounds a year."

The two young women looked at one another in dismay.

"That won't take you very far," Chloe said at last. "I presume you can continue to live with your family."

"Yes, but they do expect me to marry. Not to be rid of me, like my mother, but because they think it is best for a woman to marry." She sighed. "They are probably right. What is the alternative? Hal will marry eventually, and his wife may not wish to have a sister-in-law foisted on her."

"I am lucky that Julian is already married, and I love Rosa. I like living with them. But forever? It would be a hanger-on sort of existence wouldn't it? You would never be the mistress of the house."

"That wouldn't worry me," Ann said. "I may have to marry in the end, Chloe, but I don't want to marry as a matter of expediency; not yet at any rate."

"So you want a love match?"

"Yes—but it seems to me, to gamble on the likelihood of this happening is too great a risk. We should be able to stand on our own feet, as gentlemen can, and not be dependent on marriage.

After all, we cannot be sure we will fall in love, or that he will love us in return, or that it would be a suitable match."

"A gentleman can embrace one of the professions if necessary, but there are no real opportunities for ladies; a governess or companion generally earns only pin money and her keep. But I have not given up the hope of finding love. Look at Cynthia and Marfield. The other night they were positively glowing."

"She said it started the first time they danced together." Ann looked at Chloe. "He is a very good dancer, I agree, but…"

"He doesn't have you all atremble?" Chloe laughed. "Me neither, which is just as well, I suppose."

"You felt it with Thomas, didn't you?"

Chloe bit her lip. "Yes, but the attraction is/was one-sided—he treats me like a sister. You saw the way he looked at Miss Barlow. What about you and Mr Prescott? I thought there was something there."

"Initially there was."

"What changed?"

"I overheard the gentlemen talking about me one day at the Forbes's. One said I would be the ideal wife for a musician. Prescott agreed. I would be a true helpmeet, composing organ voluntaries and new choral settings for his choir. In addition to my wifely duties, of course."

"*He for God only, she for God in him?*"

"Precisely."

"What effrontery! But at least he would not complain about your devoting your time to music, as another man might."

Anne sniffed. "He is not so wealthy that his wife would have very few domestic duties, and I do not imagine he would put my music before his comfort. He is quite selfish."

"All gentlemen are."

"I am too, when it comes to music," Ann said fairly.

"If you are reluctant to marry, you must see if you can make music pay," Chloe said. "Can you sell your compositions to a publisher?"

"I intend to try."

"Or, what about teaching? You are very good at explaining things."

"I don't think I could teach while I live with my grandmother. She wouldn't feel it suitable for me to visit pupils or for them to come to the house."

"I can see that that would be awkward. Would you consider a post as music mistress in a select girls' school? Teachers frequently live at the school, so you would have bed and board, and company."

"I had never thought of that. Did Rosa not go to school in Bath?"

"Mrs Ellicott's. She is still in contact with her. I am sure she would recommend you."

Ann seemed quite happy at the thought of servitude as a teacher, provided she was teaching music.

"Much of your time would not be your own," Rosa warned when she was consulted, "however I imagine Mrs Ellicott would welcome a lady who has not only had a Season but was presented to her Majesty. It would be easier for you, too, for no one could throw at your head that you had no experience of the *ton*."

"Did that happen to you?" Chloe asked.

"Not to me, for I only taught the youngest class, but I know it happened to others. A school is not all sweetness and light, you know. Some of the girls regard themselves as superior to the teachers who have to earn their living. Girls can be quite cattish to one another, and some of the older instructresses might resent you, especially if you become popular with the pupils, as is very likely. Singing is almost always preferable to syntax."

"It cannot be worse than living with my mother," Ann said wryly. "Pray write to Mrs Ellicott when you have a moment, Rosa."

Chapter Twenty-Three

"Now we are on the Great North Road," Rafe said after he had safely guided his team past a coach emerging from the *Angel Inn* at Islington. "Are you sure you are warm enough? Remember you can join my parents any time we change horses. You only have to say the word and we'll wait for them."

Cynthia shook her head. The cashmere shawl that, he had admitted, had been especially purchased for her, had been folded as usual on the seat of the curricle, but in addition there was a luxurious lap-rug in case she felt chilled on the long drive in an open carriage.

"I am perfectly comfortable, thank you. I have been looking forward to the journey; these past days have been so busy. If I had fully appreciated the ramifications of planning a *ton* wedding, I should have begged you to elope."

"Indeed? I am at your service, ma'am, now and always. Scotland it shall be."

"It's too late, I fear."

He laughed at her mournful tone. "My mother insisted that the arrangements were best left to the ladies, who would keep me abreast of what was required of me which is chiefly, I understand, to turn up on time and not to forget the ring. It is not as simple for you, I take it."

The Husband Criteria

"I blame Princess Charlotte. Last year, the ladies' journals devoted months to her wedding, culminating in blow-by-blow accounts of the ceremony, the drawing-room that followed it, and ten or more of her new dresses. Because you are heir to an earldom, there seems to be an assumption that we shall do everything on a similarly grand scale."

"What nonsense! It is nobody's business but our own."

"I know. But to be constantly questioned about it is very wearing."

"What sort of questions?"

"When and where? Would we marry here in town or in the country? Generally one marries in the bride's parish, but the Benton heir should marry at their seat, your Aunt Georgina informed Mamma."

"Surely she was not consulted?"

"That did not stop her voicing her opinion at the ball."

"I hope your mother sent her to the right-about."

"She told me she just said, 'oh, indeed?' and then, 'pray excuse me,' and walked away. But afterwards we—our two mothers and I—agreed that with everybody concerned in town, it would be ridiculous to require them to travel."

"Very sensible."

"My mother was insistent that everything was agreed before we left for Ailesthorpe as the style of gown depends on the time and place and she wants them to work on my bride clothes while I am away. What is suitable for a morning, church wedding would not do for a private evening wedding by special licence, as the princess had. Your mother would have preferred that, but I wouldn't feel married if the wedding were not in a church."

She glanced up at him. "Besides, I thought it would be too like any other evening party, and I want the wedding breakfast to be at home. My present home, I mean. It will mark the end of this part of my life."

He freed his left hand to clasp hers. "I understand."

"Then your mother said a special licence would be better than waiting our turn in St George's in Hanover Square. As all weddings must be held between the hours of eight in the morning and noon, it can be like a coaching inn there some mornings, she said, with everyone vying for the next pair of horses, celebrant, I mean, and the different parties mingling indiscriminately. I could see her point. That is why I proposed St Margaret's. It is the parish church of the House of Commons, where we frequently attend service. I feel at home there."

"An excellent suggestion." He leaned down to pay the toll, then put the ticket into the pocket of his caped greatcoat. "Was everybody in favour?"

"Yes. To be sure it is before Parliament rises, we settled on the last Thursday of June, at eleven o'clock."

"Hmm. Breakfast at twelve, and we should be able to leave by two. It's seventy-one miles to Dover. We'll hardly make it that evening."

"Oh. I hadn't thought of that. Should I try and change it?"

"It doesn't matter," he said quickly. "We haven't really talked about our wedding journey yet, have we? We'll have time to do so in peace this week. We have the rest of our lives ahead of us. No need to be rushed."

'No need to be rushed.' Cynthia had never heard more beautiful words. Why was she getting so worked up about it? She should be enjoying this special time in her life. Mamma was

The Husband Criteria

determined she should have trunks of bride-clothes, but they were going to Paris, weren't they? She would talk to Mamma about giving her the money to have half of them made there. And she would try not to listen to all the 'advice' that was poured into a bride-to-be's ears. So many girls and ladies seemed determined to repeat stories of demanding or neglectful husbands. She could not imagine Rafe in either role. She would use this week to get on more familiar terms with him, and his parents, she decided, and if she had any reservations or questions she would consult someone sensible like Rosa or worldly-wise like Chloe's mother. Mamma, to whom she would always be first and foremost her daughter, would be inclined to avoid any difficult or embarrassing discussions.

The greys had picked up speed, as had the other vehicles on the toll-road, making conversation difficult if one did not want to shout over the clatter of hooves and wheels. She spread out the rug to protect her skirts from dust and debris. Alone here in the curricle, side by side with her future husband, her nurse's adage, 'there is more to marriage than four bare legs in a bed,' rose in her mind. She glanced sideways at Rafe and cautiously moved her leg so that it touched his. He looked down at her at once; their eyes met and his lips curved as she felt a gentle pressure in return.

"All right?" The coachman's question after every change; were all the harnesses and trappings in order?

"All's right." She smiled as she returned the ostler's confirmation, then lay back against the squabs and let herself be rocked into a comfortable doze.

~~~

Ailesthorpe House was a nicely proportioned house of three storeys over the rustic basement level. Its red brick had mellowed to a soft rose offset by pale quoins delineating the different sections of the façade. A flight of shallow stone steps led to the central front door.

They were greeted by the tenant's man of business, one Ezekiel Jones, and the estate steward, John Fletcher. His principal had already left, Jones informed them. A handful of servants had been retained on board wages until the expiry of the lease at midsummer, including the housekeeper, Mrs Pilcher, who would be happy to answer any questions the ladies might have, while he himself was authorised to discuss the schedule of dilapidations with their lordships' representative who had, he understood, already inspected the property.

"I suggest we walk through the house together," Lady Benton said, "then, Mr Jones, we shall leave you, Mr Fletcher, and Mr Hancock to your discussions while we talk to Mrs Pilcher."

Cynthia liked the house at once. The rooms were of a good size, comfortable for a family; not cavernous, but with connecting doors should one wish to entertain a greater number of people.

Faded curtains and window blinds had been left in place, as had heavy furniture in the style of the last century. Old-fashioned though it may be, it had been well kept, the wooden surfaces gleaming with decades of polishing.

"Does the furniture remain here?" Rafe asked.

"If you want it," his father said. "I believe my grandfather was one of Chippendale's first patrons. He and my grandmother moved here when they wed. The manor has been in her family for centuries and this house was built as part of her dowry. All their personal belongings were removed, of course, after they died, but the furniture was left. I imagine it was easier to let the house furnished."

"There is no need to decide now if you want to keep it," his mother said. "However, it does mean that you need not do everything at once, but can move in and take your time to decide how you want things."

The bedrooms, too, were spacious and airy, with old-fashioned four-poster beds. Two side-by-side bedrooms with adjoining dressing-rooms were clearly intended for the master and mistress, and there was a handful of spare bedrooms. The top floor was partly nursery and schoolroom, and partly servants' bedrooms, with generous attic space above.

"What do you think?" Rafe murmured to Cynthia as they began their descent.

"I like it. We must inspect the offices, including the necessary," she whispered back. "I wonder can they be modernised—water closets added, for example."

"I don't know. There will be no such thing as a high-water service here, as there is in London. I'll ask Hancock to make a point of inspecting the offices, and enquiring whether there are any difficulties with water supply, for example. Do they have their own well?"

Mrs Pilcher was an affable-looking woman of middle age, neither so plump as to suggest indolence nor so thin as to suggest a lack of interest in creature comforts. When they had returned to the ground floor, she said, "My lady, if I may be so bold as to offer you some tea and freshly-baked tarts in the small drawing-room? It is most pleasant there at this time of the day."

"Thank you, Mrs Pilcher," Lady Benton said graciously.

After the housekeeper had shown them to a restful room painted in a pale green and decorated with panels of roses and birds, she excused herself to go to the kitchen. "Cook was let go, my lady, and while Betty, the maid, does her best, I prefer to keep an eye on her. I made the tarts myself, earlier."

"Do you think she might be interested in staying on?" Cynthia said when the door had closed behind the housekeeper. "It would be a big help to have good servants who know the house and the neighbourhood."

"She makes a good impression," Lady Benton said. "I wonder if the previous tenant left a character for her and the other servants. Even to leave them here as caretakers on board wages suggests a certain level of trust."

"It's an excellent idea. I am also interested in what you said about my great-grandmother's family, sir," Rafe said to his father. "Do they still hold the manor?"

"The Darseys? Yes, I think so. The present line is a collateral one. The entail covered only the original estate which is why your great-great-grandfather was able to carve out this one for his only child; the manor house went to a second cousin, I believe. The connection to us would now be pretty remote."

"Nonetheless, we should call if they still live there."

Mrs Pilcher, whose strawberry tarts proved delicious, confirmed that the Darsey family, with the squire, Sir Anselm, at its head, lived at the manor.

"Are they in residence at the moment?" Lady Benton asked.

"Why, yes, my lady."

"Is there a groom or footman who can take a note over and wait for a reply?"

"Yes, my lady. It will take him two hours or so, depending on how long he has to wait."

"That will give us the opportunity to view the offices and the gardens."

~~~

Sir Anselm professed himself delighted to 'receive his cousin and family' the next day. Before calling at the manor, they would revisit Ailesthorpe House, they decided. Conscious of a day well-spent, the four returned in good spirits to *The Angel* in Grantham where Lord Benton had reserved a suite. Having enjoyed an excellent dinner in their private parlour, they were now addressing a decanter of port. Lady Benton had surprised her son by admitting to being partial to a glass, adding that when she and her husband dined alone, they always sat together over the port. Cynthia had accepted the offer of a glass but confessed that she found it too sweet.

"To sum up, it is a fine building that would reward generous refurbishment but the offices are merely adequate; the stables are in good condition, the gardens attractive but old-fashioned, and the avenue and carriage-sweep need attention," Rafe said. "The fabric is generally sound although some repairs are needed, the hangings and some of the wall-papers are shabby, and the furniture will do for the moment at least."

"The Chinese wall-paper in the morning-room is very pretty," Cynthia said. "I would like to keep it."

"Then we shall," he said promptly.

"Sometimes it is possible to transfer the panels to another room," his mother said. "It would be lovely in a boudoir." She stood. "It has been a long day. I think I'll retire."

"A good idea," her husband said.

"It's too early for us," Rafe said firmly. "Good night, Mother, good night, sir."

His mother looked at him, opened her mouth, and shut it again. "Good night, good night, Cynthia."

Cynthia rose to her feet. "Good night, ma'am, good night, sir."

Rafe shut the parlour door behind his parents. "That went well. I thought we would never get a moment to ourselves."

"I thought your mother was going to baulk, or order me to bed," Cynthia said. "If anyone knew, it would be very scandalous, but even then what could they do? They could hardly stop the marriage." She dropped back down onto the sofa and patted the seat beside her. "Let us talk about the house, and what we need to consider tomorrow. Do you have any idea of the sums involved, and what is at our disposal?"

"I don't know—I have never done anything like this before. My father said he would pay for anything that was necessary over and above what is included in the schedule of dilapidations, which the former tenant must cover."

"That is very generous, but we should still have a general idea of how much we may spend—how else are we to make plans?"

"How practical you are," he said, slipping an arm around her waist.

"I like planning, and figures and so on," she said defensively. "I often sit with my grandfather, discussing various schemes and investments, and deciding what improvements are needed on the estate in the coming year."

The Husband Criteria

"Next you will be saying you can calculate compound interest."

"Yes, of course. Can't you?"

"With a lot of counting on my fingers," he confessed.

She leaned against his shoulder. "It's not as though you will be required to do it regularly. One thing I have learnt is to start with any structural matters—those that are purely decorative can come later. We should list things in order of priority, and also consider what major changes we would like—in the kitchen, for example, and whether water-closets are feasible."

"We won't be able to do that properly in two days."

"I know. I was wondering—Rafe, supposing we came here first for a couple of months, and only went to France in September? It would be a more pleasant time to travel—the summer months can be very hot there."

"I was thinking the same. We could manage here for a few weeks, couldn't we? I'm sure Hancock would supervise the work in our absence, especially if we keep Fletcher on. We'll see what Hancock has to say about him."

"And Mrs Pilcher. I think we should keep the remaining servants if possible. I'll bring my maid, Cotter, of course. What servants will come with you?"

"Bates, my valet and major-domo, my tiger, and a groom. The others came with the house, and I doubt if they would wish to move to the country."

"We'll need a cook at once. I'll talk to Mrs Pilcher tomorrow, if you agree."

"Whatever you think best, my dear," he said solemnly and then laughed at her look of surprise. "Anna says it is the most useful phrase for a husband."

263

"As long as you mean it, and are not trying to fob me off with a feigned agreement. I would rather we disagreed honestly than that."

He caught her face in his hands. "I can see you are going to be a rare treasure of a wife," he said and kissed her deeply. As soon as he felt her response, he let his hands slide down over her shoulders and caught her to him. She willingly returned his embrace, sweetly following his lead until they broke the kiss, gasping for breath.

"Tell me, sweetheart, was there anything about this in your Husband Criteria?"

She blushed. "Not specifically, but we agreed there must be an attraction between you. My nurse used say, 'there is more to marriage than four bare legs in a bed,'—that was the starting point for the list, but at the end, it all boils down to that, doesn't it? You do not want to find him distasteful."

He touched her cheek then stroked his fingers over the top of her breasts. "So you do not find me distasteful, Miss Glazebrook?"

"Not at all; not since our first dance together. What about you? When did you first feel the attraction?"

He laughed. "Will you believe me when I say that first day at Gunter's, when you rose so ably to Miss Loring's defence?"

"Oh."

"But that was attraction. It soon became fascination and now—I love you very much, Cynthia."

"Oh, Rafe!" She raised her face for another kiss, saying afterwards, when she was able, "I love you too."

Chapter Twenty-Four

"Who are the Dugdales, Aunt?" Chloe asked Lady Ransford as that lady's carriage drew away from Swanmere House.

"Emily Gasson, as she was then, and I came out together. As our fathers were both baronets, we frequently found ourselves near one another and soon made friends. We married the same year, too. John Dugdale, who was a younger son, died within ten years of their wedding and she never remarried. She remains on the fringes of the *ton*, one might say, but I have always kept up the connection, inviting her to my routs, and to dinner if I need someone to balance the table. She never takes offence at a late invitation."

"Does she entertain much?" Ann asked.

"Yes, but to smaller gatherings, tea-parties, and what she calls *conversaziones*. This *soirée musicale* is a new departure for her. I understand it is on behalf of her godson who seeks to establish himself as a composer. When she told me that, I asked if I might bring you girls. It is a pity Cynthia is out of town, but I knew you would be interested, Ann, and if Chloe came too, Rosa could have a restful evening. These early months when one is with child can be quite enervating."

Some twenty chairs were set out in Mrs Dugdale's drawing-room, facing a pianoforte and two chairs with music stands in front of them. "I shall introduce you to Frederick later; he is quite nervous, poor boy, and said he would prefer to do the pretty afterwards."

"That is very understandable," Lady Ransford replied but, her hostess having moved on, she snorted and said, "Every young lady is expected to perform at the slightest notice. They may not indulge in such sensibility."

"We are trained to it, from a very early age," Ann pointed out. "It is not the same for boys. And playing one's own compositions is very different."

"Hmph! I daresay you are right." Her ladyship turned to greet another old friend, taking the two girls with her.

It was an older group than usual, Chloe noted, about two-thirds ladies, and she and Ann were the only debutantes. They were about to take a modest seat at the back when Mrs Dugdale called them forward.

"Sit here, my dears. Give the young men something pretty to look at."

Having arranged her guests to her satisfaction, Mrs Dugdale left the room, returning in a couple of minutes, to Ann's astonishment, with Bradley and another gentleman. Bradley looked suitably bashful while his godmother sang his praises before announcing that the guests would first hear his sonata for cello and piano. He glanced around the room as he took his seat, starting visibly when he saw Ann. She smiled encouragingly. She knew this sonata, a pleasant piece that would not challenge his listeners' ears.

The pianist was more than competent and the two musicians played with an infectious enthusiasm that earned appreciative applause. The sonata was followed by a sprightly duet for violin and piano, after which Bradley joined the other two for the final work. Just when she thought they were about to begin, he addressed the audience.

"Ladies and gentlemen, thank you for your interest. With our last piece, I am delighted to present to you a new work by a fellow-composer, a piano trio that tonight receives its first public performance." He lifted his bow, nodded to the others, and they began.

Ann stiffened when she heard the opening flourish of violin and piano. Beside her, Chloe gasped then, shielded by her open fan, whispered, "But that's your trio. I couldn't mistake it."

"No. It is mine," Ann muttered back, as the cello took up the theme. Short of making the most appalling scene, there was nothing she could do. For the next twenty minutes she was torn between critical evaluation of the performance and indignation at Bradley's effrontery in appropriating her work which, she had no doubt, he had intended to pass it off as his own. He must have secretly copied the other parts at the Forbes's, for she could not imagine Mr Forbes having given them to him. At last it was over. It was the last piece and the musicians, having acknowledged the applause, came to mingle with the guests. Mrs Dugdale took charge of Bradley, shepherding him from one person to another. Ann bided her time. She would not let him escape her. Meanwhile, there were other quarries.

"That was delightful," she said to the violinist, a tall man of about Bradley's age, with black curls and an infectious smile. He was the best of the day's musicians, she thought.

"Thank you."

"I love piano trios, the way the three instruments complement each other. They are much more high-spirited than string quartets."

He laughed at this. "I agree. Like a spring bubbling forth, at least this one is."

Ann beamed at him. "A perfect description. What an honour, to give its first performance. Who is the composer, do you know?"

"I'm afraid I don't. Until he spoke, I assumed it was Bradley's, although it is not his usual style."

"Thank you again for a most enjoyable performance."

She smiled and moved on. Bradley seemed to be avoiding her; she enlisted Chloe to play the gushing admirer. Even if he remembered her from their ball, he could not give her the cold shoulder—it would be too obvious in such a small gathering.

"There you are, Cousin," she said to Chloe, standing beside her in such a way as to cut Bradley off from the rest of the room. "Bradley."

"Miss Ann." He bowed perfunctorily, his eyes looking right and left to see if he could escape.

"How dare you plagiarise my work!"

"I am shocked that you would so accuse me. You have no proof."

"No proof? It was apparent from the very first notes. My cousin, who has been party to the development of the work, recognised it at once."

"Indeed, I did," Chloe agreed. "It is unmistakable."

"If it is, and I admit nothing, I was doing you a favour."

"By obtaining the parts of my work by stealth, and planning to perform it without my knowledge or consent?"

He flushed at the contempt in her voice.

"For God's sake keep your voice down," he hissed. "You'll cause a scene."

"If you wish to avoid one, you will return all copies of my work to me before we leave."

"As you wish. We'll say no more about it?" he added hopefully.

She shook her head. "I must tell Mr Forbes. It would be very wrong of me not to."

Although the next day was not a Monday, Ann called on the Forbes as early as might be permissible. Mr Forbes's frown deepened as he listened to her tale.

"Despicable!" he said when he had heard her out. "I had a note from him this morning, saying that other commitments would prevent him from joining us on Mondays for the next weeks. I shall reply that he no longer has a place here and I'll have a general word with the others about collegiality and respect for one another's work. I am very sorry you have had this experience, Miss Ann."

So was Ann.

"I feel something precious has been tarnished," she said to Chloe when she returned home. "Don't laugh, but I felt I had been admitted to a fellowship or a guild of craftsmen where our music made us equal but now I see it was all a sham, and it is every man for himself, and no respect for a woman."

"It is very disappointing," Chloe said, "but don't let one bad apple spoil the basket. Mr Forbes is very firmly on your side."

On her return from Ailesthorpe, Cynthia was most indignant on Ann's behalf. "There is no more you can do, I suppose?"

Ann shook her head. "No. But he has lost Mr Forbes's favour and good will, and that is more of a punishment than you may realise. Now, tell us all about Ailesthorpe."

"I will, but first—you will both be my bridesmaids, will you not?"

Chapter Twenty-Five

It was Cynthia's wedding-day. Chloe and Ann had spent the previous night in Park Place and now, still in their morning-gowns, they had gathered in Cynthia's bedroom over chocolate and hot rolls to fortify themselves for the morning ahead. The room looked bare, stripped of almost all the little items that made a space personal to its occupant. They were already packed to go with her to her new life.

"It never occurred to me when we came to town that I would not return, to live there I mean," she said. "Mamma has promised she will have my things sent on to Ailesthorpe, at least anything that's worth sending."

"You won't want your girlish dresses and bonnets," Chloe agreed.

"No, but there are things I bought in France that I would like to have as well as other mementoes. I just brought what I thought I would need for the Season with me."

"If I am to be honest, I never thought that one of us would marry at the end of this Season," Chloe said.

"Nor I," Cynthia said, while Ann nodded agreement. "For all our talk of husband criteria, marriage was something that would happen 'someday', not now."

"How did you know you wanted to marry Marfield?" Ann asked. "What made you decide for him?"

"It was a mixture of things; the more I got to know him, the better I liked him. I could talk to him without watching my words. He took my concerns seriously too. And since our betrothal we have become even closer; now I cannot imagine my life without him."

"I cannot imagine my life with any man," Ann said. "Can you, Chloe?"

"Yes, but not yet. I do not feel ready to take that next step in life." She smiled at Cynthia. "You are braver than I."

"Or you just have not met the right person," Cynthia said. "If Mr Musgrave had proposed, would you have accepted him?"

"I don't know." Chloe laughed. "Looking back, I was content to yearn from afar. He was safe—it is unlikely Julian would have approved of the match, at least not this year. And, to be fair to Thomas, he never made any attempt to fix his interest with me. I think I was more in love with the idea of being in love—and such an interest protected me from real suitors."

"I can understand that," Ann said. "I am glad to have had a Season but am not anxious to have another. Rosa has heard from Mrs Ellicott. She has no vacancy for a music mistress at present, but would like to meet me, should I be in Bath."

"And shall you be?"

"I hope to convince my grandmother to go there. The Season there has ended, of course, but perhaps in October or November. I shall be glad to spend the summer at home."

"So shall I. But I hope you will come to us in August, together with Hal and Robert," Chloe said.

The Husband Criteria

"If we may. Will Robert's father not object? He did not go home in the Easter holidays either."

"I believe his step-mother is with child again," Chloe said. "Robert is too old for the nursery and there is very little to occupy him at home, he says. He and Hal always find something to do at Swanmere."

"What about next year, Chloe?" Cynthia asked. "Will you come to Town again?"

"I don't know. It will depend on Rosa, and the new baby."

"You may have a baby yourself by then, Cynthia, or at least be increasing," Ann said.

"Perhaps," Cynthia answered.

"Are you frightened of becoming a wife?" Chloe asked.

"No. A little nervous, perhaps, but I trust Rafe." Cynthia looked at the clock. "It is time we dressed. The carriage will take you, Mamma, and Martin at a quarter to eleven, then come back for Papa and me."

~~~

"Are you ready, Cynthia? Let me see you before I go. Oh, my dear!" There were tears in Mamma's eyes as she admired her daughter's gown of the palest cream silk. The low neckline and hem were embroidered with festoons of pale pink roses held by golden bows, inspired by Rafe's necklace. For morning wear, a chemisette of organdie veiled the bosom and was gathered in crisp ruffles at the throat.

"Now the pelisse." Mamma took the garment from Cotter and held it for Cynthia to slip her arms into it. "It will be just right for cool nights, when a shawl might not be warm enough."

Cynthia gazed at her reflection. After two Seasons in muslins it was strange to be opulently dressed in gold silk. The long sleeves were puffed at the shoulders and the collar allowed her ruffle to peep out. The garment was fastened with a long row of little silk-covered buttons and, confined just under her bosom by a belt of the same material fastened with a gold buckle. On each side, gold silk flowers ran inwards from her shoulders to the centre of her breasts and then continued in a line to the hem.

"Where is your bonnet?"

"Here, ma'am." The hat of cream silk trimmed with gold was deceptively simple; the crown not too high and the brim skillfully shaped to frame the bride's face. A posy of orange-blossom and rosemary was fixed to one side where the brim met the crown. Cotter set it carefully on her mistress's head, then fetched a comb to tidy a stray curl.

"Beautiful." Mamma dabbed at her eyes. "I must go. My darling child, I wish you every happiness."

A careful embrace so as not to crush their gowns, and she was gone.

Cynthia took a deep breath then picked up the delicate Limerick gloves.

"Will you tuck a handkerchief into your sleeve, Miss? Just in case…"

"I suppose I had better." Cynthia quickly slipped the lace square into the sleeve of the pelisse. It would be safe there, but easy to retrieve if she were overcome by emotion.

"I wish you joy, Miss Cynthia," Cotter said as Cynthia moved to the door.

"Thank you, Cotter. I am very pleased that you will be coming with me. It will be a big change for both of us."

"That it will, Miss."

~~~

Papa stood at the foot of the stairs. "Ready?"

"Yes, but let me say goodbye to the servants. There will probably be no time later."

Cynthia went to the little group that waited near the door to below-stairs. She had known some of them all her life. She passed from one to another, acknowledging their good wishes and thanking them for their service, then took her father's arm. "Now, Papa."

He was silent as they walked out to the carriage but once the door was closed, he turned to her. "Are you quite sure, Cynthia, that this is what you want?"

She stared at him, overwhelmed by a wave of gratitude and love, confident that he was perfectly serious, that if she said no, he would lead her back into the house and brave the worst scandal imaginable. She leaned over and kissed his cheek. "Yes, Papa, I am quite sure. But th-thank y-you." To her horror, her voice broke and she felt tears rise to her eyes.

He rapped for the coachman to drive on, then produced a handkerchief and carefully blotted her eyes. "No crying! Your mother will have my head if you arrive with reddened eyes."

Cynthia had to smile. "What do you think she would have done if I had not arrived at all?"

"She would be furious with both of us, and probably angry that you had not spoken sooner."

"Justifiably so, you must admit. If I were you, I would not tell her of your question, or not for some years at least."

"That is excellent advice."

She tucked her hand into his. After some minutes, she said, "You will come and visit us, won't you, before we go to France?"

"Of course. And you will always be welcome at your old home, Cynthia. You should know that."

Cynthia's heart skipped a beat at the sight of her bridegroom waiting patiently on the pavement in front of St Margaret's. As always, he was impeccably dressed; his coat of chocolate-brown superfine, pale inexpressibles, and cream and gold striped waistcoat might have been chosen to complement her own finery. Then he was at her door, hat in hand, to help her alight. Their eyes met and all thoughts of dress fled.

He raised her hand to his lips. "Good morning, my love."

"Good morning, Rafe." She tucked her hand into the crook of his arm.

"You're somewhat premature, Marfield," her father said as they rounded the carriage. "She is still my daughter."

"And always will be, sir," Rafe said. "I hope that today you will regard your family as enlarged rather than reduced. The ladies await you inside."

He yielded Cynthia to him and, accompanied by Mr Nugent, led the way into the church where Mamma, Chloe, Ann, and Martin waited.

Although dwarfed by its huge Abbey neighbour, once you entered St Margaret's you could not but be overawed by the series of gothic arches, today lit by sunlight streaming through the clerestory and the beautiful window of painted glass. A handful of wedding guests—the Bentons, with Lady Anna and her husband, Rosa and Julian, the Ransfords, and her great-grandmother and

Lord Swanmere—stood near the altar where Rafe now had taken up his position with Mr Nugent and the clergyman. Martin had escorted their mother to the front of the church. It was time.

Cynthia gave Chloe her gloves then held out her right hand to her father. He clasped it lightly and they walked slowly up the aisle, followed by the bridesmaids.

"Who giveth this woman to this man?"

Papa's grip tightened before he released her to the minister who in turn placed her hand in Rafe's. His ungloved hand was warm and firm, his voice deeper than usual as he made his vows. Her own, lighter tones—she stumbled at 'obey' but, reassured by his slight nod, continued to the end. The unaccustomed weight of a gold ring on her finger, Rafe gently holding it at the first knuckle. "With this Ring I thee wed, with my body I thee worship, and with all my worldly goods I thee endow: In the Name of the Father, and of the Son, and of the Holy Ghost."

He slid the ring home to the murmured amens of the little congregation.

Now they knelt shoulder to shoulder while the minister prayed before again joining their right hands. "Those whom God hath joined together, let no man put asunder." And, finally, he addressed all present, "I pronounce that they be Man and Wife together."

It was done. They were married until death did them part.

The remaining prayers and readings, even the minister's sermon, passed over her head. She was conscious only of the reassuring bulk of Rafe beside her. Her husband. The gleam of gold that said she was Lady Marfield.

The service over, Rafe helped her stand.

The verger came to lead them into the sacristy to sign the marriage register. "First you, my lord," then, "You sign with your maiden name, my lady."

For the last time she wrote *Cynthia Amelia Glazebrook* and rose to allow their fathers and the two witnesses to sign too.

"My felicitations, Lady Marfield."

The minister's prosaic tone pierced the daze that enveloped her. Soon she was being passed from arm to arm—her parents, the Bentons, Martin, Chloe and Ann, and finally Mr Nugent who also claimed the privilege of kissing the bride. Then Rafe, after concluding his own round of embraces, reclaimed her to lead the little bridal procession out of the church.

"Now, Mamma?"

Resplendent in silk coat and knee-breeches, Jack emerged from the cluster of wedding guests clutching a small basket and advanced before them, scattering rose-petals as he went. He was so serious and business-like that it was hard not to laugh, especially when Rafe called, "Not so fast, Jack. This is not a gallop."

"I think he is afraid that he will run out of blossoms if he tarries," Cynthia murmured. "You must admit he behaved perfectly during the ceremony. I had not realised he was there."

Outside, the carriages waited. Rafe's greys were harnessed to a brand-new black and gold travelling chariot emblazoned with the Marfield crest on the door. Inside it was luxuriously fitted out with dull gold upholstery.

"A gift from my father," Rafe explained. "He said I could not expect you to travel to Paris in a curricle or, indeed, rely on the fact that the weather would always be pleasant enough to take an open carriage to Ailesthorpe."

"How generous of him!"

"Yes. It has all sorts of clever fittings. We can explore them at our leisure. But now I want to give you this." He pressed a ring box into her hand.

She opened it to see a gold ring set all around with diamonds. "Rafe. It is beautiful! But another ring?"

"I am told it is called a guard ring, to protect your wedding ring." He took it from the box and slid it onto her finger. "I like the sentiment that it is the plain gold ring, the symbol of our love, that is worthy of protection."

"And by such brilliants. I shall always wear them together." She touched his hand. "I wish this chariot did not have so many windows. I am sure it will make for pleasant travelling, but now I want to kiss you and I fear it is far too public."

"I could pull down the blinds."

She smiled at his hopeful look. "In town? That would be just as scandalous. And here we are at Park Place. You shall have to wait to be thanked, sir."

Finale

Some hours later, the new travelling chariot drew up in Dover Street. The question of where to spend their wedding night had exercised them considerably. The formal departure of the bride from her parents' home marked the end of the wedding festivities. The long journey to Ailesthorpe House meant at least one night on the road, more likely two if they had left after the wedding breakfast.

"I wish we didn't have to set out immediately," Cynthia had said. "Either we drive late into the evening, or must stop after four or five stages. Could we go to a hotel here in town, the Pulteney, perhaps?"

"If you wish. Or would you object to coming to Dover Street? I have the whole house, not just a set of rooms. We would be private."

"Have you entertained other females there? I should not like to be one of many in your bed."

"No, I promise you," he assured her quickly. "You would be the first—and the last."

"What will your valet make of it?"

"He must get used to it, just as your maid must."

"I do hope they get on with one another. I wonder will he remember attempting to turn us from the door."

When he frowned, she had added quickly, "Pray don't remind him. I think it is best that we pretend it never happened. I shall tell Cotter the same."

~~~

She was never to know whether Bates had recognised her or not. He was waiting in the hall to bow her into the house and present the other servants before handing her over to Mrs Paxon, the cook/housekeeper, who led her upstairs to the back bedroom, a square room that looked down onto the usual offices, built around a yard that presumably led to the mews. As Cynthia watched, Cotter appeared carrying her own box together with a footman bearing the small trunk containing the items her mistress would need for the next days.

Cynthia turned back into the room. The furniture was a peculiar mixture of old and new—to an old-fashioned oak armoire and four-poster bed had been added an elegant lady's dressing-table made of gilt-ornamented rosewood, a matching cheval mirror, and a small table and two chairs. A bowl of red and white roses scented the air. A chinoiserie screen painted with flowering roses and birds, reminiscent of the Chinese room at Ailesthorpe, was angled across one corner, concealing a rosewood commode chair and wash stand. The bed-hangings also had a Chinese pattern, unlike the heavy red damask of the window-curtains.

"That is all new, my lady, ordered by my lord specially," announced Paxon, with an encompassing wave of her hand. "It doesn't come with the house. We are to send it on after you have left. The same with the bed linen, blankets, and hangings. All was to be new for you, he said."

"I see," Cynthia said, touched by this consideration. The entrance of Cotter saved her from having to say anymore. She dismissed the housekeeper and was sitting at the dressing-table, about to remove her bonnet when there was a tap at the side door.

"Enter."

At Rafe's appearance, Cotter whisked herself out of the room. Cynthia looked at the closing door, slightly disconcerted. "Do you think she will do that every time you appear?"

"I don't know. It is very tactful of her, you must admit."

"I wonder if she sought advice from Mamma's maid."

"I don't know. I came to ask if you have everything you need."

"I think so. You have gone to so much trouble, just for one or two nights."

"When I looked at the room, it seemed quite shabby, certainly not fit for you. I hope you like it."

"It is beautiful. I always wanted a dressing-table with so many drawers and compartments."

"I'm glad to have hit the mark," he said. "Would you like to see the rest of the house?"

"Yes. I'll just take off my bonnet and pelisse."

"Let me."

He brushed away the hands she had raised to the ribbons of her bonnet and carefully untied the bow before lifting the hat from her head. "You are so beautiful. When I saw you this morning, you took my breath away. All I wanted to do was this." He framed her face in his hands and bent to kiss her. "Good morning, Cynthia." And then, "Good morning, wife." This was a deeper kiss that had her clinging to him, and looking at him with dazed eyes when he raised his head.

The Husband Criteria

He carefully unfastened the gold buckle of her pelisse, then started work on its buttons, dropping to his knees when he reached her waist. "How many are there?"

"I don't know. I didn't count them." She could feel his head touch her breasts as he bent to his task, causing her nipples to pebble as if it were an icy morning. She shivered.

"Almost there." He rose to his feet and drew the pelisse away from her shoulders and carefully laid it over one of the chairs. "You are still wearing your gloves."

These too were stripped from her and her hands kissed, not the back, as was usual, but turned so that he could kiss the palms. She shivered again. What next? Surely he was not going to bed her in the middle of the day? Cotter had not even unpacked for her.

Something of her concern must have shown in her face, for he laughed softly. "We'll take our time, shall we?"

At her nod, he put his arm around her shoulders and ushered her into his own room.

While her own apartment showed no sign of previous occupancy, his spoke of comfort tailored to one individual. She recognised the lingering, faint, spicy scent. His soap, perhaps, or some unguent for his hair.

The bed and window hangings were of dark green damask, trimmed with gold. A low, deep armchair beside the fireplace suggested that he liked to linger there, perhaps to read, judging by the side table on which stood an oil lamp, a couple of leather-bound volumes, and a decanter and glasses. An elaborate shaving stand stood between the two windows, to get the best light, she presumed. Beside the roomy armoire, a rack supported several pairs of highly polished boots, soles up.

"You seem very comfortable here," she remarked.

"I believe in comfort," he answered. "I don't need luxury or opulence, but I like to feel at ease in my own four walls."

"You do not spend your time in your clubs, then?"

"Sometimes for company—a hand of cards or a game of chess. But now I shall have better company at home, shall I not?"

She smiled. "I certainly hope you will find it so."

The drawing-room was down one flight of stairs. "I hardly use this room," he said. "An odd time, for a card party, but that is all. Here"—he opened a connecting door—"is where I spend most of my time when at home."

The walls of the back room were lined with book-cases. Comfortable armchairs stood either side of the hearth and a desk was set under the window. On it were a pipe rack, tobacco jar, and tray of decanters. That accounted for the aromatic scent that filled the room, Cynthia thought. A selection of newspapers and journals waited on a round table. "Are they all your books, or did some come with the house?"

"They are all mine except the volumes of sermons and theological discourses."

"And you will have them sent to Ailesthorpe with your other possessions?"

"Yes. Paxon will see to it once we have left."

In the dining room downstairs, the walls were hung with vivid landscapes instead of family portraits.

"How beautiful." Cynthia went to inspect a painting of Venice more closely. "Are these yours or the landlords?"

"Mine."

"I am beginning to realise how much fun it will be to make our own home. So many things to think of. I am sorry now that I did not consider the paintings at the Exhibition more closely. They are for sale, after all."

"We could go again tomorrow," he offered.

"Would people not think it odd to see us there, the day after our wedding?"

"Let them think!"

"I am no longer bound by all the young lady restrictions, you mean." Suddenly she twirled, skirts flying. "I am a married lady now; I can make my own decisions. I am free!"

"Now that you are entitled to wear a cap, you are not going to throw it over a windmill, I trust."

She leaned back in his embrace to look up at him. "No, because I have no intention of wearing one. Not until I am thirty, at least. Horrible things!"

"I agree. I would much rather see your pretty hair."

~~~

Rafe looked impatiently at the clock. How long should he give his bride to get ready for bed? His father had warned him to allow her to go upstairs first. "Females need time to make themselves comfortable, as they put it." At Rafe's interrogative glance, he had added, "Make water. A young bride won't wish to do it with her husband in the room, not even if she has gone behind a screen."

At least she had gone upstairs at half-past nine. He smiled to himself. These things, too, would get easier with time. He rubbed a reflective hand over his jaw. He had better shave, he supposed. He snuffed the candles and went upstairs.

Cynthia lay back against her pillows. Mamma had advised her not to sit up too late. 'A gentleman will take his cue from you, but you should not keep him waiting either. A false modesty has no place in marriage, my dear. Your husband must be welcome in your bed—do not regard it as a duty to be endured.'

There was a light tap on the connecting door. "May I come in?"

He wore the red dressing-gown she had seen the morning she had called to his door but this time his hair was neatly tamed.

"Well, here we are, wife." He crossed the room to sit on the bed and took her hand in his, raising it to his lips. "Are you frightened?"

"No. A little apprehensive, perhaps."

"There's no need to be. May I join you?"

She lifted the bed-clothes, inviting him in. "Please do."

Beneath the dressing-gown, he wore a white night-shirt, open at the neck and coming just to his knees. His legs were bare. She suppressed a giggle. This was what it came down to, bare legs in a bed.

He quirked an eyebrow then, leaving the candles burning, slid into the bed and took her into his arms.

"Home, at last."

Home. That was it. Here, in each other's arms. Cynthia stopped thinking, concentrating on his whispered endearments and the new sensations, touches, caresses, that she instinctively began to return, nipping at his lips, stroking her tongue against his, sinking more and more into him. When he lifted his head, she lay there, dazed, the sheet and blanket pooled at their waists. His lips curved, then he sat up and pulled his nightshirt over his head. As she gazed, fascinated by his muscular torso—she never knew men had hair there as well—he dropped the garment onto the floor and reached for her nightgown, drawing it up until it caught at her hips.

"May I?"

"Yes." She sat up facing him as he carefully manoeuvred the folds of linen past her breasts and lifted it away from her, letting her hair spill down over her shoulders, his gaze intent.

All thought of modesty had fled. She reached out and he caught her to him. They both gasped. Slowly, he began to explore her body with his lips and hands. In turn, she caressed his shoulders and chest, smoothed his chest hair, and was surprised by his gasp when she found male nipples.

When she felt his hands mould her derriere, she slid hers down to cup his backside. He jerked beneath her hands and pressed against her firm belly.

"Cynthia?"

"Mmm?"

"Do you know… did your mother explain?"

"Yes."

"Then, open for me."

Following his urging, she spread her legs. His touch on her most intimate flesh had her shiver and raise her hips in silent demand. His long fingers slipped into her, stretching her, making her long for more. Then he rose over her, and she felt his member at her entrance, nudging in and withdrawing, in again, and again until he surged into her.

"Oh!"

"I'm sorry," he whispered. "There, it is done now." Holding still, he bent and kissed her mouth until the slight sting eased.

"Better?"

"Mmm."

He began to move again, quicker, harder, until she felt a sudden, strange quivering, there, where they were joined. She moaned.

"Rafe!"

"Cynthia!"

He jerked, and surged even deeper. He was at the very heart of her, moving faster, faster, until with a long groan he collapsed on her. She held him to her, gently stroking his hair back from his forehead.

After some moments, he rolled to the side, but continued to hold her close, their legs tangled together.

"My love," then, "did I hurt you?"

"No. In fact, it should be at the top of the Husband Criteria," she murmured drowsily.

"What should?"

"Four bare legs in a bed. It's impossible to imagine—but with the right man it is…" she paused, searching for the right word. Then it came to her. "It is completion."

"Completion." He repeated the word, as if tasting it. "Yes. Completion."

Background Notes

This is a work of fiction but set in a real time and place. While it would not be possible to list all the sources consulted or comment on interesting trivia, I wish to mention the following:

London Fog and Smog

From the mid-1600s, London ill-health was attributed to coal smoke from both domestic and industrial chimneys combining with the mists and fogs of the Thames Valley. In *The Climate of London* (1818–1820) Luke Howard, coined the term 'city fog' when describing the heat island effect which concentrated the accumulation of smog over the city. The Miseries of an Artist (1820) describes "having opened your window at going out, to find the stink of the paint rendered worse, if possible, by the entrance of the fog, which, being a compound from the effusions of gas pipes, tan yards, chimneys, dyers, blanket scourers, breweries, sugar bakers, and soap boilers, may easily be imagined not to improve the smell of a painting room!"
It was only after the passing of the first *Clean Air Act* in 1956 that the quality of London air was really improved.

Dominos and Loo Masks

A domino is a hooded cloak. When worn as part of a disguise or masquerade, a mask was added. A narrow mask covering the eyes was called a domino or loo mask.

The Plural of Couple

Strange as it may sound to our ears, the plural of couple during the Regency was couple e.g., Our ball on Thursday was a very poor one, only eight couple (Jane Austen to Cassandra Austen).

Stairs in Large Georgian Houses

Why did Marfield have to go up five or six flights of stairs to the nursery on the third floor of Benton House? In Europe, the ground level in a building is counted as 0 so the first floor is the one above it. As Georgian houses have very high ceilings, especially on the ground and first floors, there are double staircases between them. The first flight ends halfway up at a small landing called the return. Instead of continuing straight up from there, the second flight continues in the opposite direction so that the person ascending must complete an 180° turn. Marfield goes up three levels. Cynthia knows there will be two flights each up to the first and second floors, but does not know whether it is one or two between the second and third floors, as that varies from house to house.

The Royal Academy of Arts at Somerset House

For information on the Royal Academy at Somerset House during the Regency, I am indebted to the RA's excellent website, Adam Waterton, Librarian, Royal Academy, and *Art on the Line - The Royal Academy Exhibitions At Somerset House*, edited by David H. Solkin, 2001.

Regency Wedding Etiquette

Weddings during the Regency were small affairs and I have not been able to find a contemporary source describing the etiquette in detail. The earliest description I have discovered is from Volume Two of *The Family Friend*, 1850, i.e., thirty years after the end of the Regency and twenty years after the death of King George IV. However, given the slow pace of change in such matters even today, I think it can be assumed that there will not have been significant changes in custom in the intervening years. The most surprising detail to me was the statement that *The bridegroom shows his gallantry by handing the bride from her carriage.* In other words, he is waiting outside the church to greet her and her entourage. Perhaps this is to assure her that he is there and she will not be left waiting for him to appear.

A Handbook of Etiquette from 1860 says *The bridegroom should receive the bride in the vestry and, later, the father of the bride advances with her from the vestry to the altar, followed by the bridesmaids.* This precludes any bridal grand entrance and procession up the aisle. In describing Cynthia's and Rafe's wedding, I have opted for him to meet her on the pavement outside the church and then to go alone to the altar.

If you enjoyed reading The Husband Criteria, you will love the other books in The Lorings saga.

Book One A Suggestion of Scandal

If only he could find a lady who was tall enough to meet his eyes, intelligent enough not to bore him and had that certain something that meant he could imagine spending the rest of his life with her.

As Sir Julian Loring returns to his father's home, he never dreams that 'that lady' could be Rosa Fancourt, his half-sister Chloe's governess. They first met ten years ago but Rosa is no longer a gawky girl fresh from a Bath Academy. Today, she intrigues him. Just as they begin to draw closer, she disappears—in very dubious circumstances. Julian cannot bring himself to believe the worst, but if Rosa is innocent, the real truth is even more shocking and not without repercussions for his own family, especially for Chloe.

Driven by her concern for Chloe, Rosa accepts an invitation to spend some weeks at Castle Swanmere, home of Julian's maternal grandfather. The widowed Meg Overton has also been invited and she is determined not to let such an eligible match as Julian slip through her fingers again.

When a ghost from Rosa's past rises to haunt her, and Meg discredits Rosa publicly, Julian must decide where his loyalties lie.

"*A smooth read; providing laughs and gasps in turns. Readers will enjoy the cool-headed Miss Fancourt, while hoping that Sir Julian puts the pieces of the puzzle together quickly! A host of other loveable and detestable characters keep the entertainment moving through the trials, tribulations, and victories of love.*"
Historical Novels Review

http://mybook.to/suggestionofscandal

Book Two Lady Loring's Dilemma

Must she pay indefinitely for her indiscretion?

England, 1814

Delia, Lady Loring has long accepted that a wife has few legal rights and little say in the direction of her life. When she is caught in compromising circumstances, her furious husband, Sir Edward, banishes her to Harrogate where she is to live quietly with her mother and behave at all times in a seemly manner. All contact with their sixteen-year-old daughter, Chloe is forbidden.

In Harrogate, she finds small joys, makes friends and rediscovers a long-forgotten freedom. Most important of all, she meets Lord Stephen FitzCharles, her first love of some twenty years ago. The separation from Chloe grieves her, and she worries about what will become of her daughter but a mother has only the rights her husband allows her and Sir Edward shows no sign of relenting.
Delia resolves to place her trust in Stephen who offers her a new life on the Continent. They leave for Paris, then travel on to Nice.

But Sir Edward, determined that his erring wife pays for her misdeeds, counters with new measures.

Napoleon's escape from Elba and march on Paris to oust the newly-restored French king, bring further complications as Delia must face the most unexpected of decisions. Can she retain her freedom and reconcile fully with her daughter? Or will her wings be clipped forever? mybook.to/LadyLoringsDilemma

About the Author

Catherine Kullmann was born and educated in Dublin. Following a three-year courtship conducted mostly by letter, she moved to Germany where she lived for twenty-five years before returning to Ireland. She has worked in the Irish and New Zealand public services and in the private sector. Widowed, she has three adult sons and two grandchildren.

Catherine has always been interested in the extended Regency period, a time when the foundations of our modern world were laid. She loves writing and is particularly interested in what happens after the first happy end—how life goes on for the protagonists and sometimes catches up with them. Her books are set against a background of the offstage, Napoleonic wars and consider in particular the situation of women trapped in a patriarchal society.

She is the author of <u>The Murmur of Masks</u>, <u>Perception & Illusion</u>, <u>A Suggestion of Scandal</u>, <u>The Duke's Regret</u>, <u>The Potential for Love</u>, <u>A Comfortable Alliance</u> and <u>Lady Loring's Dilemma</u>

Catherine also blogs about historical facts and trivia related to this era. You can find out more about her books and read her blog (My Scrap Album) at her website. You can contact her via her Facebook page or on Twitter

Printed in Great Britain
by Amazon

45246062R00169